LORD EDGINGTON I

BOOK 4

THE
MYSTERY
OF
MISTLETOE
HALL

A 1920s MYSTERY

BENEDICT BROWN

COPYRIGHT

For my father, Kevin,
I hope you would have liked this book an awful lot.

WELCOME NOTE

Hello readers, new and old. This book is a spoiler-free Christmas story in the "Lord Edgington Investigates…" series. I wanted to write it as a standalone so that anyone who fancies a shot of Christmassy mystery can dive in without discovering the secrets of the other novels. I hope that new readers will enjoy it so much that you go back to read the previous books and crack Lord Edgington's earlier cases.

At the back of the book, you'll find a character list, a glossary of antiquated and unusual words, a link to a free novella, a list of interesting historical titbits and an explanation of my inspiration and reasons for writing.

Merry Christmas and happy reading!

PROLOGUE

When they found the final corpse, we left the house in one large group. No one said a word as we followed the brass-buttoned officer through the snow. The high banks that had accumulated the day before were turning to ice, and the ground crunched and compacted underfoot as the parade of mourners thinned out into one long line.

It was a grim moment, but my grandfather's golden retriever wasn't to know that. Delilah took big flouncing jumps and stopped from time to time to roll about in the fluffy white stuff. I must admit, I was jealous. With everything that had occurred since we'd arrived at Mistletoe Hall, I'd had very little time to play in the snow. I found myself copying Delilah and bounded ahead of the group, until my grandfather gave me a disapproving look to remind me why we'd gone outside in the first place. I fell back and allowed the old man to set the pace.

Mother wore a melancholy expression as I took her hand to help negotiate a patch of slippery ground, and we walked along arm in arm through the forest. When we arrived at our destination, the sight was both more macabre and more mundane than I could have imagined. The body had been suspended from the lowest branch of a beech tree. The eyes were tightly closed, as though in the middle of a nap, and I found myself crossing my fingers that the sleeper would awake at any moment to break the spell. I was old enough to know that wishing wouldn't get me far.

There was blood on the ground, but I could see no obvious wounds on the limp body. I tried not to look at the noose because I didn't want to see the swollen red marks where the rope had bitten into flesh. We'd reached the end of our torturous Christmas holiday, and it no longer seemed important whether the killer would be punished or justice would be served. The only thing that mattered was the people who had died, and that there was nothing we could do to bring them back.

A second police officer arrived from the house with a saw. He worked for a few seconds at the rope before the body landed down gently in the snow. I let out a gasp as those bulging eyes came involuntarily open and the poor soul stared out at us one last time.

CHAPTER ONE

Surrey, England,
1925

Christmas was upon us, and the final days of Oakton Academy's term were drawing to a close. For once, they did not drag along incessantly, but were filled with excitement and nervous chatter as every boy speculated on what that year's festivities might deliver. Even the staff seemed quite jolly on the matter. My games teacher, Mr Bath, eschewed our usual five laps around the cold, muddy field, for four laps around the cold, muddy field and a cup of minestrone soup at the end.

While Oakton was largely free of yuletide trappings, our acting headmaster, Mr Mayfield, had made an overture to the season by placing a rather pretty pine branch at the main entrance. Some lower-school boys had decorated it with pieces of silver foil and long colourful paper chains. It made me cheerful every time I passed.

For a boy at boarding school, summer and Christmas stand out like lush islands in the middle of shark-infested seas. I was paddling up to the last day of term with great energy – this is a particularly poor metaphor, however, as, in reality, I am an abysmal swimmer.

Along with my gang of friends – Marmaduke and the three Williams – I went without a wink of sleep on the night before we were due to head home. Thanks to the recent cull of some of the school's more aggressive teachers, midnight feasts were no longer such a dangerous endeavour. In slippered feet and pyjamaed bodies, we sneaked out into the cold night in search of leftovers from the end-of-term lunch.

"We could still get caught," Bill, or possibly Billy, said. It was awfully dark, and the three Williams looked and sounded almost identical at the best of times. "Just because we've got a nice friendly cook, instead of the monster who worked here before, that doesn't mean that we won't get into trouble."

"Stop being such an absolute poltroon." Marmaduke was always the one to buoy us up and gee us along. "Just think of all the delights that await us beyond the kitchen doors."

There was a coating of frost on the ground, and the air was so cold that it nipped at my nose like a lobster's claw. I wished I'd taken a moment to retrieve my dressing gown, and perhaps a balaclava.

I'd rarely been out of the dormitory at night, but I was seventeen now. It was about time I bent some rules and lived a little. My grandfather was always telling me that I wouldn't get far in life if I never came out of my shell, and, though every bone in my body was rattling with fear, I kept walking.

We reached the door to the dining hall and two of the Williams leant back against the wall, like miners about to set off a stick of dynamite. William number three pulled the handle.

"It's locked. We'd better go back to bed." He didn't sound too disappointed about his discovery and, with glum faces barely visible in the moonlight, we moved to leave.

Marmaduke soon rounded us up again. "Not so fast, you cowards. I've never seen such streaks of yellow in three fellows."

"It is terribly cold out here," I said in our defence. "And if the kitchens are locked, we're not likely to get much out of them."

"Oh ye of little faith," my carrot-topped friend replied and, with a quick glance around, in case of any stray teachers, he climbed onto the windowsill behind us. "Didn't you think I would plan ahead?"

Marmaduke Adelaide was the fastest and most agile boy in the school. He could do things that defied comprehension and, right at that moment, he managed to scale a brick wall like a spider. In six and a half seconds, he had made it to the window above the door, which he'd evidently wedged ajar earlier in the day. In no time at all, the snick was pulled back, the door swung open and the four of us were free to enter that (comparatively) sweltering space.

"Welcome to the party," Marmaduke proudly declared. He moved further into the shadows to bow and offered a florid wave as we passed.

"Welcome to our very own private festive feast," I said, carried along by his positivity.

I wasn't the only one smiling, either. As Billy lit a candle, William whistled 'God Rest Ye Merry Gentlemen', and Bill led us forwards with a spring in his step.

The candle wavered and sputtered, casting its warm light across the gloomy space as best it could. It was strange to be in the dining hall at night. Though I must have eaten there a thousand times, it looked alien to me. I felt like an intrepid explorer, discovering a new land.

"This way, boys," Marmaduke yelled without fear, as he disappeared off into the darkness. By the time we next saw him, he was pulling trays of food from the larder and had a chicken leg between his teeth.

"Delicious," he said in a muffled mumble.

Billy lit more candles around the kitchen and the rest of us helped Marmaduke to assemble the illicit banquet. There were roast potatoes, whole steak and kidney pies, sausage rolls and neatly cut sandwiches. The end-of-term meal was a real treat compared to the slop that Oakton Academy normally served its inmates. Though our new cook was a great deal friendlier than the previous scoundrel, she was no more adept at her profession, and primarily dealt in dubious stews.

We climbed onto the wide wooden table that was usually reserved for preparing food rather than serving it. There was just enough space for the five of us to sit in a circle and, at first, no one spoke. We were too busy filling our hungry stomachs with the goodies in front of us.

"Food always tastes best when it's been pilfered." Marmaduke had lived a far riskier existence than the rest of us, and we giggled like nervous sheep.

"Food always tastes best when I'm the one eating it," Bill added.

"I wish there was cake," was all that I had to contribute to the discussion.

Billy had a huge grin on his face and held a pork chop up to the sky in celebration. "Merry Christmas, gentlemen. May the coming year be our best yet."

"That's a given." Marmaduke laughed before explaining himself. "1926 will be the year we finally leave school."

This led to a roar of conversation as the five of us offered our own thoughts on the matter. We'd been at Oakton since we were little more than infants, and the very idea that there could be a life to look forward to beyond those red-brick walls was thrilling and terrifying in equal measure.

Marmaduke soon produced a bottle of cooking sherry that smelt like vinegar. Pulled along once more by his wild, wicked, though most welcome influence, we all had a glass. It was terrible, but we loved it.

And that is how we spent the final night of the Christmas term. Eating, drinking and talking. Time went both very fast and very slowly. Conversations spiralled around one another before lurching off on incredible tangents and, just as the chapel bell rang for six o'clock, the topic turned to Christmas itself.

"My father always wakes me at the most ridiculous hour on Christmas Day." William rubbed his tired eyes as he spoke. "He gets more excited about the presents than I do."

Bill was lying on his side on the table. "In my family, we spend the whole day eating. From the moment I wake up, there's some sort of pastry shoved into my hand which leads to cake, followed by some sandwiches, then breakfast, elevenses, lunch, afternoon tea, Christmas dinner itself, and any number of delectable treats to round off the proceedings. We rarely get to the task of opening presents until Boxing Day."

"You lucky thing," Billy replied, his eyelids now fully closed. "I have to go to my grandmother's house, and I'm not allowed a morsel to eat before she serves her figgy pudding. Though, I must say… it's worth the wait."

As they talked, I noticed that Marmaduke – who was normally the liveliest of the bunch – had fallen deathly quiet.

"What about you, old chum?" I considered giving him a playful punch on the arm, but was worried he might return it with interest. "What sort of things do you get up to at Chez Adelaide?"

He looked down at the chicken bones and pie crust that remained on his plate, and I doubted he would answer. There was a feeling in the air that I'd said the wrong thing. Billy even opened his eyes a crack to see what was happening.

"Oh, we don't do anything interesting," Marmaduke finally replied in a low murmur. "To tell the truth, I've never been much of a fan of Christmas."

"How is that even possible?" William's voice was run through with shock.

Marmaduke smiled then, as though pretending that the whole thing was rather funny. "It's all right for my sisters. My father spoils them with pretty dresses and all sorts of wonderful gifts…" He fell silent once more and the smile he'd tried so hard to fashion disappeared. "The thing is, my father doesn't seem to like me an awful lot. My reports from school are normally so bad that I'm not allowed any presents, and I almost invariably play some silly trick on my mother. Come the twenty-fifth, I'm lucky if anyone is still talking to me."

We were knocked awake by his confession. Everyone knew the stories of Marmaduke's father's criminal past. I'd crossed paths with the infamous Horatio Adelaide on a number of occasions and the prickly chap made my own sullen father look like a font of love and affection.

We peered about at one another, wondering who could possibly respond to such a sad story. Inevitably, I was the only one stupid enough to try.

"But this year will be different. Don't you think?" I attempted to sound sure of myself. "Your marks haven't been nearly so bad this term, and–"

He must have taken pity on me, as he interrupted before I could ramble on any more. "No. I doubt it will change anything. My father isn't like other people. He'd rather give me a good thrashing than take me fishing or have a conversation. I'm sure he sees the school holidays as a punishment for his past sins. To be perfectly honest, I find that Christmas is the worst time of year to be with him. At least in the summer I can escape outdoors."

I looked around at my friends in the hope that one of them could find a silver lining to tack onto his tragic tale, but they couldn't even meet my gaze.

I racked my brains for something to make it better and then spoke without thinking. "In which case, we must ring in the new year together." I had to swallow then, as I didn't actually have permission to organise such an event at Cranley Hall. It was too late now, though, and I pressed on confidently. "My grandfather's always keen to let his hair down. I think a New Year's Eve celebration will be just his cup of tea."

Marmaduke was instantly cheered by the proposal. "Top notch, I'll bring the punch!"

Two of the Williams were similarly enthused, but Bill crossed his arms and, with a sorrowful sigh revealed, "I'll be at my great-aunt's house in Tunbridge Wells. She looks about one hundred and two. Nobody is allowed to make any noise and we all have to be in bed by nine o'clock. I'm sure there are more festive gaols in Britain than Auntie Sally's house."

"Well, I'll be there," Billy said.

"Me too," William agreed.

"Me three." Marmaduke was all smiles by this point and we raised our glasses to celebrate the season and a plan well made. Now I just had to hope that no one in my family would object.

CHAPTER TWO

There is no happier day on the calendar than the last day of Christmas term. The normally restrained atmosphere of my boarding school was alive with the sound of chirping boys' voices and heavy trunks being lugged downstairs, one crashing bump after another.

Sticking with tradition, my fellow Oaktonians engaged in all sorts of hijinks. Thaddeus de Montfort broke into the new head's office and wished us all a merry Christmas over the Marconi loudspeaker system. Robert Alders launched a small flour bomb across the dining hall, and Derek McGeorge confessed his love to our new matron. Unlike the previous holder of that position – who would surely have locked him in the store cupboard for the holiday as punishment – the smiley lady just laughed, wagged her finger and called him a scamp. The old place had improved a lot in a few short months.

With our final, excruciating lessons completed, and every boy packed and ready to leave, we filed out to the front of the school to be collected by our parents (or their servants). I was sad to have to say goodbye to my pals. We'd become closer than ever since the previously intimidating Marmaduke Adelaide had joined our select group. I was confident I could cope without them for ten days, though, especially when that time would be filled with feasts, games and merriment.

I was expecting to find Todd, my grandfather's chauffer, waiting in the Silver Ghost Rolls Royce, but there was no sign of him. I couldn't help feeling rather forgotten and was just cursing my luck when there was a toot at the end of the long driveway. I raised a hand to my eyes to see a strange vehicle shoot towards me. It looked like a bright orange bullet, flying in reverse.

Grandfather had to beep his horn a good few times more as, evidently, he was worried that people would not notice the near-luminous sports car without this audible clue. I stood in staggered wonder as he pulled to a halt in front of me with a spray of gravel.

"What is that?" I managed to ask.

"A Christmas present to myself." The former superintendent's head wobbled with pride as he spoke.

"I can see that from the bow you've wrapped around the bonnet.

But what is it?"

Somewhat stiffly –he was seventy-five years old, after all – he opened the small, penny-shaped door and stepped out to admire his new toy.

"It's a Hispano Suiza H6C Speedster."

He already had far too many cars, and I was struggling to understand why he'd bought another. "But… where has it come from?"

"Their factory in Paris, obviously." I'd rarely seen him with such a smile on his face, as several boys, and even a few parents, gathered around to admire the spaceship that he'd just landed. "Well, I had the carriagework done here in England to the specifications of Andre Dubonnet's entry into last year's Targa Florio in Sicily."

He might as well have been speaking Mongolian for all this meant to me. In reply, I nodded and said, "It's very… pretty."

This drew a laugh from a few of my classmates, and Lord Edgington looked a little horrified. "Pretty? Did you genuinely just call it pretty?" He actually tutted at me then. "It's not pretty, my boy. It's a torpedo on wheels; a thing of art, beauty and science. The pinnacle of human engineering and craftsmanship, and the result of four European nations working together to–"

He would have continued like that all day if I hadn't interrupted him. "Yes, yes, but it's only got two seats."

He did not see the problem. "Well, racing drivers don't tend to take their families along with them."

"Where is my trunk supposed to go?"

He looked at me, and then at the large box I was still perched on. "Ahh, I see." He considered the issue for a moment, before conceding, "Well… I may not have fully considered the ramifications of bringing such a small automobile to collect you." He clapped his hands together and cheered right back up again. "Not to worry, I'll send Todd to collect it. He's dying to take my new beauty for a spin."

I was overjoyed to see the old chap, but still rather sorry that he would be the one driving. Though our chauffeur was just as much of a car fanatic, he was far more careful on the road than my wild grandfather.

"Come along, Christopher." He tossed me a pair of goggles from the glove compartment – which is never a good sign. "Your mother will be at Cranley soon, and I want to be there when she arrives."

He climbed aboard the capsule-shaped vehicle and I reluctantly did the same. There were several school prefects on duty, so I had every reason to believe that my trunk would be rifled through within minutes.

Grandfather pulled his tan leather gloves on and raised his eyebrows, as though challenging me to be scared. At least he exited the school grounds at a reasonable speed.

"Let me tell you, my boy. I have so many plans for this holiday. Not just for the festivities themselves, but every day until you return to Oakton in the new year."

This was another reason to be afraid. So far that year, my re-energised grandfather – or the Marquess of Edgington, to give him his full title – had thrown a grand ball, taken me up in a hydrogen balloon and charted an elaborate tour across Great Britain (finding any number of corpses and killers along the way). I could only imagine the unique plan he had hatched for our Christmas holiday.

And yet, far from being worried what new dangers he would place me in, I was excited for the coming days.

"It sounds wonderful, Grandfather. "I can't waaaaaaaaaaaaah!" He'd slammed down on the zippy car's accelerator and sent us hurtling along the road.

"This is heaven!" the mad chap screamed over the noise of the growling engine.

"This is hell!" I didn't actually say these words, but you can be sure I was thinking them.

I suppose it was a good thing that my grandfather was a former policeman and knew the officers in our area. As my teacher Mr Arthurs had gone to great pains to explain in my end-of-year report, I'm no whizz at mathematics, but I'm fairly sure that the eighty miles an hour that the speedometer was showing is quite a bit more than the national speed limit of twenty.

There was no sense in pointing out such a minor consideration to my grandfather. He was too busy yelping with unrestrained joy.

"This is the life, my boy! This is the life!"

I'm happy to say that we made it back to Cranley without killing anyone, or ourselves. Admittedly, my hair was frazzled, my heartbeat kept changing between very fast and not at all, and my skin felt like someone had been throwing ice darts at me for the last fifteen minutes, but I was alive… more or less.

When my ancestral home came into view, I wasn't just happy to be home; I was filled with Christmas spirit. The mansion's looming towers looked rather inviting against the dim winter sky. Though not a leaf clung to the trees in Cranley Woods, and no birds flew in the gardens, the scene reminded me of the joys that were to come. Even on the darkest days, the wondrous estate, which I had spent so much of my childhood exploring, exuded a warmth that made it the perfect place to pass the holiday with my family.

"I'm terribly sad and I don't want to talk to anyone," my brother informed me as soon as he arrived. Grandfather had left me at the front of the house while he parked his ridiculously fast car in the garage.

"Now, now, Albert." Our dear mother is the best in the family at healing wounds, both physical and emotional. "We've discussed this. You promised that you wouldn't darken our time here with your bad mood."

He cast a scornful look at her as Halfpenny, our ancient footman, and Big Dorie, our new maid-cum-weightlifter unloaded their bags. "I'm not in a *bad mood*, Mother. My heart is broken!"

My brother was forever having his heart broken, and it was phenomenally difficult for me to remember which young lady he was in love with at any given moment.

"I thought you'd got over Evie," I said, in the hope of clarification.

"It wasn't Evie!" He crashed down on the running board of our father's Bentley.

"Izzy then?"

"No." He really did look depressed, even for him. "Her name is Bessie, and I don't want to talk about it." There was a moment's silence as he looked between my mother and me, clearly hoping that one of us would persuade him to do just that.

"It's so wonderful to see you, Chrissy," she declared, and we ignored my sulky brother. She gave me a brief embrace and stood back to look at me. "I think you've grown."

"Mummy!"

"No, really. I'm certain that you're taller than the last time I saw you."

I didn't see how this could be true and told her just that. "You came here to visit less than a month ago. You can't possibly notice any difference."

"You're becoming quite the handsome gentleman."

I was probably blushing by then. Mother is a genius at making me feel better about the world.

"Bessie said that I was handsome, before she ripped my heart out with her bare hands and…" Unable to produce any crocodile tears for our benefit, Albert looked distraught, then ran into the house.

"Don't worry about him, darling." My mother took another moment to smooth down my hair after my harrowing journey. "Your brother will be fine as soon as the family is gathered, and he sees there are plenty of presents to open. He's just like a toddler; he needs something to distract him and then he'll be as right as rain."

I laughed at this and felt jolly wonderful to be in my home from home. Sadly, my good spirits didn't last long. Walking into the house, I noticed a distinct lack of festive decoration. The ballroom, dining room and salons (both petit and grand) looked just as they always did. There was not a stick of holly or a sprig of mistletoe to be seen.

"It's the twenty-second of December," I complained. "Why does it still look so gloomy in here?" I was marching up and down the long corridor in the western wing, hoping that if I peered into enough rooms, one of them would offer up the wonderland in which I had pictured myself spending Christmas.

"Do calm down, boy," Grandfather said, just as my favourite maid appeared with an envelope for him. "Ah, jolly good. I'll open this in the library. I do so love receiving Christmas cards." Without another glance in my direction – or an explanation for why he had failed in his duties to provide an impressionable young chap with a suitably cosy environment to pass the Christmas season – he turned and fled.

Lovely Irish Alice looked far more sympathetic to my plight than my grandfather, and it was at this moment I formed a resolution.

"All right, this simply won't do. We can't have Christmas without decorations and, at the very least, a tree. Alice, I'm terribly sorry to order you about as though I have any influence in this house, but there comes a time in a man's life when he has to take stock of the important–"

I was rambling and so she interrupted me. "What is it I can do for you, Master Christopher?"

She'd thrown me a little, but I soon found my train of thought. "Right… Yes… Good. Or rather, no, it's not good. You must collect up every last member of staff who isn't otherwise far too busy and follow me to the gardens."

I turned on my heel and marched off towards the kitchen like a soldier heading to the wars. I walked along that near-endless corridor and the strangest thing occurred. Servants seemed to pop out of every door we passed. Having finished his previous task, Halfpenny fell into step with me, a few younger maids got their instructions from Alice and joined the back of the parade and even our part-time butler, a normally most contrary fellow, was willing to heed my demands. It made me feel quite grown up, I can tell you.

"Where do you think you're going?" I asked our chauffeur once I'd navigated our way through the kitchens and outside to the old barn where Grandfather kept his ever-expanding collection of luxury cars.

"I'm off to Oakton to pick up your trunk, Master Christopher."

"The trunk can wait. We have more important business to discuss." The power had evidently gone to my head; I was barking out orders in all directions by this point. "I'm sure you're terribly overworked at this time of year, but I really must insist that we head to the woods and collect all the holly, ivy, pine branches and mistletoe we can find. We're going to transform Cranley Hall."

Surprisingly, they all seemed rather inspired by my announcement and chattered amongst themselves as we made our way onwards. The gardeners, Danny and Driscoll, had joined us and our battalion was ready for battle. Even Grandfather's dear golden retriever had given up her spot on the hearth in the kitchen to brave the cold and was jumping and barking at my heels.

When we arrived at the woods, I put big Dorie in charge of uprooting a pine tree, while I helped the servants pull up long chains of ivy from the forest floor. Driscoll, the head gardener, had cleverly brought some secateurs with him and cut down any number of holly branches covered in bright red berries. Todd, meanwhile, climbed the bare apple trees in the orchard to harvest sprigs of mistletoe.

"I've always found mistletoe ever so romantic," one of the younger maids exclaimed, looking up at the strapping chauffeur.

"It's poisonous if you swallow it, mind," he replied, apparently oblivious to her batted eyelids and mooning expression.

With the work done and our arms laden, we hurried back to the house, eager to engage with the next stage of my stunning plan.

"Should I drive to your school to collect your trunk now, sir?" Todd asked, and an idea occurred to me.

"That's right. And, on your way, stop at the florist in St Mary-under-Twine to order some Christmas roses."

He stopped walking and looked a little doubtful. "How many should I buy?"

"Oh, I'd say… half a field?"

He did not show much confidence in my judgement. "With all due respect, Master Christopher, you do remember what happened the last time you ordered flowers? The house was full to bursting."

"Ah, yes. You're probably right. Perhaps it would be wise to ask the florist how many she'd recommend."

Suitably reassured, he strode off ahead, and the rest of us nattered and joked on the way back to the house. Dorie lugged the tree over her shoulder like it was a twig, and we could barely see Driscoll for the number of holly branches he was carrying.

Once inside, we spent the afternoon making Cranley Hall's state rooms look suitably seasonal. The smell of pine needles and sap mingled with the scent of advent candles and the brandy my brother had poured to drink away his sorrows. He sat in the corner of the ballroom feeling sorry for himself and occasionally letting out an anguished moan as the staff and I worked our magic.

I was terribly happy when Mother appeared with fine Bohemian glass ornaments to decorate the tree. There were angels and kings, stars and mangers and they sparkled in the light of the grand chandelier. When the work was complete, and I could stand back to admire a job well done, the kitchen staff begged a visit. Two at a time, as there was so much work to do getting everything ready for the weeks of feasting ahead, they joined their colleagues to marvel at the scene we'd set in the dining room, the two salons and ballroom.

"You've worked wonders, Master Christopher," Cook told me, and I blushed as red as a robin.

"What on earth is all this for?" Grandfather did not sound quite so pleased when he appeared soon after.

"Well… it's Christmas," I replied, as I really couldn't fathom what he'd failed to understand. "Don't you like it?"

He reflected on this for a moment, then showed his softer side with a brief smile. "No, no. It's rather lovely in fact. Only…"

Seeing that he was struggling to express himself, my mother went over to the doorway to ensure that he was not having some sort of medical dilemma. "What is it, Father? Is something the matter?"

He burst out laughing then. "I'm so sorry, I really am. You've all done such a wonderful job and Cranley hasn't looked so festive in a decade. But…" He laughed guiltily once more. "But, I'm afraid we won't be staying here for Christmas after all."

CHAPTER THREE

"It's rather late notice, don't you think?" Even my mother looked upset with him.

At least it gave Albert a chance to show how grumpy he was. "That's typical. Not only have I had my every last romantic fibre ripped from my body by an unfeeling succubus, now we have to head out into the cold to spend Christmas in some distant foreign realm."

"You know," Grandfather replied somewhat pensively, "I'm not sure that Gloucestershire counts as a 'foreign realm.'"

I was secretly hoping his announcement might mean we could avoid spending Boxing Day at my grandmother's house, but I would have no such luck.

"It's only until Christmas Eve," he continued, having evidently read my mind. "And I very much doubt you'll be cold where we're going. Old Ollie Mountfalcon normally throws a good shindig. His house up in the Cotswolds really is the jolliest place to be at this time of year."

"Who's Ollie Mountfalcon?" I felt I should ask, when no one else did.

"Lord Oliver Mountfalcon?" he replied, as though this would explain everything. "He was my commissioner for a long time in the Metropolitan Police. Jovial chap, I've always been fond of him. We usually exchange Christmas cards, but this year he's sent me an invitation to a party at Mistletoe Hall."

"Mistletoe Hall?" Albert sighed. "Is this some kind of joke? Are you trying to underline the paucity of kisses I will be receiving this year?"

Grandfather was suddenly animated and, swishing his amethyst-topped cane through the air, sauntered further into the room. The servants had left us by this point, in that almost preternaturally discreet manner they had.

"I thought you'd be excited. I fired off a letter to him as soon as I received his card. He's promised a veritable celebration. I doubt we'll be the only ones there. Who knows, there may even be some young ladies invited."

This made Albert sit up. He took a sip of his brandy and straightened his posture. "Well, I suppose if you've accepted the invitation, there's not much I can do about it."

"That's the spirit." Grandfather tried to inject some enthusiasm into my brother's really very half-hearted support for the plan.

Mother still looked a little concerned. "Will we be going to Trevelyan Place to meet the rest of the family for Christmas Day, as usual?"

My Uncle Gregor's house was almost as big as Cranley and, though he and his wife were now deceased, we were sticking to tradition and spending Christmas there with our many million distant relatives.

"Yes, and you can go on to meet Walter's family as planned the next day." Grandfather had done a good job of reassuring my mother and disappointing me. My paternal grandmother was something of a monster and I was not looking forward to spending yet another Boxing Day being told that I mustn't have any more pudding or that I looked rounder than ever.

"Well, I am fond of dear Ollie Mountfalcon." Mother attempted a smile and then muttered to herself as she bustled off. "I'll have to ring the City to explain the change of plans."

The old lord waited until his daughter had left before toddling over to me with a wicked look on his face. "It will be just like it was in the summer, eh, boy? You and I on the road, on a course set for adventure – with plenty of staff in tow. I simply cannot wait to depart!"

I think I might have turned a shade of green previously only spotted on parrots and people suffering from severe anaemia. The thought of sitting beside my ancient forebear as we navigated one hundred miles of icy roads in his four-wheel rocket did not bear contemplating.

"I believe it might snow," he added, as though this would make me any more enthusiastic about getting in a car with him. "We'll be leaving first thing."

I camped out in the kitchen for the rest of the day, as the news had left me feeling rather cold. There was nowhere in Cranley quite so toasty as Cook's kingdom below stairs. Dorie's sister, our equally massive new scullery maid, was forever dropping things and getting in the others' way, but the staff still managed to produce several sweet-smelling desserts whilst I was there. Delilah sat on my feet to keep me even warmer, and I luxuriated in the smell of cinnamon, cloves and several types of fruit, which were macerating in a bowl alongside me.

I nodded off into peaceful oblivion as I read 'A Christmas Carol'. Charles Dickens wasn't to blame, of course. I was simply so comfortable there it would have taken a man of far greater mental fortitude to resist. I doubt that even my worthy grandfather would have managed it.

The problem with going away was that, having just returned to Cranley, I was required to pack once more. After a dinner of traditional braised pork with, far less traditional, spiced chicken hearts – another of our cook's more experimental combinations – I spent the evening in my room, organising clothes to take for the trip. I'm not the most decisive person and, after an hour struggling to choose between slippers and loafers, plaid and checks, I ended up taking five of everything in my wardrobe.

Come the morning, I was rather looking forward to our winter voyage. No snow had fallen overnight, but a pure white frost had consumed the Cranley estate. Every bush, tree and blade of grass had been repainted in time for Christ's birthday and the world itself looked as though it had been reborn.

Out at the front of the property, Delilah was barking and running around in circles. Nothing made her quite so happy as when we were setting off on a journey. She was a puppy once more.

The only regret I had was that I would not be at home to receive a Christmas card from a certain young lady to whom I may or may not have been writing on a weekly basis for the last few months. A fortnight had passed since I'd heard from her, and I just had to hope that the recipe for mince pies I'd sent wasn't in some way insulting. I must admit, I was unfamiliar with the best way to woo one's paramour and now felt terribly concerned that I had hobbled our relationship before it had begun.

"This is the stuff." Grandfather clapped his hands together as he caught sight of the impressive convoy in which we would be travelling. "This is the very stuff indeed."

Very little of his body was visible, shrouded as it was by several thick, woollen scarves over motorist's leathers. His eyes peeked out through his goggles and he wore a deerstalker on his head to complete the outfit. If he hadn't spoken, I may not have recognised him.

Cook and Dorie were already packed into Halfpenny's Austin Twenty. Though it may have been an 'all-weather' coupé, I can't say I would have chosen to travel in such a draughty contraption in the cold of December. My mother and brother were far more comfortable in the royal blue Rolls Royce. With Todd behind the wheel in his full chauffeur's livery, and a thick fur blanket over their laps, they looked perfectly content in the back of the plush limousine.

I was just about to join them when my grandfather spoke again.

"Come along, boy, we'll take the Aston Martin."

I ignored him and walked in the other direction as, though perfectly pleasant to drive in the summer, the sporty grey vehicle barely had a roof. He did not agree with my choice and placed his hand on my shoulder to correct my course.

"Mother! Save me, mother!" I screamed, as I tried to wriggle free from his surprisingly forceful grip. "I won't survive another journey with Grandfather at the wheel. At best I'll freeze to death."

She apparently didn't hear me, or pretended that she hadn't, and waved through the window before the stately vehicle pulled way.

"I don't know what you're complaining about, Chrissy," the old man said as he tugged me, still kicking, towards the drophead sports car.

"You wouldn't. You're dressed up like some sort of highland sheep that's impervious to the cold. You'll still be smiling long after my blood freezes."

"Stuff and nonsense," he said, and I'm sure I detected a faint laugh in his voice. "If anything, with the roof in place, we'll be too hot."

The one saving grace was that Delilah had jumped aboard before me and warmed the cold leather upholstery. The downside of this was that she refused to move over to the dickey seat, and so I was fairly certain that I would have her ever-so-active tail whipping against my face for the next three hours.

To my amazement, the old man's prediction came true. Once the three of us were inside the vehicle, it was remarkably warm. The windscreen lived up to its name and protected us from the harsh weather, and Delilah was her very own heating element. In fact, the windows soon became steamed up, which meant we had to engage in a never-ending cycle of opening the flaps in the roof and closing them again whenever it got too cold. I can tell you, there was not a dull minute the whole way there.

We shot past Guildford and out of Surrey before driving on to Windsor, Henley and Oxford. Of course, Grandfather could have simply taken the new A-road north of Newbury, but he insisted on "seeing what this remarkable county has to offer three courageous voyagers on a winter's morning."

He was in an exceedingly talkative mood. Not only did he regale me with the story of a number of old cases from his days working as a bobby in London, he even cast his mind back to his childhood. "Christmas was very different in the Victorian age, you know?"

I assumed this was a rhetorical question but, when he hadn't continued after ten long seconds, I prepared an answer. "No, I–"

"I was born halfway through the last century. In 1850 would you believe it?" This time I was sure it was rhetorical and kept my mouth bolted shut. "And though the last twenty-five years have broken down social barriers like nothing that came before, I grew up in a thoroughly Victorian household. My parents were typical of their age. They only had children out of a duty to Queen and country. On the odd occasion I was in their presence, they looked at me as though someone had let one of the hunting hounds into the house by mistake."

"Thank goodness my parents are nothing like yours. I know I don't get to see much of my father these days, but Mother can always be relied upon to make up the shortfall."

"And the reason for that, young Christopher…" He raised one finger and looked at me keenly. I rather wished he would keep his eyes on the road. "…is that she is my daughter."

I wasn't sure what this fact implied, but he soon continued speaking. "The one period of the year when my parents seemed to enjoy having children was Christmastime. We'd get excited about it by the end of October, and it wasn't just the presents we would anticipate, oh no. It was the games and the feasts, the decorations and songs of the season."

His voice caught a note of sadness then, and his pace slowed. "More than anything, though, it was being together. When the four of us ate dinner as a family, my brother and I were actually allowed to speak. It was the only time when I didn't feel like an expensive curiosity for my parents to take out and display. It was the only time I can remember when I really felt loved by them."

As he finished his account, his tone became increasingly hushed. It faded out into silence and it took me a good minute before I felt confident enough to put a question of my own to him.

"So what happened after Christmas? With your parents, I mean."

He glanced at me, as though all the explanation he needed was there on my face. "The sherry would wear off, the two of them would recover from their brief spate of joy and they'd readopt their normal frosty demeanours. It was quite dramatic to see the change, in fact; a true wonder of nineteenth century society. They were Fezziwig one day and Scrooge the next." He motioned to the book by my side, which I hadn't opened since we'd entered the car. "But the glow of that magical period would stay with us through the year."

I often dream that I could have seen Charles Dickens performing one of his readings on the London stage, but I can't imagine he would have been any greater a raconteur than my beloved grandfather. The way the old man spun his tales, so that people and places danced about in my mind, was surely quite Dickensian, and I was hungry to hear his next story.

There was another plot unfolding, however, as we travelled north-west past fields, forests and villages. The weather had deteriorated. The frost had made way for slush, which soon became snow, and Grandfather had to slow his rapid vehicle to avoid skidding off the road. The further we drove from Cranley, the colder it got and the thicker the ashen dusting upon the trees and buildings became.

I thought, perhaps, that Albert's prediction wasn't too far off the mark after all. This really was a foreign realm to me; an older, quieter place, filled with the memory of our pagan past and the nineteen hundred Christmases that had occurred there. Even the towns on the road signs sounded different from the names I was used to at home. I saw Lower Slaughter, Milton-under-Wychwood and Temple Guiting, all of which made me wonder whether the pagans had ever left.

And, just as these thoughts became manifest, Grandfather was forced to stop the car. It was not for the snow, which lay about in high banks on either side of us, but for a parade of cloaked, singing figures who had occupied the road.

Though gone midday, we'd reached a particularly dark spot in a tunnel of trees and the procession before us was illuminated by candles. The most remarkable thing about the scene, though, was what the carollers wore on their heads. It took me a moment to understand what I was seeing, but, sure enough, the slowly shuffling individuals were adorned with crowns of mistletoe.

"It's a local festival," Grandfather explained. "This region has been associated with mistletoe for centuries. They have auctions for the stuff at the beginning of December and, at some point, this procession grew out of it."

I didn't respond, but raised the canvas flap that functioned as the car's side window and listened to the mournful song they were singing.

> **"Herod the king, in his raging,**
> **Chargèd he hath this day**
> **His men of might in his own sight**
> **All young children to slay."**

Delilah let out a tuneful howl to join in with their hymn.

I must admit, I've always found the 'Coventry Carol' to be one of the most frightening songs associated with an otherwise joyous time of year. It's all murdered infants and rivers of blood and, in a rare feat for a Christmas carol, manages to be both horrifying and depressing at the same time. Hearing it there in the eerie darkness did nothing to dispel this sensation.

Grandfather gently revved his engine to get the singers' attention. One young woman, her green velvet cloak wrapped around her against the cold, glanced back at us, but the others continued their slow, sorrowful journey undisturbed.

"What exactly are they doing?" I eventually had to ask, but Grandfather seemed just as affected by the moment as I was and took his time to reply.

"I suppose, in a way, it's a kind of prayer. Ollie told me about the tradition once, but I don't remember the details. I believe they crown one of the young women as the queen of Mistletoe, but first and foremost, they walk from the village here up to the crest of the hill and light a beacon to welcome the coming season."

"It gives me the willies," I admitted, and, with a slight shudder, Grandfather nodded.

When the space opened, and his moment arrived, he drove us around the parade and back into the light.

The next village we came to was called Snowshill, which I thought rather appropriate. It was little more than a hamlet of forty houses, each built in the same Cotswold stone as every other picturesque parish we had passed through for the last hour. The sun had come out to illuminate the brilliant white on the roofs of the houses and the rising hills in the distance. It was a lovely little place that was almost bright enough to wipe away the memory of the macabre procession we had witnessed.

In fact, I was really most content when Grandfather pulled the car off the road on the outskirts of the town.

"This is as far as we go," he told me, and jumped from the vehicle before I could ask why.

CHAPTER FOUR

Leaving our warm bubble within the car reminded me just how cold the outside world was. Despite the pale light that reflected off the snow, the air was humid and sharp at the same time. The snow was up to my knees in places and a sign on the path told me that we'd arrived at Mistletoe Hall. How we would complete the final part of our journey was anyone's guess.

"The house is a good mile down this road." Grandfather did not manage to sound too cheerful on the matter. "I'd imagined there would be someone here to greet us, or that they'd have cleared the path at least. Never mind, I'm sure we'll find a way through."

I didn't have his confidence and could see that the snow drifts were even deeper up ahead. Luckily, I wasn't the one who needed to solve this problem and, in the end, help came from an unexpected source.

"Woof," Delilah said, and then she said it again in case she hadn't made herself clear. "Woof."

She'd run off into the snow, but now peeked her head back out to explain where she'd gone.

"Oh, you clever beast." Grandfather beamed with pride as he realised what his hound had discovered. "The stables! Of course!"

Delilah disappeared once more, and it was something of a sight to see my seventy-five-year-old grandfather go bounding after her.

"But it's cold and wet," I complained to no one.

I soon gave in and traced the wise old fool's footsteps through the snow. I was glad that I did as, on arriving at the rickety barn which was hidden behind a copse of trees, I encountered quite the most magnificent sight.

"I knew that Ollie wouldn't let us down." Grandfather rubbed his hands together, his eyes as wide as any child's on Christmas morning.

As Delilah ran up and down the barn with pure elation writ large on her face, Grandfather seized a handful of hay from an open bale to feed the two snow-white geldings in their pen. On the other side of the dusty old space was a sleigh that wouldn't have looked out of place in the sky on Christmas Eve.

"What a strange thing to possess in England." I couldn't help giggling at the sight of it. "You'd be lucky to get five days of use out of it in any given year."

Lord Edgington laughed too, his fervour still burning brightly on his face. "Yes, but you don't know Ollie. You see, he's a collector."

I was hoping he might expand on this point. Instead, he nodded to himself, then shook his head, then nodded once more as though he couldn't believe what he was seeing. "You'll find out about that soon enough, my boy. For now, we must hitch up the horses. Then we'll return to the car to load our bags and head to the house. We can come back later for the others when they arrive."

I could tell he would enjoy the challenge that his friend had apparently set him, and he immediately got to work. I know as much about horses as I do about cars, which is to say, not very much at all. I stroked Snowy and Sherbet (I thought the names I chose were rather perfect for them) while he sought out reins and harnesses and several pieces of apparatus I couldn't begin to describe. One was a yoke, maybe? Who's to say?

Working with his usual vim and concentration, he soon wrangled the horses over to the sleigh and connected everything for our journey.

"I haven't been on one of these since I was a young man. It used to snow a lot more back then. This is nothing compared to the winter of 1875. There was snow on the ground for months and something like this would have come in very handy indeed."

He was already climbing on the sleigh, whereas Delilah looked like she wanted to stretch her legs after all those hours in the car. He held his gloved hand down to me and I climbed aboard for the two horses to lurch forward into the snow. Despite his enthusiasm, it did not seem as though my grandfather had the first idea about how to steer such a contraption and so, rather than stopping off at the car first, Snowy and Sherbet instinctively turned left onto the long track towards the manor house.

"Oh, well…" He did not seem flustered. "It can't be helped. We can send someone back for the luggage later on, I suppose."

Delilah yelped and bounced about in the snow. Much like her master, she was getting on in life, but still had the heart of a much younger animal. As the snow got thicker, even she struggled to keep up with the sleigh and she finally jumped on board. With the extensive tunnel she'd made through the frosty layer, we might not have seen her for days otherwise.

We eventually took a diagonal bend through the woods and Mistletoe Hall came into view. The path was lined with beech trees which had been decorated with a thick coating of frost and snow, so that little of the foliage underneath was visible. As the wind caught them, they seemed to wave us onwards towards the house.

And what a house it was! Though minute in comparison to Cranley Hall's palatial splendour, the manor before me was a singularly welcoming sight. Constructed from red bricks that burned bright against the white landscape, it was quite the most festive abode in which to spend our holiday.

Despite my quiet wonder at the place, there was something a little odd about it, too. Out there in the wilderness of a snowy forest, it was as though it had been misplaced and its rightful owner would be along at any moment to collect it.

It was just then that I noticed a clear discrepancy. "Where's all the mistletoe?" I couldn't see a single twig of the stuff in the high, bare trees and, to be perfectly honest, I felt rather swindled.

"I beg your pardon?"

"It's called Mistletoe Hall. Why isn't there any mistletoe in the forest?"

He had a good laugh at his naïve grandson. "Mistletoe prefers light, open spaces. It doesn't tend to grow in woodland." I was about to complain that this was really very unfair, when he spoke again to reassure me. "Don't worry, Christopher. If it's poisonous parasitic plants you're after, there'll be no end of the stuff in the orchard behind the house."

This made me feel a little better and, as it turned out, we wouldn't have to wait long. Snowy and Sherbet trotted along with great determination and soon deposited at the front door. We climbed the front steps and rang the bell to await the no doubt warm welcome that was well overdue.

But… nothing. Not a sound came from the house, and the door remained firmly shut. With a whinny, Snowy and Sherbet made a wide circle in the clearing and returned to the stable before we could do anything about it.

"Where could everyone be?" Grandfather sounded more concerned about our hosts than the errant horses.

"Perhaps they've gone into the village?" I suggested.

Grandfather glanced around the front of the building and then back along the path. "That's a nice simple answer, but there are no tracks of any kind except our own. We'd surely have seen some sign of life if that were the case. The snow was fresh last night."

I was tempted to ask how he could tell fresh snow from any other, but I'd long since learnt that, even at his most enigmatic, my grandfather normally knows what's what.

A rush of bravery surged up within me, and I threw caution to the wind. Well, I opened the door at least. I turned the large brass handle, and to my surprise, it wasn't locked.

My lordly companion sent forth his stentorian voice into the bowels of the house. "Hello… Ollie?" I'm fairly certain he had a special tone that he reserved for just such occasions. It was both deeper and more commanding than normal and it echoed back to us as we stepped inside. "Commissioner Mountfalcon? It's Superintendent Edgington, as summoned."

The hall we now entered certainly looked as though it was ready for guests. A kissing bough was hanging over the threshold and the bannisters leading upstairs were decorated with ivy, holly and the odd satin bow. This was good news, as I didn't think I had the energy to decorate yet another house for Christmas.

While this was my first thought, my second was, *what an unusual place!* Every wall in the room was lined with glass cases which were stuffed to the brim with, well… ummm… things.

"I imagine you understand what I mean now about Lord Mountfalcon being a collector."

I walked a little closer to inspect the first cabinet. Each shelf was piled with toys of varying antiquity and design. One large space held forty different dolls' heads. Another displayed small wind-up devices, of the sort a child might purchase on Brighton pier. There were brightly coloured carousels, steamboats and swings, all with their keys in place, waiting to be enjoyed.

"It's rather creepy," I muttered, as my grandfather wandered off along the corridor.

"That's nothing," he called back to me. "Come and see this."

I must say that it was with some trepidation that I approached him. "Well, what do you think?"

I had come to an absolute stop as I gazed around a ballroom filled with quite the most unusual scene I could have imagined. There were twenty-six of them – I know because I counted. Twenty-six terrifying figures, and every last one was staring at me with the most intimidating expression on their masked faces.

"Aren't they wonderful?" Grandfather whistled through his teeth as he wondered at these otherworldly artefacts.

"What in heavens are they?"

He tutted and walked over to inspect the nearest figure. "They're samurais, boy. Japanese warriors. Well, the ceremonial armour that once belonged to them, at least. You'll be happy to know that there's no one inside."

Behind my back – so that he couldn't see and call me superstitious – I crossed my fingers that he was telling the truth. Though the costumes appeared to be hollow, I was sure that someone could have hidden inside one without our knowing. Many had curved swords at the ready over their heads, while others bowed at the waist, as if addressing a master. To a man, they were deeply disturbing.

"That's Ollie for you," he said with affection. "After he retired from the force, he travelled around the world and sent back countless treasures and keepsakes to be displayed here in the hall upon his return. What a hero he really is. Now, if we could only find him."

I thought I heard the sound of distant bells just then and ran to see who would be joining us. Coming around the bend, halfway along the track, was Todd, with Mother and Albert behind him on the sleigh. He was on his feet, with the reins in one hand, urging on the gallant steeds. It made me wonder how anyone could be more capable than our spirited chauffeur. Driving, fishing, charming young ladies, and now sleigh riding; I'd yet to find a talent he hadn't mastered. My grandfather was impressive with his ability to solve crimes and whatnot, but Todd had a style of his own that made me want to be just like him.

I suppose it was no wonder that the girl who'd captured my heart that summer hadn't written to me. With gents like Todd about, what chance would a podgy boy with no apparent abilities have of winning fair maiden?

"Darling!" my equally fair mother beamed when Todd brought them to a stop in front of the house. "Isn't this place wonderful?"

Albert was still moping. "It's all right, I suppose. Though it doesn't look like there are any pretty young ladies here. Grandfather promised me young ladies."

Mother fussed over her elder son before Todd helped them down onto the front steps of the property to avoid the worst of the snow.

"It's not just ladies that are missing," I informed them. "It looks as though the place is empty. Grandfather is conducting a search."

As I said this, an upstairs window flew open, snow showered down upon my head and the old chap looked out. "There's not a soul to be found. I simply don't understand what could have happened."

"Have we perhaps come on the wrong day?" His daughter put forward this suggestion. "I did think it odd that he would invite you at the last minute."

Grandfather was scanning the tree tops for signs of… actually, I haven't the faintest idea what he was looking for. Smoke signals?

"That's because you don't know Ollie as I do. He's always been spontaneous. I remember when he turned up at Cranley Hall at ten to twelve on New Year's Eve one year. He had a crate of champagne and an omnibus full of revellers with him. He hadn't thought to telegram ahead and didn't even know whether I was home. My great-aunt Hortensia got a real shock, I can tell you."

"There must have been someone here recently though," I said, pointing through the front window to a sitting room we were yet to enter. "The embers in the fire are still glowing."

"How puzzling." Grandfather had vanished from his vantage point before the words were out of his mouth, and I listened as he crashed around upstairs in search of some clue as to our host's location.

In the meantime, we retreated from the cold into the warm surrounds of Mistletoe Hall and I settled down with Delilah beside the still toasty fire. The room was perfect for the season, with deep burgundy walls and pine-green curtains, sofas and chairs. It was also less cluttered than the other spaces I'd seen. There were shelves on one wall, but the weapons, busts and figurines that were on them were spaced out more freely. It looked less like a rag and bone man's yard and more like a typical gentleman's salon.

Grandfather finally joined us, his face streaked with concern.

"There are signs all over the house that someone's been here, and yet I can't find Ollie or any staff." It was a rare moment when the superlative detective displayed a hint of fear. "I am truly mystified."

CHAPTER FIVE

Todd set about getting the house ready for the arrival of the rest of the staff. I decided to investigate more of Lord Mountfalcon's esoteric collection, and Albert found a comfy armchair in which to have a good sob.

It wasn't long before the final car arrived and the well-trained horses transported our staff to the house. Sadly, no one thought of tying the pretty beasts up again before they could run back to their stables.

"Stop," I shouted past our footman, Halfpenny, who instantly froze on the spot. "No, stop the horses from getting away. We'll be stuck here otherwise."

He quickly turned around and, as he was rather a decrepit fellow, simply collapsed into the snow. Big Dorie charged over to tug him back up by the collar, as though he weighed less than a china doll.

"My apologies, Master Christopher," he said as he brushed the snow from his face. "But perhaps someone will be along soon to join us."

I didn't like our chances, especially as the snow had started falling once more and the visibility was almost non-existent. It would be dark before long and, if I wasn't nervous enough already, that was sure to set me on edge.

"You're probably right," I lied. "There's bound to be someone. Grandfather made it sound as though there would be more guests for the party at least."

This seemed to make the old chap feel better, and our cheery cook, Henrietta, put her arm through his to go looking for the kitchens.

"I knew it would come in handy to bring so many servants with us." Grandfather had stuck his head out of another sash window on the first floor of the house; he sounded quite smug.

Todd and Dorie carted the rest of the luggage in from the sleigh – much of which appeared to be made up of food hampers and boxes of utensils. Cook had brought half her kitchen with her. She clearly held to a similar philosophy as my grandfather and came prepared for any eventuality.

With the staff hard at work, my family and I settled down in the sitting room to enjoy our respective tomes. Mother was reading the poems of Christina Rossetti for the thousandth time, Grandfather had a huge, thick book with a Latin title I couldn't decipher and I'd reached the third ghost in Dickens' tale.

"Excuse me, Lord Edgington," Todd said upon entering. "I believe I've solved one part of the mystery." He held out a piece of folded paper. "I found it on a desk in the servants' quarters. I imagine that all the staff would have received one."

Grandfather perused the note for a moment, without giving away any hint of what it might mean. His face still inscrutable, he passed it on to me, his designated assistant.

> **Dear Cook,**
>
> **My uncle has asked me to inform you that your services will not be required over the Christmas holiday, as I am coming to stay. I have enclosed a £2 bonus in honour of your untiring service and wish you the very merriest of Christmases.**
>
> **Sincerely,**
>
> **Milly Bowen**

"Was there an envelope?" he asked our designated jack of all trades.

"Yes, M'Lord." The wily chap had kept his hand behind his back this whole time and now produced the second piece of evidence for my grandfather to examine. "I found it in the wastepaper basket in the same room."

"Excellent work, Todd. Truly excellent." Lord Edgington paused to examine the stamp and post marks. "There's only one problem with this. The last I heard, Ollie Mountfalcon's remaining family lived in South Africa. This letter was clearly sent from London."

"She could be here visiting for the holiday," I suggested – as it's generally my job to come to the wrong conclusion in our investigations.

"I very much doubt it. Ollie hadn't talked to anyone on that side of the family in thirty years. He fell out with his brother over their parents' will. And, more importantly, why would his niece write a letter to the staff here and not come to see them in person?"

42

"Maybe she… Perhaps if…" I didn't actually have an answer to his question.

"And why wouldn't Ollie have told them himself?"

Todd's far smarter than me and had something useful to add. "Isn't it rather strange that the staff would disappear like that without their boss telling them in person, M'Lord?"

Grandfather looked up at the smart chap. "I suppose that the money and some extra time off at Christmas would have ensured that they didn't raise a fuss."

"So now all we need to work out is where Lord Mountfalcon could have gone. It's a mystery within a mystery." I thought this sounded rather clever. Or, at least, I hope it did.

"Well put, my boy." Grandfather took the note back from me and read it through once more.

"Can you learn anything from the handwriting, Grandfather?"

"Hmmm… graphology is an art form in itself, and one in which I do not entirely believe. I refuse to accept that we can determine a suspect's gender or age from the way they hold a pen. I've met forgers who could make you believe that Queen Victoria had risen from the dead to write Prince Albert a Christmas card. Still, it's an interesting concept."

I noticed that he hadn't answered my question, so took this as a *no*. He faded out of the room, transfixed by the simple note in his hand. Todd took his leave, and I heard the horses clipping through the snow again, with their bells a-jingling, and decided to follow him out.

"Inspector Blunt?" I shouted with more than a hint of surprise in my voice as I spotted the sullen officer on the sleigh.

"Christopher Prentiss? What are you doing here?"

"I was about to ask you the same thing."

Inspector Blunt had assisted (if that's the word for it) on a number of our investigations that year and I had come to know him as, well… a bit of a grump, actually. I waited for him to arrive so that we didn't need to strain our voices any more than we already had.

"As it happens, I was invited by Commissioner Mountfalcon." The frozen chap informed me once he'd disembarked. He fished about in the satchel over his shoulder and produced a card with a pretty picture of a coach and horses riding through a snowy night-time scene. "Awfully gratified I was that he'd even think of asking me to his Christmas party.

To be perfectly honest, I never expected the Commissioner of the Metropolitan Police to remember a lowly inspector such as myself."

"Blunt?" My grandfather must have heard our new arrival as the downstairs window was once more pushed open and he poked his head out to interrogate his former subordinate. "Why in his right mind would Lord Mountfalcon have invited you?"

"Oh, that's charming, that is." Blunt was not amused. He wiped the layer of snow from his shiny bald head and threw it towards the house. I can't imagine why he'd set off from home without a hat. "I thought I was coming for a luxurious stay in the country with fine conversation and even better food. I did not picture myself locked up here with you lot."

The two men had served in the police together, but to say that Blunt was no fan of former Superintendent Edgington was an understatement.

My grandfather, meanwhile, was at least a touch more magnanimous. "Oh, put a cork in it, man, and come in for a drink. There's no sense in us screaming our heads off and ruining the holiday for everyone else. How about a Christmas truce?"

Blunt shook off his long mac and considered the proposal. "What sort of tipple have you got for me?"

"Cook is preparing some mulled wine as we speak." Sensing that this wasn't enough to convince the man, Grandfather upped his offer. "And I've brought a rather nice Glenturret Scotch you might enjoy."

In his usual ungrateful manner, Blunt seemed reluctant to accept, but finally went with, "It had better be a good year."

"It's vintage, man. What do you take me for?"

Blunt finally allowed himself a smile. "I wouldn't like to say with the boy present."

My grandfather wasn't one for self-deprecation, but even he had to laugh at this. "All right, you've said your piece. Come in out of the cold. Perhaps you can help solve our conundrum." This was quite possibly the nicest thing he'd ever said to the thorn in his side, which it seemed he'd never be able to extract.

I was determined to tie the horses up so that we would at least be able to leave the house in an emergency. Sadly, I had no idea how or with what to secure them, so I simply stood there, stroking Snowy and Sherbet until Todd appeared and found a solution.

"That should keep them in place," he said, looping their reins around the nearest tree in his usual competent manner. "Though we'll have to find somewhere warm for them for the night. They'll catch their deaths out here, just as you or I would."

Horses were clearly one of the things about which Todd knew an awful lot. Personally, I was yet to discover my area of expertise. I suppose I was a dab hand at decorating for Christmas, though I doubted it would help me find a suitable career. Grandfather insisted I was improving my skills of deduction with each case we'd investigated, and I had to believe him because he was much cleverer than me.

By the time I got back inside, the adults appeared to have drunk all the mulled wine and half the bottle of whisky, too. Grandfather and Blunt actually seemed to be getting on rather well for once. I can't imagine why.

"Todd has is looking after the horses, so they shouldn't get away this time. But I notice there's something missing here in the house which I really must address," I announced and, before the sentence was complete, Blunt had nodded off in his armchair.

Grandfather wasn't looking a great deal brighter himself. "Jolly good, my boy, you do that."

"I haven't told you my plan yet. I was thinking I'd have a look around the grounds for a Christmas tree."

He attempted to open his eyes wider, but the alcohol in his veins and the warm air from the fire had left his head foggy. "As I predicted, a sterling idea. I, meanwhile, might have a nap."

Blunt suddenly sat bolt upright and, coming to his senses, said, "It was rather a long journey. I think it's time I laid down."

He wobbled from the room, off in search of a nice comfy bed, leaving my grandfather to his own devices. I would have given my prestigious relative a tut, as I rarely get to be so condescending, but he was already fast asleep.

CHAPTER SIX

As pretty as the house was, all polished and decorated to the nines, it seemed a terrible shame that there was no tree. I put my warmest clothes on and walked around the house in search of a tool shed or garage. Sure enough, there was a small collection of outhouses, and I found just what I was looking for. I also spotted a number of footprints in the snow, though I assumed that one of the staff had been out there getting the lay of the land. With my high boots on and my saw in hand, I set off through the gardens in search of the perfect Christmas tree.

I'd never been anywhere quite like Mistletoe Hall before. The house itself wasn't unusual for an English Palladian manor, but the gardens were unique. Rather than laying the grounds out based on the species of plant or international fashions, they were dotted with various types of constructions and architectural features that were visible even in the thick snow.

I walked through an ornate arch with the inscription above it that read 'Mystery is most valuable in design: never show all there is at once.' The sentiment didn't mean a lot to me at first, but as I followed the snow-laden paths deeper into the maze of strange features, I think I came to understand it.

I was fairly certain that Lord Mountfalcon himself must have designed this curious world of half-human sculptures, mock-Tudor follies and gatehouses. There were large frozen ponds and terraces with benches and stone cabins split amongst them. I could quite happily have spent the day exploring, but the one thing I couldn't find was a pine tree.

Following the paths around, like Mary Lennox in her secret garden, I finally discovered a gap in the sculpted hedge which surrounded the labyrinthine space. I tipped my woolly hat to the large topiary peacock above the archway and disappeared through it into a substantial orchard. Mistletoe abounded, just as my grandfather had promised. Every tree there held several large balls of the stuff, complete with juicy white berries that looked good enough to eat – though I knew I really shouldn't.

I had almost given up my search for a Christmas tree when I spotted a patch of woodland beyond the garden walls and stomped off towards it through the falling snow. The majority of the trees there were old oaks or towering beech, but around the edges of the forest, a few small spruce had been planted – as though the gardener had known that, one day, some young lad would come looking for just such a tree.

I took my time selecting the right specimen; these things need thought and consideration. Some of the trees were bushy at the bottom and skinny at the top and others vice versa, but I finally landed on two perfect options. They were both so pretty it was hard to choose between them. Still, I wasn't the sort to waste a lot of time worrying over such things. I was seventeen now and practically a man; I knew just what to do.

Pointing back and forth between the two, I deployed a counting rhyme to help me decide.

> **"Ip dip sky's blue**
> **Which tree shall I choose?**
> **Between you and you**
> **I wish I could take the two**
> **But you will have to do!"**

I closed my eyes at the end and, when I opened them again, discovered I was pointing at the slightly taller tree – which was good because that was the one I'd secretly hoped to pick. It felt awfully cruel to choose a favourite, of course, but this was no time to be sentimental. I raised my saw to free the lucky winner from its trunk and pretended not to notice the other tree's disappointment.

Not being particularly experienced in the art of sawing, I had no idea how difficult such a task could be. After a couple of minutes, I'd barely scratched the bark, so I bent lower to get a better angle. That helped a little, but my arms were incredibly tired. I switched hands for a while until that gave me a blister and I had to change back.

I thought I'd never manage it, but I finally reached the key point, just a little beyond halfway, and tried to push the tree over so that it snapped at the base. Well, that didn't work either. He was clearly a tough fellow, and I returned to my graft. Within ten minutes, I was almost all the way through, but it still wouldn't go. I decided to check around on the other side of the tree to make sure that nothing was blocking it.

It pays to be thorough when completing a task and, just as I'd cleared the snow, and made sure there really were no obstacles in the way, the tree fell down smack bang on top of me.

It hurt my nose.

"Oh, come along, tree," I begged. "This is terribly unfair after I chose you ahead of your prickly brethren."

It wasn't just that the thing was heavy – though I did now wish I'd picked a smaller one – with the icy ground underneath me being quite so slippery, I struggled to stand back up again.

"Can anyone hear me? I appear to be stuck," I uttered in a half-hearted shout, as I knew how far from the house I was. "Anyone?"

I remembered the story of Captain Scott, who had frozen to death in his tent mere miles from safety, and I was determined to escape. I rolled from side to side as much as I could, but that just made me sink lower in the snow. After a few minutes of lying there like a trapped eel, I decided that the only solution was to slide out from under the tree and fight my way up to standing.

I wriggled, then pushed, eventually crawled and, with a little help from a handy tree stump, got to my feet. I was just about to congratulate myself on a job well done, when I spotted something over by the orchard wall. There was a wooden awning with a carved cross on the top of it. It looked ancient and out of place, and I had to assume that this was another of the unusual artefacts that Lord Mountfalcon had sent home from his travels.

Of course, that wasn't what made me walk over to see it. The reason that I felt I should examine this unusual object a little more carefully was the fact there was somebody sitting on a bench underneath it.

A good few years older than my grandfather, he was an elderly man with a walrus-like moustache, a patch over one eye and he was stone cold dead.

CHAPTER SEVEN

I would have stuck around to find out a little more, but I felt the strangest sensation phase over me and I was quite certain that I was being watched.

It's hard to say whether, in such moments, a sixth sense engages, or whether some part of my mind can pick up on gentle noises or the faintest of scents. Either way, after a quick search around, I spotted a figure dressed all in black near the door to the orchard.

He stayed completely still and, for the briefest of moments, I was afraid it was not a man I was looking at, but some kind of devilish beast. He wore a hood and I could make out nothing of his features, but I knew that he was the killer.

To be perfectly honest, I have no idea what came over me then. All I can say is that, without uttering a word, I sprang towards him. My legs pumped their way through the snow and I was desperate to apprehend the villain. I haven't a clue what I would have done had I caught the chap, and so it was a good thing that he decided to turn and run.

"I'll get you, you swine!" I bellowed after him as I traced his tracks through a corridor of apple trees back to the main gardens.

He appeared to know the path well enough, and I had to wonder whether he'd been camped out in one of the small cottages since we'd arrived. We looped along the twisting path and it surprised me to realise that he was heading straight for the house.

"Todd, Grandfather, Dorie, Cook," I yelled in the hope of getting someone's attention, when it became clear that the brute was getting away from me. "Blunt, Albert, Mother, anyone! Stop the wicked fellow before he gets away."

I was running as fast as I could – I promise I was – but I've never been much of an athlete. I've always considered myself more of a *curl-up-in-an-armchair-with-a-ripping-book* than a *puff-your-lungs-out-for-no-good-reason* sort of person and never expected to match the chap for speed. My one hope was that the deeper snow out in the clearing would slow him down or he'd run himself into a dead end. But then I've never been a particularly lucky person and, by the time I arrived at the front of the house, he'd got away.

"What's all that shouting for?" Grandfather asked from the front step.

There was barely a breath left in my exhausted body by now and I could do nothing but wheeze and point at the sleigh that our culprit had stolen.

"Oh, not again. I thought we'd tied them up."

I responded with some more desperate gestures.

I was quite expecting my grandfather to tell me to stop flapping my arms about like an albatross and speak some sense. To my surprise, he grasped my meaning precisely.

"Somebody stole them?"

Though I could probably have managed a few words by then, I was rather enjoying myself and continued with the miming.

"And you found something that you need to show me?" I think he was just as impressed with my silent skills as I was. "You found…"

I waved my hands through the air to communicate the vital piece of information.

"…a large blue cow?"

"No, Grandfather," I said, still panting. "I've found a body. A dead body, in the woods beyond the gardens. I think you should come with me, right now."

The old policeman didn't need telling twice – well, I suppose he did in one sense, but that's not the point. He ducked into the house to retrieve his long grey morning coat, which he most rebelliously chose to wear at all hours of the day, and followed me back into the gardens.

My grandfather was far too accustomed to dead bodies to be in any way silenced by my discovery. "Ollie built all of this, you know. He designed the gardens himself with a famous landscape artist. He likes to say that each of the areas represents a different space in the house. There are dining rooms and salons, a games room and even a summer kitchen. I've always thought it was his greatest contribution to the place. Quite remarkable."

"Remarkable," I said without feeling, as I was still susceptible to nerves when coming across a corpse.

We followed my footprints through the snow and I wondered whether the killer had walked over them to hide his own. In no time, we reached the woodland, whence I would still have to retrieve my tree before it got dark. The awning with the corpse was set back into the wall, and I entertained a brief fantasy that we would find it empty. It wasn't to be. Even from some yards away, I could see the dead man's legs protruding. There were no footprints visible other than my own, and I thought it bore mentioning.

"He must have been killed here before it snowed."

Grandfather had fallen quiet, but now spoke up. "I was thinking the same thing, my boy. That's very good detective work." He paused a moment for the words to have their impact. "A simple conclusion to form, but good work nonetheless."

When we were face to face with the dead man, Grandfather sucked his moustachioed lips into his mouth and let out a single sad sigh. "I was worried that would be the case."

"Is it Lord Mountfalcon, Grandfather?"

He answered with a near imperceptible nod.

"I'm sorry," I began. "I mean to say… I know the two of you were friends. I'm sorry that such a thing would happen…" I was rambling, so I stopped myself.

He emitted a brief cough, straightened his back and, as though he'd just received orders from his superior, erased all signs of emotion from his face. "Commissioner Mountfalcon would have been the first to say that this is no time for tears. No matter what I felt for the man, we have a job to do. A murder has been committed and we must examine the evidence."

"He was definitely murdered then? He couldn't have come for a walk and died of the cold? After all, he was a very old man, he–"

"He was five years younger than me!" My grandfather made no attempt to disguise how offended he was. I often forgot that he was so much older than he looked. I would have sworn that the dead commissioner had a decade on my sprightly companion.

"Oh… ummm… whoops. Death can't have done him any favours."

Grandfather ignored my efforts at diplomacy, but responded to my original question. "And as for your assumption that he died of the cold, that would seem to be ruled out by the rather large bullet hole in his breast pocket."

Mountfalcon was dressed in a red braided jacket that looked almost military in its composition. It had epaulettes on the shoulder, large, shiny buttons and, indeed, a scorched bullet hole through the breast pocket. I felt quite foolish for having missed it.

"He looks like an eccentric sort of cove." I laughed nervously, and Grandfather once more turned his disapproving eyes upon me. "Or rather, I wish I'd had the chance to meet him."

"He was a great man and, yes, quite the eccentric. I'm sure he would have loved to meet my youngest grandson too."

It was his ability to switch between stern and affectionate, from one moment to the next, which meant I never quite knew what the old chap was thinking. For all he'd said about putting the investigation before his emotions, I noticed a weariness to his actions. His eyes scanned the corpse, and he tried to make sense of the scene.

He had a peek behind the dead man's back and pouted a little, as if unimpressed with what he found there. "In fact, I think he was shot somewhere else and then moved here. As there is no sign of blood on the bench, the logical explanation is that he was killed closer to the house and moved to a spot where the killer didn't expect anyone to find him. We'll have to wait until the snow melts to get the whole picture."

It occurred to me that something didn't fit together in what he'd said. "He's not very well concealed. The police would have come across the body whenever they had a good search."

Grandfather nodded. "Yes, you're perfectly right. Which means that our culprit wasn't worried about the police. He was only concerned with us."

I was a little confused and couldn't imagine to what he was referring. "Us? But why would he… How would he even know that we'd be here?"

He turned away from the body to smile at me. "Don't you see it yet, Chrissy? Don't you see what's happening?"

I tried my darnedest. I honestly did. I racked my brains for an answer; I even tried to recall some of the advice my peerless mentor had shared on previous investigations, but nothing came. Until…

"The letters to the staff and the Christmas cards you and inspector Blunt received must have come from the same person."

He slapped one hand across his thigh most theatrically. I had to hope this meant he agreed with me.

"Exactly. That's exactly it. Ollie here didn't invite us to come to his house this Christmas. In fact, I'm sure he was dead when the invitation was sent."

I took a step back as the force of his words impacted upon me. The snow crunched beneath my feet, but I felt something else as well and looked down at the ground.

"Grandfather? I think I've just found the murder weapon."

CHAPTER EIGHT

My grandfather normally has a handkerchief about his person for such moments. We wrapped up the ancient pistol and carried it back to the house to examine it. Well, Grandfather carried it. I still had a tree to lug behind me.

"For goodness' sake, boy." He did not seem happy with my technique. "Would you at least attempt not to wipe away the suspect's footprints? They could be the key piece of evidence that solves the crime once the police get here."

"Sorry, Grandfather. I really am," I said, trying to lift the thing higher. "The path isn't very wide though, and there must be plenty more footprints over by the house. And besides, with the way the snow is falling, you'll be lucky if there's anything left of them when the police arrive."

"You may have a point," he begrudgingly accepted. "We should look for a camera in the house to take a likeness of them. They're quite large. Size eleven at the very least I'd say."

I thought about what he'd said for a moment. "You know, I got the impression that the chap I was following was… well… a chap."

He looked back along the path at me as though trying to translate what I'd just said. "You mean he was probably a man?" He made it sound quite absurd.

"Yes, a man or… Well, perhaps a large woman. Or a fairly normal-sized woman with high-heeled boots, or–"

"So we can rule out midgets then?"

I considered the possibility. "Oh, yes. Definitely. Unless two of them stood on one another's–"

"Thank you, Christopher."

I didn't say anything after that until we were back in the warmth of Mistletoe Hall.

The elegant white flakes, which descended from heaven like wishes made real, had grown larger than at any time that day. I'd never seen such snow before. It lay thick on the ground and I was sure it would be up to my knees come the morning.

Grandfather rushed into the hall, shouting out commands to our all-weather chauffeur. "Todd, we'll need to find a camera in the house. I've no doubt that sounds like a tall order, especially with Ollie's extensive collection of bric-a-brac, but I know for a fact that he collected the things. I imagine they'll all be together somewhere and therefore impossible to miss." He turned to me soon after. "Christopher, you go too. Many hands make light work, etcetera, etcetera."

Instead of answering him with a nice, rude *I have a Christmas tree to decorate!* I merely glanced down at the spruce that was still in my hand, dripping melted snow all over the carpet.

"Oh, fine," he said and left the room to search for my mopey brother instead. "Albert, make yourself useful for once and help Todd."

My big brother responded with a weary grunt before he trundled off to do as requested.

Mother was sitting talking to the inspector, who had risen from his nap and now looked very comfortable with his hands wrapped around a tankard of steaming-hot mulled wine. The drink filled the air with the scent of sweet fruit and spices.

"What a lovely… tree." Mother at least attempted to sound earnest. "What are you going to do with it?"

"I'm going to decorate it, of course. And, oh yes, I found a body in the woods."

Blunt nearly spilt his drink. "A body? Was it dead?"

"That's right; a dead body. You got it in one." I realised that I sounded a little too chirpy on the matter and altered my tone. "It was poor Lord Mountfalcon, may he rest in peace."

"Has anyone called the police?" Mother asked, just as Grandfather re-entered the room to answer her.

"The line in the hall is dead." He hurried over to another telephone on a small table in front of one of the immense museum cabinets. "This one too."

"Do you think it's the weather?" I asked. This seemed like a sensible, undramatic conclusion to make, but my grandfather had other ideas.

"I believe the line has been cut to stop us calling the police." He held up the mouth piece as though it were a weapon. Speaking of which, he was also holding a gun.

"I don't understand what's happening." It wasn't me, or even my mother, but Inspector Blunt who uttered these words (then had a nice long sip of his warming tonic).

"What's happening, Blunt, is that a madman summoned us both here, murdered our host, cut the telephone connection and raced off on our only means of transport through the snow. What's happening is that we're stuck in Mistletoe Hall."

This would have been a very dramatic moment to conclude the conversation. Instead, Blunt nodded and said, "Right you are then," and went back to peering at the fire.

As exciting as all this evidently was, I was hoping there would be some new arrivals to meet by now. Gruff, pernickety Inspector Blunt was unlikely to turn my family gathering into a roaring party, but sadly he was the only other guest to show his face. With the night soon to fall, I very much doubted anyone else would come.

Grandfather had laid the pistol down upon a small table and scanned the cupboard in front of him. "I thought I'd spotted a gap when I was in here earlier." He pointed to a shelf at head height and, still using his handkerchief, prized the cabinet open.

"What are you looking for, Grandfather?" I couldn't resist asking him.

"Fingerprints in the dust, of course. But the killer is cleverer than I'd reckoned. He wouldn't have gone to all this trouble and then given himself away so easily."

Walking over to him, with the tree still dragging along behind me, I examined the pistol in the light of a green favrile table lamp. I didn't really know what it would reveal. It was a gun. It fired bullets, and it had shot one straight at Oliver Mountfalcon. Perhaps my grandfather would have better luck, but the nineteenth century percussion pistol – with its filigree hammer and carved stock – told me nothing.

"You don't think we should bring Lord Mountfalcon in from the snow?" Blunt suggested.

Grandfather did not look up. "He's dead, man. He's not going to get any deader. If anything, the cold will preserve potential evidence."

Blunt just nodded, as his former superior produced a magnifying glass and continued his careful examination.

"Christopher, what are you hoping to do with that tree?" my mother asked, closing the book that she'd been largely ignoring anyway.

"I'm hoping to decorate it."

"I know that." She got up from her chair and came over to advise me. "But perhaps we should look for something to put it in first."

I had to hand it to her. "That's a jolly good idea."

"Let's see what we can find, shall we?" She put her arm through mine and led me out of the sitting room.

"Such a funny old house," I said as we wound through a long twisting corridor past countless cluttered rooms.

I noticed that my mother appeared to know where she was going, and she soon explained why. "I remember coming here when I was young and imagining it was haunted. If you think this place is odd, you should have met Lord Mountfalcon. He was such a character that he made your grandfather look quite normal. He was forever hosting parties here, and he usually ended up quite drunk before any of his guests arrived." She looked up towards the ceiling as she reminisced, but the smile she'd worn was slowly fading. "The stories he could tell of his travels in the far East, Africa and the Americas were extraordinary."

We paused at the top of a discreet staircase that descended steeply off the corridor. I didn't know what the matter was, but there was a tear faintly visible in one corner of one eye.

"Mother, are you all right?"

She wiped it away with the back of her hand. "Oh, yes, yes. I'm fine. You know what I'm like at this time of year. Your silly old mater is a jingling ball of emotions, just like a sleigh bell." She laughed at this, but I'm not quite so silly that I believed her.

My mother was normally a headstrong, confident sort of person and it was rare to see her so unnerved.

"You don't have to worry," I promised. "Grandfather's here and he wouldn't let any harm come to us."

She put one hand on the side of my face and regarded me for a moment. "Oh, it's not that. I just wish we weren't halfway across the country without your father. Trapped out here in the snow, I feel quite lonely all of a sudden."

Having previously wanted to reassure her, I now found myself wishing she'd be a bit more scared of our predicament after all. "Well, there is a killer on the loose, Mother. It only makes sense that you would feel a little apprehensive."

She straightened up then and seemed to find her confidence.

"You're quite right, Christopher. We must be vigilant." She paused and looked at me once more as though she didn't recognise me. "My baby boy, you are so grown up all of a sudden. What happened to the little fellow who spent all his free time looking for birds in the gardens and reading storybooks?"

It was rare for a member of my family to pay me such a compliment. I didn't like to point out that I really hadn't changed so very much and still enjoyed ornithology and reading my favourite novels.

Before I could reply, she turned to descend the stairs, and I hurried after her. We came out in a homely kitchen. It was half the size of the large, well-equipped space at Cranley Hall, but it was filled with modern gadgets and gleaming dishes. There was already the mouth-watering aroma of a goose roasting.

Our cook, Henrietta, seemed rather alarmed to see us there. "Oh, M'Lady and young Christopher. I wasn't expecting you."

My mother offered one of her warmest smiles in response. I knew for a fact that the staff appreciated Lord Edgington's youngest child for her kindness and joyful manner. She certainly never suffered in comparison with her brutish brother and sister (may they rest in peace).

"Christopher would like to put a Christmas tree up in the sitting room and so we've come looking for a container to hold it."

The three of us scanned about the room in search of the necessary utensil and we all spotted it at the same moment. An enormous oval brass casserole, with a looping handle on either side, sat on a shelf on the wall. I reached up to take it as, although I'd never noticed before this very moment, I was an inch or two taller than either of them.

"That will be perfect, thank you, Cook."

Henrietta curtsied to me. To be perfectly honest, I wasn't used to such formality from the staff. Since I'd gone to live in Cranley earlier that year, they'd largely treated me as one of their own.

Helpfully forgetting the fact that our lives could be in danger, I felt quite overjoyed to have completed my own small mission. I might not have thought of the dead body in the forest again that day if the bell in the kitchen hadn't rung at that moment and we all jumped out of our skin.

CHAPTER NINE

I rushed back through the house (with casserole in hand) to see who was ringing the doorbell. Todd was still busy looking for the camera and so only Halfpenny and my grandfather beat me there.

It was nearly dark outside, and all I could see through the open door was a gloomy figure and the outline of the sleigh. Our footman fumbled around for a switch and the scene was suddenly flooded with gaslight.

"Dicky Prowse!" I heard a voice bellow from upstairs and we turned to look at Albert, who, as was the way with men in my family that day, had poked his head out of a bedroom window to see who had arrived. "I'll be right down."

The man standing in a long cashmere coat and galoshes looked a little embarrassed. He had a thin, Spanish-style moustache on his lip and his un-hatted bonce bore a full head of thick black hair, slicked back with grease. I wouldn't have recognised the man, but I certainly knew his name.

"Dicky Prowse, the cricketer!" Halfpenny beamed as brightly as the lamp above the door, and my grandfather turned his critical gaze upon the footman, but said nothing.

"I hope we've come to the right place," our guest replied in a tentative voice. "I was awfully worried this was some wild goose chase."

"In fact, we're having goose for dinner," I replied completely unnecessarily, and then felt rather fatuous and hid the casserole behind my back.

Though I noticed there were two other figures keeping warm on the sleigh, it was Prowse who held our attention.

"You received an invitation to come here, I suspect," my grandfather predicted, but his point would go unanswered as Albert shot past us, out into the snow.

"Dicky Prowse," my brother repeated, seizing the man's hand with a look of wonder on his face. "The best fast bowler alive, by my reckoning. Your Yorkers are a thing of beauty. What was it? Thirteen wickets in a day at Lord's this summer? Eight for thirty-four in a morning session?"

Don't worry if you don't understand a word he said. Neither did I.

"It's nice to meet you all," Prowse responded diplomatically. "I bumped into some other guests lurking near the cars when I arrived." He sent a thumb over his shoulder and, perhaps feeling welcome by this point, his fellow passengers climbed down from the sleigh.

A jolly, rotund fellow, in an ill-fitting three-piece suit and dented bowler hat, let out a peculiar laugh. "Evenin' gents. You must know me; I'm Harry Crump of Bermondsey!"

He managed to get tangled in the reins and fall face first into the snow. I suspected that he had been drinking, but then he lifted the hat from his head and gave us a wink before jumping to his feet.

"Harry Crump!" I said with quite the same joy as Albert. "Hilarious Harry Crump. I saw you in a revue at the Alhambra Theatre on my fourteenth birthday. I've never laughed so hard in my life."

He bowed low and swept his hat from his head once more. I looked at Grandfather with great excitement as – though I have very little interest in famous cricketers – having a genuine comedian there for Christmas was a dream come true. Perhaps unsurprisingly, he did not seem too impressed.

"And madam?" he asked the final passenger. "May we have your name?"

She was a small, fragile creature, wrapped in a thin mackintosh that can't have done much to keep her warm. She peered between the various faces and then up at the grand mansion in the snow.

"It's Sophy Viner, if you must know." She seemed awfully ill at ease there. I suppose she feared what might happen to her, all alone in the woods with a herd of old gents and lunatics.

"Of the Dorset Viners, I imagine?" Grandfather put to her, but she did not accept his supposition.

"No, no. I'm no high-flown type. Just a school teacher and governess. Nothing special at all."

Grandfather's voice grew a little sterner, as though he was offended by her brittle tone. "Forgive me, madam. I did not mean to insult you."

To make up for his mistake, he waded out into the snow to help her from the sleigh. Halfpenny stepped forward to do the same. I didn't want the old chap's arthritis to play up in the cold, so I handed him the casserole to look after while I collected Miss Viner's bags.

"Very kind of you, sirs." She sounded a little more confident now.

"If you'll direct me to my room to get settled. I can start my duties this evening if necessary."

"Your duties?" I asked.

Her head twitched about, and she looked most perturbed once more. "With the children? This is Lord Mountfalcon's house, is it not? I was told to come for the holidays to look after two boys. I have references if you'd like to see them."

Grandfather surveyed her face for a moment and, remembering his manners, said, "We can see to that once you've warmed up a little. Please, come into the sitting room with the others and we'll call for more mulled wine."

He ushered her towards the house, and she hesitated for a moment before smiling uncertainly and acceding.

"Wine, you say?" the clown in our midst responded. "Where there's booze, Harry Crump will happily go."

Prowse shook his head in bemusement at the cheerful comedian's gag, and all three guests climbed the steps to go inside.

"There were more people arriving as we left," the cricketer turned back to say. "Perhaps someone should take the sleigh back and–" As he spoke, the horses took their cue and looped around the snowbound driveway to return to the stables. "How remarkable!" For a man of the world and some fame, he was awfully impressed by the instincts of the poor, cold beasts.

"Yes, impressive," I replied, less enthusiastically. "I suppose the old lord must have trained them."

"Oh, quite possibly. Ollie is a real character. Where is he, by the way?"

His familiarity with Lord Mountfalcon surprised me. I didn't know how to answer, though, so I stuttered out a foolish response. "Oh, he's off in the gardens… somewhere. I'm sure he'll turn up."

He nodded his thanks and turned to go inside. I, meanwhile, couldn't decide whether to wait for the horses to return or listen in on our new guests' conversation. As I was dithering, Todd appeared with a camera so light and small that, if he'd had three, he could have juggled them.

"It has thirty-five-millimetre film!" he explained with glee. "It's from Germany. Must be brand new. I've never seen such a tiny thing."

The man might just as well have been talking about cricket for all this meant to me. I looked at the lens in the light streaming from the porch and noticed the name Hektor Leitz on the front.

"Jolly good," I replied. "Take some wonderful photos now, won't you?"

"Of footprints, Master Christopher? Yes, of course." Good old Todd didn't make me feel like a fool, but winked and went to traverse the house in search of the murderer's tracks.

I loitered for a moment, but, as there was no sign of the sleigh, or even the distant sound of bells, I decided to head back inside. The sitting room was really buzzing now. Near every last chair was occupied around the fire and, having all those chapped faces there with us, it was beginning to feel an awful lot like Christmas.

"Quite remarkable," Albert was saying. He was sitting far too close to Dicky Prowse on a chaise longue from which, I'm fairly certain, the sportsman would have liked to retreat. "And where did you pick up your skills with bat and ball? Don't tell me… you were at Eton, weren't you!"

Prowse released a disbelieving note of laughter. "Eton? Goodness me no. I couldn't have grown up further from such luxury. I'm very much a player, not a gentleman. A humble working man, not an idle amateur."

Standing with his arm extended along the mantlepiece and an unlit pipe in his mouth, my grandfather considered his response before replying. "So how did you know Lord Mountfalcon? Ollie was no fan of cricket."

Dorie bashed her way into the room with a tray and instantly looked out of place. It added to the awkwardness of my grandfather's suspicious enquiry. With Halfpenny busy trying to get my tree to stand up straight in the casserole, I distributed the drinks myself. Dorie really wasn't a *front-of-house* worker, and I wondered whether my grandfather had brought her along as a bodyguard more than anything else.

"If you must know, I first met Oliver Mountfalcon when he arrested my father." Prowse was the only person in the room who looked comfortable with this statement, and he soon continued. "I'm not ashamed of it. I come from humble beginnings and my father was a swindler. I've never hidden my background and I never will."

"Hear hear!" Harry Crump agreed, only he had a habit of dropping his Hs and it took me a moment to work out what he was implying. "All the best people started low and reached for the skies. Ain't that right, Sally?" He addressed the young teacher with a leer.

"It's Sophy. And I'm sure I wouldn't know."

Until this moment, Grandfather had seemed content to observe the interaction of our guests, but now took the opportunity to speak. "As it doesn't look like the other members of our party are arriving just yet, I feel I should introduce myself."

I'd delivered all the drinks by this point and, as there were so few seats available, I sat on the floor beside our very sleepy golden retriever. There wasn't enough mulled wine for me, either, but Delilah can always be relied on to warm cold hands on a winter's day, and I set about giving her a good stroke.

Grandfather waited until I had settled before continuing with his introduction. "I am the Marquess of Edgington. I served as superintendent of the Metropolitan Police under Commissioner Mountfalcon. Along with my family and staff, I believed I was coming here this weekend to celebrate Christmas with one of my dearest friends."

"Me too," Blunt put in, as he didn't like to be excluded.

I could see that he had that much in common with our clown, Harry Crump. "That's right. And Lord Mountsparrow hired me to entertain you all!" He voiced his trademark giggle and hiccup.

"I'm sorry to say that I find that hard to believe." Grandfather did not hide his distaste for the man. Personally, I thought he was very witty. "Not only does my dear friend Oliver prefer the work of great artists such as Wagner and Byron to passing entertainers of the day, I'm afraid to tell you that you have been duped. In fact, we all have."

"I don't understand," Prowse responded. "I had a letter from Uncle Ollie asking me to come up for the holiday to spend some time here. There's not many people I would drop everything for, but he's certainly one of them."

"And I was promised a month's wages," Sophy added in little more than a tragic whisper. "My friend in London told me it was too good to be true."

Grandfather ran a careless hand through his long silver hair. "May I ask how your services were contracted?"

The poor woman was shaking by now. "It was all done by post. I'd had a position with a good family in Clapham until November, but they let me go without notice. I begged them to tell me what I'd done wrong, but they wouldn't say a word. So when I received Lord Mountfalcon's letter…" She paused to open her pocketbook and search for the aforementioned missive. "Well, I jumped at the chance of an extra month's pay for just a few days' work. He even mentioned that it might become a regular arrangement if he were happy with me." Slightly flustered, she failed to find what she was looking for and felt the need to apologise. "I'm terribly sorry, but I don't appear to have brought it with me after all."

Something about Sophy didn't quite add up. Though her clothes were shabby and totally unsuitable for the winter months, her voice was rather polished, and she had an accent I couldn't place. She was nervous when responding to my grandfather's questions, and yet she displayed hints of underlying confidence once her words began to flow.

"Here's mine," Prowse said, reaching into the pocket of his suave black evening coat.

Grandfather inspected the letter that the cricketer held out to him. "Yes, it's the same hand as the Christmas card I received. A very good imitation of Ollie's, but not quite perfect." He clicked two fingers on his free hand and tutted to himself. "What a fool I am. I noticed the slight change in the writing, of course, but put it down to his advanced years. I'm willing to bet the forger relied upon that fact to confound me."

"Sorry, Guv'nor." A note of bemusement, perhaps even fear had entered Crump's voice. "But what exactly are you suggesting?"

"So… I'm not going to be paid, after all." Two tears had prepared themselves in the corners of Sophy's eyes and were waiting for the order to descend her cheeks.

My mother was quick to comfort the poor woman. "Don't you worry about that, dear. We'll make sure you don't go out of pocket."

"This has gone on long enough, Lord Edgington." Dicky Prowse shot to his feet. "What on earth is all this about?"

He wasn't the only one with questions. As we'd been talking, the remaining guests had appeared and an impressively forthright young woman bounded into the room. She wore driving goggles and a rough afghan shawl over thick woollen tights and hiking boots.

"I'd like to know the same thing," she said, grabbing the glass of mulled wine from Crump's hand and knocking it down her throat. "We turned up here in the snow, at the turn of night, and there was no one to greet us but a pair of horses. It's not on, I tell you. I had several invitations I could have taken up this year, but I chose this one as everyone says that Lord Mountfalcon throws a damned good party. So tell me where the old fellow's got to right now or I'm leaving."

"I'm afraid he's not here," Grandfather responded with his usual calm detachment.

Three other people had entered the room by this stage. One was a pale, slightly effete chap in slacks, a tightly fitted shirt, striped jacket and bowtie, and the other two were already familiar to me. My schoolfriend Marmaduke Adelaide and his father Horatio had arrived. No one paid them any attention as the bold woman held forth.

"Then where the devil is he?"

My grandfather smiled and then paused to light his pipe. He waited until the tobacco had fully ignited and took two long drags on it before letting out a cloud of smoke into the air above his head. "Oliver Mountfalcon is dead."

CHAPTER TEN

In an instant, the room came alive. The only person who seemed capable of keeping his opinion to himself was our cricketing hero. As everyone else rose to make their thoughts known on the matter, he collapsed back down into his seat. The poor chap looked distraught.

"What do you mean he's dead?" The skinny fellow who was the last to arrive had the loudest voice.

"I'm here to put on a show." Crump was equally furious. "I've done a performance on Christmas Eve every year since pagan times. That's a tradition that is. And some dead lord ain't going to put an end to none of Harry Crump's traditions." If you imagine that there was barely an H or a T in that outburst, you'll have some idea of how the man spoke.

"I've been bilked!" Sophy exclaimed. "I knew I should never have trusted my luck."

"What I want to know is what this means for dinner!" Inspector Blunt – who thought of his stomach before all other things – was perhaps the angriest of the lot.

"And where can I get one of those drinks you're all keeping to yourselves?" For his trouble, my classmate Marmaduke received a slap around the back of the head from his father.

"It's just not on, I'm telling you!" My brother Albert was on his feet too. Though I doubt he had any specific grievance to address, he can never pass up the chance to have a good old moan.

"Excuse me!" Grandfather's voice was like the horn of a small cruise liner. "Ladies and gentlemen, if we could have a little decorum, I will explain what I believe has occurred." This went some way to calming the scene, but there was one person who would not be silenced.

"Did you not hear me?" The fiercer of the two women bellowed out. "Did you not notice I was even speaking? My name is–" before she could say anything more, Lord Edgington had interrupted.

"Yes, I know who you are." He followed up his claim with a few seconds of silence, as though determined to hold his knowledge over her. "You're Idris Levitt, 'the Valkyrie of the motor car', 'the fastest girl on Earth'."

That soothed her fury a little. "Yes, I am. How did you–"

"I read the papers, Miss Levitt." Grandfather had diffused her anger and steered her into one of the few remaining seats. The wild woman was purring like a kitten by the time he continued. "And, I must say, I'm very impressed by all of your many endeavours. Motor racing, land speed records, ballooning and even piloting a plane. You make Sir Ernest Shackleton look positively unadventurous."

"Oh, I don't know about that," she said with far less humility than her words might have suggested.

There was a question that had been weighing on my mind since she'd entered the room. "I'm sorry, but did you happen to tie up the horses?"

Even sitting down, she had a fierce presence, and peered down at me like a vulture from a high perch. "Of course I did, boy. I'm not a fool."

"Please." The pale chap entered the middle of the circle. He was the one figure in the room whose name we still hadn't learnt. "You said that Lord Mountfalcon is dead. Please tell us what happened."

I wondered if my grandfather had failed to notice the gaunt figure before, as he now considered him keenly. "Your name, sir?"

"Wentworth Ogilby."

"Ogilby?" He turned this over in his mind for a moment. "From London?"

The petite fellow shook his head. "No, my people are from the north. Do you know any of the Newcastle Ogilbys?" He certainly didn't sound like any Geordie I'd heard on Father's Gecophone crystal detector radio.

"I can't say that I do. May I ask upon what business you were summoned here this evening?"

Ogilby reached into the inside pocket of his jacket and handed Lord Edgington a neat visiting card. "That should explain it."

"You're a musician?" Grandfather sought to confirm.

"And singer. I often get invited to such parties at this time of year. People like to spend time with artists." He had a rather arrogant air about him, but his bohemian aesthetic was certainly intriguing. "We tell the best stories and can be relied upon to provide after-dinner entertainment."

"Ogilby!" Harry Crump said between slugs of his drink. "There was an Ogilby who sung sea shanties upstairs at the George in Stepney. Was that your old man?"

"My father was certainly no public-house entertainer." The musician in our midst looked distraught at the allusion and stamped one foot. "Could we not get back to the matter at hand? What happened to Lord Mountfalcon?"

All eyes returned to my grandfather, and with a brief nod of the head, he obliged. "Perhaps you should all sit down. Halfpenny, could you please bring two extra chairs from another room?"

Our footman was balancing on one knee at an awkward angle beneath my Christmas tree, so I thought it best if I ran to the adjoining salon in his stead. I soon returned, wheeling two armchairs in front of me. Horatio Adelaide had already found a chair, so I gave Ogilby one of them and plumped myself down in the other to listen to my grandfather's tale.

"It seems as though we have been brought here under false pretences," he began and, though the young teacher had worked this out for herself, she let out a dispirited sigh. "I was led to believe that my old friend Ollie was throwing one of his famous parties. Several of you were told the same thing."

"I did think it odd that Mountfalcon would have had anything to do with me." Horatio Adelaide was a commanding presence in the room. Broad and quietly powerful, there was an intensity to him that I had not encountered in many other people, and his muscular frame promised any amount of danger. I could well understand why his son was so afraid of him. "The last time I saw the commissioner, he was testifying against me at the Old Bailey."

"But you came here for the party, too?" I asked.

Without moving his head, his eyes clicked onto me, and he considered his answer. "Yes... Something like that."

"Father, shouldn't you–" Marmaduke began, but Horatio silenced him with one raised hand.

The interruption over, Grandfather continued his account. "My family and I were the first to arrive this afternoon, before my ex-colleague from the Metropolitan Police, Inspector Isambard Blunt, joined us."

The crumpled-up inspector nodded repeatedly to the assembled crowd.

"Soon after that, my grandson, Christopher, was poking around the gardens and discovered a body."

"I was looking for a Christmas tree," I felt I had to say, as he'd made my actions sound terribly sordid. On cue, Halfpenny stood up to admire his handiwork, only for the tree to lurch sideways.

Grandfather glared at me, as though to say, *Priorities, Christopher! Priorities!* He managed to keep his tone of voice neutral, though. "That's right. My grandson found a fine example of a Northern Spruce, which our head footman Halfpenny is currently securing. He also discovered the body of Lord Oliver Mountfalcon."

This was news to no one by this point, and it drew little reaction.

"So how did he die?" the scorcher Idris Levitt asked to move things forward.

"Was it the cold that got the poor chap?" Prowse suggested.

"No, it was a bullet. He was shot through the heart." Grandfather revelled in their shock for a moment. "But knowing all this hasn't brought us any closer to the killer. I believe he has set us a puzzle and, to conclude this party with the right man in handcuffs, it is our task to solve it."

There was a rash of murmuring then as several of the guests discussed what this could mean with their neighbours. I wasn't sitting close enough to anyone, so I leaned down to talk to our faithful hound.

"What do you think, Delilah? Is Grandfather suggesting that the killer planned this whole strange situation?" I was the last person to finish talking, and some furrowed brows turned in my direction. Happily, Lord Edgington soon resumed his speech.

"I don't believe for a second that we have been invited here at random. Both Blunt and I worked with Commissioner Mountfalcon during his days running the Metropolitan Police."

"And I've already told you of my connection to him," Prowse reminded us.

Grandfather bowed gratefully. "That's right and, if you don't mind me asking, what exactly did your father do to get arrested?"

The cricketer was a hard man to read. Though he'd claimed to feel no shame over his father's colourful past, he had to inhale a sharp breath through pursed lips before responding to the question. "He was a gambler. He borrowed money from too many people and eventually stole from his work to pay his debts."

Grandfather listened carefully but offered no judgement. "Like any one of a thousand cases I came across in my career, no doubt."

"No doubt," Prowse replied, perhaps a little heartened by his compassion.

Grandfather opened the discussion to the rest of us once more. "Can anyone else here claim to have known Lord Mountfalcon in person?"

The speed demon Levitt was quick to reply. "He came to see me race once. It was a speed trial on the flats at Bexhill-on-Sea. He sought me out after and told me how much he admired my driving. I set a record that day."

"And that was your only contact with him?"

She craned her head to think. "Yes, just that one occasion. But the press was there, and they took our photo for The Times. I assumed that was why he'd invited me, you see. Though that was years ago now."

I hadn't put the pieces together at first, but the more that Idris spoke of herself, the clearer the picture in my head became. She was one of a set of female motorists who were forever popping up in Father's papers. She'd broken records for the fastest car over a certain distance and that sort of thing. Though her real draw was the scandal that accompanied her wherever she went. She'd been linked with a string of bachelor aristocrats and became quite the bête noire of polite society. I thought all such exciting people were thoroughly wonderful – though I know that my father didn't approve of women drivers – or women painters, doctors, scientists or most professions as it happens.

"That's very interesting," Grandfather responded, but would not explain why. "What about the rest of you?"

"I had nothing to do with the man until I received his letter." The note of panic was back in Sophy Viner's voice. "That's not to say that I wasn't grateful, of course. But I'd certainly never had any dealings with him in person."

"Yeah, same here," Crump added and then gazed around the room as though he were bored and was waiting for something more interesting to fill the time.

"I'm trying to see what the connection could be." With his cheeks drawn, Grandfather looked quite perturbed by the state of affairs.

"What about fame?" Horatio suggested. "It sounds like we might all have had our names in the paper at one time or another."

The esteemed detective shook his head. "Except for Miss Viner. I'm afraid to say that teachers don't get the press that sportsmen, entertainers and notorious criminals receive."

Horatio crossed his huge arms across his chest, perhaps objecting to this last description. Though he'd long since left the more scandalous elements of his criminal career behind him, my friend's father had never shed his notoriety.

"The arts then," Ogilby suggested. "What's your speciality, Sophy? What do you teach?"

"A bit of everything, really. But languages are my speciality."

Grandfather was quick to pounce on this. "Have you lived abroad?"

She wouldn't look at him then, but kept her eyes on the far less threatening Ogilby. "Not for long. The continent a little." I wondered if this could explain her constantly shifting accent. I thought perhaps that I'd caught a hint of Dutch in it at times.

"This is getting us nowhere," Idris said, rising from her armchair. "I think it's time we—"

"It's time we dressed for dinner," Grandfather interrupted with a deferential smile, and his announcement was well met by all.

CHAPTER ELEVEN

Idris Levitt confidently led us up the stairs. I hadn't set foot up there until then and was intrigued to find that it was quite a different world. The upper floors were… well… really rather neat. There was a small cabinet in each room with a selection of Lord Mountfalcon's treasures, but otherwise, it was as spick and span as any fine house I'd visited.

Even more surprisingly, the whole place was ready for guests. I had to conclude that the staff had been given instructions to prepare the house before they left, unless the killer himself had been hard at work cleaning and making beds. Many of the bedroom doors had paper signs pinned to them. On my grandfather's door, the symbol of a looking glass had been placed. On Idris Levitt's there was a speeding car, while Dicky Prowse's had a cricket bat. There was a bowler hat for Crump, a pencil and compass for Miss Viner, and a violin for Wentworth Ogilby. Each room was immaculate.

My mother, brother, schoolfriend and I – or the uninvited extras as I spent the day referring to us – made do with the left-over rooms. We hadn't brought nearly enough staff for so many guests, and so I had to unpack my own bag. Well, I tipped everything out in the wardrobe at least. In any event, I'm not sure that Dorie would have done a much better job. I quickly changed into my dinner suit and hurried back to the action.

Marmaduke had a similar idea and was already waiting at the bottom of the stairs when I got down there. He hadn't taken the time to dress for dinner. "Chrissy, has anyone thought to call the police?"

"The line is dead." I decided to hide exactly how much this frightened me, and quickly added, "It's probably just the inclement weather. Nothing to worry about."

Below his ginger brows, Marmaduke narrowed his eyes to regard me. "Who said I was worried? Though I doubt that Neanderthal Blunt will do much to catch the killer, I'm sure your grandfather will do a good job." My former bully had admired Lord Edgington's knack for solving crimes ever since he'd got him out of a spot of bother of his own.

"Master Christopher?" our very cold-looking chauffeur entered the house to enquire. I wondered if he'd had trouble getting the camera to work as he'd been outside for an age. "Did no one think to tie up the horses?"

Striding out to the porch, Marmaduke answered for me. "We certainly did. I helped that mad driver woman secure them myself."

"Well, they're not at the front of the house." Todd had to hug himself to recover from the arctic blast outside. It wasn't the most servant-like behaviour, but I didn't blame the poor chap. His fingers were as pink as uncooked sausages. "Perhaps their desire to be warm was greater than your skills with a knot."

Marmaduke did not appreciate the aspersion and stepped outside into the snow. I followed after him and, standing at the top of the front steps, we analysed the scene.

"They were right there half an hour ago." My friend peered about the place as though the horses could be hiding behind a tree or out of sight under the steps.

I examined the tracks they'd left behind. I could see where everyone had dismounted the sleigh and where the animals had been securely tied. "There are four sets of footprints. Yours, your father's, Idris Levitt's and another person's that lead from the back of the house."

Marmaduke descended a few more steps to get a better view. "I think the killer is still out here. First, he'll isolate us and then he'll pick us off one by one." He sounded positively gleeful at this violent idea. "Come the morning, we'll be lucky if there's a single maid or footman left."

While we'd been speaking, someone had joined us without me hearing.

"This is becoming ridiculous." The singer, Wentworth Ogilby, spoke in a confident tenor voice. "I'm not going to wait around here to be murdered."

He disappeared back into the house and returned a minute later with a thick fur coat on, which looked like it had been borrowed from a Russian general. He sat on the bannister wall and pulled on a pair of huge leather boots.

"I'm going for help, boys."

"You'll freeze to death," I protested, but I could tell from the look on his face that he wouldn't be dissuaded.

"Better that than shot through the heart." I hadn't taken him for the brave type before, but there was an impressive determination to him just then. "You needn't worry about me. The snow may be coming down, but it's only a couple of miles to the village. Once I'm there, I'll call the police and come back with the sleigh. To be honest, I'd rather stay in the local pub tonight, thank you very much."

I think we were both awfully impressed with his speech. In fact, Marmaduke stood up a little straighter and said, "Wait there just one moment, I've something that might help you." With all his usual speed, he shot back upstairs and returned a minute later with a gift for Ogilby. "I stole it from a boy at school. It gives an awfully good light." He handed over the electric torch, which looked a lot like one I'd recently lost.

"You're good lads. Maybe one day I'll write a song about this moment." The singer gave us a wink and turned to the snowbound path to descend the front steps. "Save me some goose, boys. I'll be back in time for dessert!"

We stood and watched him disappear into the storm. I couldn't help thinking of Captain Lawrence Oates sacrificing himself in a blizzard to save his companions on their way back from the South Pole. In that instance, the whole party ended up dying. I had to hope that the same would not be true for us.

"So, goose, eh?" Marmaduke said, his wicked smile on full display.

As we stepped inside, his father appeared at the top of the stairs in a well-tailored suit. "Was that you stomping about upstairs a moment ago, Marmaduke?" The man had a special growl reserved for his son.

My friend traversed the entrance hall to reply. "Yes, father. Sorry, father. It won't happen again."

Still attaching his cufflink as he strolled down the stairs towards us, Horatio was not convinced. "And how many times have I heard that before? You're not at school now, boy. Don't embarrass me in front of Lord Edgington."

It wasn't just his past as the head of a criminal gang that made the man frightening. Horatio's physical presence was enough to leave anyone ill at ease. I was positively terrified of the fellow, and I can only imagine how Marmaduke felt. His eyes fell to the red woollen carpet and he wouldn't make another sound in his father's presence for some time. If only I'd adopted a similar approach.

"Why do you hold the man who arrested you in such high esteem?"

Even as I spoke, my teeth were chattering, and it wasn't because of the cold we'd just endured. I don't know how I could have entertained the idea of addressing him like that. Perhaps my brain had frozen. But, even worse than uttering this question, waiting for the answer nearly killed me.

"I wouldn't say I esteem the man." There was a note of defensiveness to Horatio's voice. "Unlike most people, he knows who I was before… this, but does not condemn me because of it." He held out his arms to show his exquisitely assembled suit. I had no doubt that it was custom made by one of the tailors on Savile Row – not because I know anything about clothes or design, but simply because Horatio wanted the world to see just how much he possessed. "A wise man once told me that we only know what we have become because of who we once were."

With this riddle delivered, he turned to prod his son along back upstairs to get changed. I stood where I was, attempting to make sense of the encounter. Horatio Adelaide may have ended up a rich landowner, but he'd started out as a lackey for a London gang. If we were considering who would have a grudge against the police, he would surely be at the top of the list.

It wasn't the first time Horatio had cropped up soon after the appearance of a dead body. Though there was nothing to connect him to the previous unfortunate souls, I had to wonder whether he'd learnt something from our culprits' mistakes and decided he could do a better job himself. The very fact that he'd sent his son to the same school as his old rival's grandson could be more than just a coincidence. Perhaps he'd been plotting his revenge for years.

I chastised myself for letting my mind run away with the idea. But, as Grandfather had often explained, the first step to becoming a good detective is thinking like one.

I believe I had just have taken my first step.

CHAPTER TWELVE

"You look lovely, Chrissy," my mother said to break into my thoughts. She'd arrived in a black and purple pleated gown that was replete with marcasite and dark crystals sewn into the bodice. The colours of the fabric shifted as she passed the glass-shaded wall lamps above the stairs.

"Thank you, Mother. You look quite presentable yourself."

She laughed at my casual compliment, and I offered her my arm to escort her into the dining room. Aside from the attendant staff, the only other figure in there was Harry Crump. He had not changed his clothes and still wore the tatty suit that was clearly two sizes too small for him. I had to wonder if it was part of his act, or he simply couldn't afford anything more suitable.

As soon as I saw the table laid out for dinner, I had a question for our footman. "Halfpenny, was the table already prepared when we arrived?"

The old fellow looked at me with a rather pleased expression. "That it was, sir."

I counted the places and there were just enough for all of us, including the recently departed musician. "But the killer can't have known the exact number of people coming. I, for one, merely tagged on to Grandfather's invitation."

He tapped his head as though he'd just remembered something. "That's right, sir. In fact, the room was originally prepared for eight diners."

I did some quick counting in my head, then had to count a second time as I've never been very good at maths and I'd got a little muddled. "There were eight invitations sent. Grandfather, Inspector Blunt, Miss Viner, Miss Levitt, Wentworth Ogilby, Dicky Prowse, Horatio Adelaide and Harry Crump."

Though he wasn't wearing his hat at that moment, Crump pretended to raise it. "And much obliged I am too." There was no food on the table, but he was somehow already tucking into a bread roll. His presence there before the other diners made me wonder if he'd been the one to sneak out through the back of the house and release the horses.

"That's right, sir," Halfpenny continued. "Eight invitations and eight places laid. I must say that it struck me as odd, though. There were in fact nine chairs around the table."

"It's not so strange." My mother is always quick off the mark. "The empty seat was for our absent host. I believe that the killer must have planned this evening in incredible detail."

I looked at her a little sorely then, as I was about to draw a similar conclusion. "Mo-ther!"

"Oh, sorry, darling. Don't mind me."

This was not the moment to impress everybody with my detective work, as the remainder of the guests took an age to arrive. In the meantime, Crump put on a little show for Mother and me to enjoy. He juggled five pine cones, before each one bumped him on his head, then sang us a few ditties. I have to say we were in absolute hysterics when he performed 'The Galloping Major' in his broad Cockney accent. The song was nearly unrecognisable, but we all joined in for the chorus.

"Bumpity! Bumpity! Bumpity! Bump! As if I was riding my charger.

Bumpity! Bumpity! Bumpity! Bump! As proud as an Indian rajah.

All the girls declare, that I'm a gay old stager.

Hey! hey! clear the way! Here comes the galloping major!"

I must confess, I'd never identified the bawdy hidden context to the song until I saw Crump performing it with all his winks and nudges. I think, perhaps, my innocence was lost that day.

He continued to entertain us, and I was positively starving by the time the others arrived. Dicky Prowse led in the party, with Grandfather at the rear.

"I was expecting to see Ogilby down here," the old lord explained, having rapidly registered all those in attendance. "Has anyone seen him?"

"He walked off into the snow like a true hero." Marmaduke had taken his place at the table and beamed up at my grandfather.

"He's missing out on a roast dinner?" Blunt emitted a sceptical huff of breath. "That doesn't sound heroic to me; it's downright dim-witted."

I whispered the details of the sleigh and the prints in the snow into Grandfather's ear and waited to see how he would react. I predicted a rare burst of panic, but Lord Edgington was full of surprises.

"Jolly good. Now... let's all sit down, shall we?" He was clearly a touch disconcerted that so few people had waited for him to take their places, but he showed no sign of fear at the fact we were cut off from the world with a killer nearby.

Looking on the positive side of things, the room was exquisite. Grandfather settled at the head of the long oval table that was covered with sprigs of holly and mistletoe. At different points along the table, advent rings sat prettily, with four candles blazing on each. Pine wreaths hung from the lamps on the ceiling, tied in place with red and green ribbons. The cutlery was brightly polished silver, to match the candelabra in the centre, and each place was set with a crimson ceramic charging plate.

It turned out that we weren't the only ones who'd dressed for the occasion. Our flexible chauffeur, Todd, now appeared in footman's attire, pushing a trolley with the first course upon it. I'd noticed a dumbwaiter just outside the room and Halfpenny popped out to bring sauces and drinks as necessary. We were served ris de veau sweetbreads, to which our ever-experimental cook had added a prune and brandy sauce. For once, I approved of her break with tradition. The sweet yet piquant relish helped me forget the fact that I was eating a cow's throat.

Dicky Prowse was the man to get the conversation started. "I've been thinking about it and I've come to the conclusion that the only connection between us, if there actually is one, must be the law." He let this comment hang in the air above the table.

"The law?" Idris responded. "I'm not a fan of the law. All the police ever do is stop me driving when I'm going along at a pleasant speed."

"Just think about it for a moment," the cricketer continued. "We have three policemen in our ranks – one of whom is now deceased. My father was in prison a number of times, as was Mr Adelaide here."

Horatio Adelaide did not enjoy this reference to his past and haughtily interrupted. "It's Lord Adelaide, actually."

I'd clean forgotten that he'd acquired a baronetcy for himself through some no doubt murky scheme. In fact, it was the first time I'd heard him insist on someone using his title.

Prowse was undeterred and continued with his point. "It's surely something worth considering. Don't you think, Lord Edgington?"

Grandfather had finished his first course and sat listening to the discussion. Like everything he did, he ate in a fast, efficient manner, but took his time before replying. "It has entered my mind. But again, there are exceptions to the rule." He turned to Harry Crump, who was eating his sweetbreads with quite the wrong spoon. "What about you, Crump? Do you have a dark criminal past you're concealing?"

"Not I, your lordship," he said in a quivering childish voice. "I've always been a good lad me."

"What about your family, then?" Prowse pushed. He was quite determined to solve the riddle. I wondered if this need came from his time spent on a cricket pitch, mentally calculating the best way to undo his opponent. "Has anyone you know had a run-in with Superintendent Edgington or the commissioner?"

Crump dropped the act. "Here, that's a bit much, that is. Picking on the working-class chap. Tarring every commoner with the same brush. I told you; I ain't a criminal and just because I don't speak fancy like some I could mention, it don't mean I'm descended from dirt."

My mother hates to see an injustice done and attempted to mediate between the two. "I'm sure that no one was insinuating such a thing, Mr Crump. We'd merely like to get to the truth of the matter."

Crump's clown face curled up in a lovestruck smile and his arm rolled out across the table towards my mother. "Oh, that's awful nice of you to say, ma'am. What a sweetheart you are." He stuck his tongue out, raised his invisible hat and winked with either eye. It was too much for my mother and she couldn't hold in a giggle at his silly act.

"If anything, we're getting further from the truth." Idris Levitt had a powerful voice, and her comment helped us all to focus once more. "I certainly can't fathom some mysterious, all-encompassing connection between us. As far as we know, the killer might only have required those with a connection to Mountfalcon himself to come this weekend. Perhaps the rest of us are… what do you call them, red mackerels."

"I think you mean herring," I said, but she wasn't the kind of person who could be distracted.

"The point is, it would be rather clever of him to disguise his motives like that, don't you agree?"

We all turned to look at my grandfather. Normally this would have upset Inspector Blunt who, after all, was the only serving police officer in the room, but he was still enjoying his starter.

"You both make relevant points." Sitting with one hand to his chin, he tapped his finger against his cheek three times before continuing. "And I have racked my brains for a significant case from my past that could explain what we're all doing here. Some unfinished business with a criminal who would now seek revenge against Ollie or myself."

His words faded away to nothing, and I could see that he would need some prompting to get out what he had to say. "And so, Grandfather?" I asked, far more hesitantly than I'd intended. "What did you recall?"

He glanced around the table before answering. "There is one case in particular that comes to mind. A man by the name of John Fletcher Schoolcraft murdered his maid to cover up their affair."

This brief mention of such a sordid crime was enough to silence the room entirely. Though there was a dead body on the very premises and a killer not too far away, the thought of the poor girl, whom this savage had murdered, wormed its way deep inside my head.

"What were the details of the case?" Miss Viner, who had not uttered a sound until this moment, asked with a touch of the morbid curiosity that we all exhibit at such moments.

Grandfather's eyes jumped over to her. "Schoolcraft was a nasty chap. A rogue with money and his fingers in too many pies and pockets to be a legitimate businessman. When the scandal broke, he denied his involvement, but there was no doubt in Lord Mountfalcon's or my mind that he was guilty. It was before your time, I suppose, Blunt?"

Pointing to his very full mouth, the inspector merely nodded.

"So what happened to him?" Idris Levitt looked quite distraught at the tale.

"He should have been hanged, but he was rich enough to avoid such a fate. He must have known the judge or known how to bribe him, as he got off with a short time in prison on account of 'extenuating circumstances'. Such injustices were more common fifty years ago, but I've never quite understood it. I do know that he swore revenge against the pair of us. But as far as I heard, with his life in ruins and his family having deserted him, he wasted away his fortune and died a drunk."

"Perhaps his ghost has come back to haunt you, Grandfather." Would you believe that I wasn't the one to utter this foolish comment?

The old detective glared down the table at my brother and shook his head. "Ghosts don't leave footsteps in the snow, Albert. Nor, in fact, do they exist."

Every last one of us had finished eating by this point, only for Todd to reappear with the main course. And, oh my goodness! What a meal it was. If I ever write an autobiography of my life, I will devote a whole chapter to that sumptuous feast. To quote Tiny Tim in Dickens' most festive of tales, "There never was such a goose." Halfpenny cut the bird open at the table to unleash the wondrous smells of sage and onion stuffing, and every jaw fell low in anticipation.

It came with pommes duchesse (pureed potatoes, piped into florets and baked in the oven). Rich apple gravy was served by the jugful to drown our plates in meaty goodness and, as this food had been produced in the travelling kitchen of our cook, Henrietta, there were contrasting flavours of pomegranate seeds, marjoram and ginger to bring out the essence of the bird. By the end of the meal, much like the Cratchit family after their own humble banquet, we "were steeped in sage and onion to the eyebrows!"

Conversation waxed and waned depending on the speed and ferocity with which we devoured our dinner. For all the good breeding of the Edgington clan, I'm afraid to say it was hard to stick to our usual refined manners when Crump and Blunt were gnawing on bones alongside us. Even Grandfather looked less upright and correct than normal, but no less happy for it. I suppose his days on the police, mixing with people from all levels of society, had provided him with a flexible outlook on life, but I was quite amazed when he picked up a goose leg with his bare hands and stripped it clean.

"Don't look so shocked, Christopher. Would you rather I wasted the meat?"

I didn't have any reply for him and continued to eat my meal with my knife and fork, just as God and King George would expect. The only disappointment I faced was the realisation that we would not be enjoying Cook's legendary Christmas pudding until the following evening. I suffered in silence and had to make do with a chocolate buche de noel instead. Admittedly, I allowed myself a second portion to ease the pain.

Dessert was followed by cheeses, cheeses by fruit and fruit by something stronger and wetter – of which I had no interest in partaking.

"It's Christmas time, boy," Harry Crump insisted, as Todd served out the Tom and Jerry cocktails. I'd never come across one before, but it turned out to be a spicy milk punch, mixed in with eggs, rum and cognac.

"I think I'll stick to my grape juice, thank you."

Everyone had a good laugh at me, and I felt a little silly. In fact, I was rather tempted to go up to my room and get started on Dickens' second Christmas novella. 'The Chimes' isn't nearly so heartwarming, festive or enjoyable to read as 'A Christmas Carol', but I'm something of a completist and read it every December. Well, that was my intention at least, but then the discussion around the table changed and I had very little interest in spending any time alone.

Crump had consumed his frothing drink as though it were cordial. "It does beg the question of where the killer is hiding in this weather." As if on cue, the wind outside howled, and the shutters rattled.

Grandfather appeared to bite the inside of his mouth in puzzlement. "What in heavens do you mean, man?"

"Well, he can't be far away, can he?" Crump signalled to Halfpenny for another drink. "I mean, he bumped off the old lord and untied the horses. He must be around here somewhere."

"The gardens have several small buildings that would do the job," I said, but Grandfather didn't take his eyes off the comedian.

"That seems quite unlikely."

"You mean he's already scarpered?" Crump emitted a few notes of laughter.

"Not at all." The old fellow smiled and tipped his head back a fraction to regard the man through down-turned eyes. "What I mean is that I suspect the killer is here with us at this very moment."

CHAPTER THIRTEEN

A hush descended.

I believe that every being in that room, from our spirited racing driver Idris Levitt to Delilah – who had curled up under the table at her master's feet – was thinking the same thing. Well, maybe not Delilah, as it appeared she was fast asleep. She let out a rather pleasant hum with each breath she exhaled.

Anyway, where was I? Yes, everyone was thinking the same thing – except Grandfather's golden retriever. We were all wondering which despicable individual had lured us to Mistletoe Hall, only to hide their murderous nature from us.

"Come along then." Dicky Prowse had his hackles up. "Out with it. Who do you think's to blame?"

Grandfather had the room in his grip and I realised then that this was exactly what he wanted. "Any name I put forward would be little more than a supposition at this stage. One thing I know for sure is that someone here has concealed his true identity."

It was Miss Viner, the teacher, who was the first to let out an anxious cry. She apparently possessed the weakest nerves of the lot of us, which is surprising if you consider the fact I once fell over backward when confronted with an unusually large sausage dog. Her eyes darted about in search of the figure Grandfather had mentioned, and I had to wonder what he'd managed to decipher from our suspects' reactions.

With a truly wooden face, he gave nothing away. "All I wish to say on the matter is that, if all this is for my benefit, I am not intimidated." My grandfather's mind was a fortress to me at the best of times. At that very moment, I couldn't have begun to imagine what was going on up there. "As we have no other option, we will spend the night here and pray the killer doesn't strike again."

"What about Ogilby?" Blunt asked. "He could be back with the police before long."

Lord Edgington fired a quick glance towards the door and relaxed into his plushly upholstered dining chair. "I very much doubt it."

We waited for him to continue, but, to respond to the killer's machinations, he had assumed his most theatrical persona and would need some prompting.

"What do you mean, father?" Mother asked, to save me from doing so. "It's quite possible that he'll return at any moment."

Grandfather pointed to the clock above the impressive fireplace with its cast iron guard in the shape of a snarling dragon. "It's been almost three hours since he left. He told Christopher that he would return on the sleigh. His continuing absence forces me to conclude that one of two things has happened. Either he saw how bad the storm had become and decided to wait in the village…"

"Or?" Prowse was rarely the most jovial figure, but now wore an expression that could have cut through a block of ice.

"Or he never reached his destination in the first place."

This drew another gasp from poor Miss Viner. Even the resilient Idris Levitt looked taken aback by Lord Edgington's supposition.

"Jumping ahead of yourself, aren't you, old fella?" Crump was halfway through his second whisky already, and was drinking the stuff like he was afraid he would be thrown out.

"Not at all. A slight, ill-equipped man walked out into a blizzard at night with temperatures well below freezing point. The snow is thick on the ground and the visibility non-existent. Even on a simple journey like the route to the village, such factors make his arrival unlikely. And besides…" I could see that he regretted saying these last two words as soon as they were out. Rather than wait for someone to prompt him, he continued all the same. "I very much doubt the killer would have let him get far."

Even my thick-skinned mother couldn't bear this and gave me her hand to comfort her. Prowse dropped his gaze to the table. Crump drank a little faster, and Miss Viner had frozen in place.

"There's a simple enough solution," Idris said, clearing her short fringe from her eyes with a long, delicate finger. "We'll simply stay together this evening. Sophy, you can bunk in with me."

"That's a wonderful idea," my brother declared, sounding quite relieved for the first time that evening. "Mummy, I'll come in your room. There's safety in numbers."

Blunt raised one hand to contradict my brother's claim. "Unless you choose your mate poorly and end up sharing a room with the killer."

My foppish sibling's face cycled through various expressions. At first he looked rather amused at the idea that our mother could be a savage murderer, then a moment's fear passed over him before disbelief won out.

"Which is why I chose my mummy!" Albert's response was both indignant and infantile.

Idris had more to say on the matter. "Well, you can take that view if you so wish, inspector. But if the killer is foolish enough to kill his own partner, we'll all know who he is, won't we?"

No one had an answer to this and so she continued. "Therefore, I repeat my offer. Miss Viner, you can come into my room. As it is, I found those images on the doors really rather sinister. Perhaps the killer wants to know exactly where we are so that he can kill us off in the right order." Her loud voice rose to a new level of confidence. "We won't be playing his game tonight. And, come the morning, things won't look nearly so bleak. Just wait and see."

Sophy Viner did not look convinced by the lady motorist's reasoning, but nodded in that mouse-like way of hers, and the two women rose.

I noticed that Grandfather had not passed judgement on the idea and, as the pair left, he merely said, "I trust you will stay warm and well, and I look forward to our breakfast together on the morrow."

They thanked him for his hospitality. Idris gave one last look at our cricketing hero, who still hadn't recovered from the recent revelations, and then led Miss Viner from the room.

"How about it, Blunt?" Crump asked while there were still partners to be claimed. "My room's got twin beds if you fancy reducing the risk of… you know…" He pulled his thumb across his neck, then stuck out his hands and tongue in imitation of a corpse.

"I reckon I'll be fine on my own, thank you very much." Blunt sounded rather offended by the idea that he would need such protection, and turned his back to the portly comic.

Crump tried again. "What about you, Dicky? I've never bunked with a sportsman before. Unlike some people around here, I didn't go to no *highfalutin'* boarding school."

"Huh! You wouldn't say that if you'd spent a night at Oakton Academy." I couldn't contain my response and the words burst out of me. "The beds are as comfortable as the floor in a Victorian dosshouse."

Crump ignored me and asked his question once more. "So, Prowse, what of it?"

The cricketer finally looked up, and the comedian's words appeared to sink in at last. "Pardon…? Oh, right. Why not. I'll be up before long, but don't feel you have to wait."

Crump didn't know what to make of this and dithered in his seat as Blunt polished off a small glass of brandy and pulled his chair back.

"Well, madam, thank you for a lovely evening. Your company here is very much appreciated." The inspector was fond of my mother, as she was the only one in my family who showed him much politeness. He turned his gaze on his former boss with far less warmth. "Edgington… you'll sleep well, I have no doubt."

In the end, Crump followed him out, but not before staging a fall over his chair leg, which turned into a forward roll and a jump back to standing. He held his invisible hat out to Lord Edgington, and our substitute host placed an imaginary coin within it, though he showed no sign of amusement.

When only my family and the newly traumatised Dicky Prowse remained, my grandfather looked very solemn. He leaned in closer to me, as though he were about to say something incredibly important. "It's time…" His mind was clearly running amok with ideas and preoccupations and I had to conclude that he was struggling to find the right way to phrase what was surely a most essential declaration. "It's time for tea. Let's retire to the sitting room."

CHAPTER FOURTEEN

The staff were below stairs, and there was little life in the corridor we now entered, but I felt a presence accompany us through the dim spaces of Mistletoe Hall. It was not real, but pure imagination. Yet, from that moment on, the killer was with me for the rest of my stay. His force was manifest; his shadow large enough to engulf that house in darkness. I could hear the wind howling outside, the snow battering against the windows like hailstone, and I knew that we were not safe in our comfortable prison.

On previous investigations with my grandfather, I had felt safely removed from danger. They were merely stories to which we had to find the ending, and at no point did I feel that my own life was directly at risk. That night in Mistletoe Hall was different. I couldn't say whether the great Lord Edgington had intentionally been stirring our fears to see what result it might produce, but as we walked through the dimly lit house on our way back to the largest salon, my hair stood on end, my skin was as cold as the air outside the house, and my whole being shivered with fear.

I kept Delilah close to me as we walked, hoping that she would sniff out any hidden assailants – though aware that her senses were largely trained to search for tasty scraps of food. When we finally entered that welcoming sitting room, it felt as though we were finally home. Todd must have fed the fire in our absence; it was roaring away, and our canine companion charted a quick circle in front of it to choose the very best spot in which to settle for the night.

I wasn't the only one who was grateful to be there. My mother breathed a sigh of relief, but pretended to be happy for my sake, and my brother would clearly have preferred to go to bed. I could only conclude that Albert was too scared to climb the stairs on his own. I normally enjoyed teasing my older sibling for his soppiness, but this was one instance when I couldn't blame him one bit.

"I have a question for you, Mr Prowse." Grandfather had naturally settled in the biggest armchair beside his golden retriever. Dressed in his evening suit with its silver watch chain and a pearl and amethyst pin in his cravat, he looked every part the king on his throne. "When you parked your car this evening to come here, had anyone arrived before you?"

Prowse still seemed oddly removed and had apparently not recovered from our after-dinner discussion. Sitting opposite Lord Edgington, he looked as though he couldn't understand why anyone would ask such a question, though I believe I had an inkling.

"I beg your pardon. My car?"

Grandfather's expression softened a touch. "Yes, that's right. When you pulled off the road and parked your car, was anyone there waiting to come to the house?"

The distant expression clung to him for a few moments longer before he finally focused on the question. "Let me think… I drove off the road into a small fenced-off enclosure where three other vehicles were already stationed. Harry Crump had arrived before me and Miss Viner was dropped off by a taxi just after I'd parked. The invitation said four o'clock, and we all seem to have got here at about the same time."

"All right, that's very good. So Crump was waiting on his own?"

Prowse glanced up at the ceiling as though this would make him surer of the facts. "Yes, that's right. I got the impression he'd only recently arrived himself. We saw some faint footprints leading through the snow, so we followed them and came to the stable with the two horses. As we were preparing to leave, another car pulled up with Miss Levitt on board. Quite the sporty number she was driving, not ideal for a snowstorm."

Grandfather looked disappointed not to have gleaned more. "So everyone you met there arrived by car? No one could have walked over from the village, for example, or out of the woods?"

There was no hesitation this time, and Prowse held Grandfather's gaze as he replied. "No, I don't believe so. Of course, I didn't see Ogilby or the Adelaides arrive. They might well have got here through some other means. Though I doubt they could have come by bicycle in this weather." He gave a brief, uncertain laugh at the idea before falling quiet.

"Thank you for answering my questions." Grandfather responded in a blunt, almost sarcastic tone, to which several people had taken exception in the past.

Silence seized the room. As there wasn't a great deal I could do to grease the wheels of conversation, I decided that I might just as well attend to my Christmas tree. By placing rocks in the shiny casserole at its base, Halfpenny had managed to stop the tree from falling over. It was very nearly (not quite) straight. The only problem left to solve was an entire lack of anything that might be described as a Christmas decoration.

Had it not been night time, in the middle of a blizzard, I could have gone outside in search of sprigs of holly with bright red berries that would have stood out nicely against the grey-green pine needles. Sadly, such a move was quite impossible, and so I sought another solution.

My mother spotted what I was doing and came to join me. "What about this?" she suggested, opening the cabinet I was peering into and selecting a small figure of an owl on a chain that would be just perfect for the tree.

"Just perfect," I replied, and we continued our search.

As we did so, Dicky Prowse seemed to rematerialise before us and donned the forthright manner he'd displayed earlier in the day. "I'm sorry to seem so nervous, but... well, the events of this evening rather brought back my first run-ins with the police when I was a boy."

Though he was a lifelong policeman and had never abandoned his detective's instincts, my grandfather was a compassionate man. I found that he always had time to listen to the stories of those less fortunate than himself.

"Were you arrested for something?"

Prowse shook his head but looked no more confident. "No, nothing like that. It was my father. When he was at his worst – when his wagering was simply out of control – a different bookie would be around every week, stirring up trouble until one of our neighbours called a bobby to keep the peace. I didn't blame them, it was as much for my father's sake as anyone else's."

My grandfather had a calm way about him that encouraged others to tell unburden their souls and, after a few moments' silence, Prowse continued with his tale. "Father was a clerk in a small mercantile law firm. We weren't wealthy, but we had a nice life when I was very young. That all changed when he was locked away, though."

Grandfather shook his head sadly. "It sounds like one of those cases to which a more compassionate legal system could have found a better solution. I've long thought that non-violent criminals should be taught how to avoid repeating their mistakes rather than being locked away from the world. I've known plenty of men who went to prison as upstanding, though unfortunate citizens and walked out as hardened criminals."

All hope and positivity had deserted Dicky Prowse once more. "My father never recovered from his time in gaol. He wasn't a bad man, but he was irresponsible and, after my mother took me away, I never saw him again. You know, I can't even tell you whether he lived or died." He looked into the famous superintendent's face, as though hoping he might provide the answer.

"It's a sad tale, but at least you came out on the other side. You should be proud of all you've achieved."

Prowse shrugged one shoulder, as though he really didn't know the truth of the statement. "Some people are good at mathematics or have the gift of the gab. I've always been rather adroit with a bat and ball." He made it sound as though his training and commitment to the sport had made very little difference to his success.

"So what about Ollie Mountfalcon? You called him Uncle Ollie, didn't you? You must have known him well."

This seemed to cheer the poor fellow just a tad. "That's right, but that was later. You see, he saw me play a match when I was about fourteen. Some friends of his had a son on my team and he'd got roped along to watch. I claimed every wicket that day and he came to ask me my name. As you said, he was no fan of sports, but he took the time to talk to me and, when I answered him, he looked me up and down and asked me who my father was."

"He remembered?" my grandfather asked with some excitement.

"That's right. I told him, 'Arnold Prowse,' and he knew the name immediately. He got my address from the secretary of the cricket club and sent me twenty pounds that Christmas and every year since. He even took me out from time to time when I was growing up. In fact, I was there the day he met Miss Levitt at the speed trials."

"What a wonderful story," my mother said from across the room. She'd found all sorts of trinkets and knickknacks for the tree by this point, whereas I'd only found a slightly bent teaspoon with a heart-shaped handle. "No wonder today has been so draining. It must feel as though you've lost a member of the family."

Grandfather breathed in loudly and gave a shake of his head. "Ollie really was a kind-hearted sort. London never had a better commissioner and likely never will."

The two men fell into silent reflection and, just as Halfpenny turned up with the tea, Prowse rose to say goodnight. "I'm afraid I must retire. Thank you... all of you, for your hospitality this evening."

"Yes, of course," Grandfather responded. "I'm only sorry it's not under happier circumstances."

He finally managed a smile in response. "As Charles Dickens would have it, 'Such is life'."

I must say that he went up in my estimations then. Who'd have thought that a cricketer would quote that great English wordsmith?

With a quiet nod of the head, he was gone for the night. Mother laid her armful of discoveries down on the table where the murder weapon was still resting and looked like she wanted to get away, too.

"If tomorrow is to be our last on earth," she began, rather darkly, "then let us enjoy a good night's rest to prepare for it."

Albert had nodded off by this point, but as her wide skirt swished past him, he woke with a start and said, "Mother, don't leave me!" and hurried out of the room after her.

For a few minutes, as I continued my fruitless search, the only sound was the crackling of the wood in the fire and the occasional scratch from Delilah. Giving up on my task, I decided to start the actual decorating, just as Grandfather spoke once more.

There was a curious thickness to his countenance, and his eyes seemed to look through me. "Do you know what's happening here, boy?" He suddenly sounded all of his seventy-five years, and I had a terrible presentiment that he would not be of this world for very much longer. Luckily, I'm no clairvoyant.

I stopped hanging my mother's carefully selected gems and sparkling shapes on the tree and answered his question. "Well... ummm. No, I'm afraid I don't. Though I do know why you asked about Dicky Prowse's arrival on the grounds."

"Oh, yes?" I'd piqued his curiosity.

"Yes... well, I think I do. I might not actually. In fact, perhaps it was a silly supposition on my part. Pretend I never said anything and–"

"Christopher," he interrupted. "We've talked about this. You must have the courage of your convictions. Tell me what you were thinking and be confident."

Just hearing these last two words helped make them a reality. I took a deep breath and began. "You wanted to know whether he had seen the killer, isn't that right?"

"It might be. Continue with your idea."

"Well, I rather had it in my head that you suspected Harry Crump. If he'd arrived before the others, he might well be our man. Perhaps, after I spotted him in the gardens, he jumped on the sleigh and raced away, then merely waited for more people to arrive."

"It's possible," Grandfather replied. "Though you said the man you saw was tall."

"No, I said he wasn't a midget. But Crump *is* tall. He doesn't look it because he hunches his shoulders so terribly, much like Inspector Blunt. I think in Crump's case though, it's just part of his act and, were he to stand up straight, he'd be quite as lofty as Dicky Prowse, or Idris Levitt even."

"Excellent work, Christopher." That morbid quality I had noticed in him had faded in the ever-dancing light from the fire. "Truly, your instincts improve with each day we spend together. So perhaps now you can answer my question."

As much as I enjoyed the compliment, I was loath to admit that I couldn't remember what he had asked. My face must have spelt this out for him, as he leaned a little closer and repeated his previous enquiry. "Do you know what's happening here? Do you know why we ended up in this place with these people?"

I didn't immediately reply, but went to sit down opposite him in the seat that Prowse had vacated. "Well, that's the vital question, isn't it?"

He turned to watch the flames in the fireplace as they jumped and swayed dramatically. "Yes, 'the vital question'."

I could tell that he was hoping for more and so I thought up a topic to reassure him. "The key thing is not to be intimidated by the task." I was parroting his words back to him. This was just the kind of advice he was always giving me. "Let's not worry about the mystery of what we're doing here and focus on the simple things."

He let out a quiet laugh, and his impressive whiskers curled up towards the elegantly moulded ceiling rose. "'The simple things'?"

"Yes. All we need to think about is who the killer might be. That shouldn't be difficult for you. We have five or so suspects and a mounting pile of evidence through which to sift."

His eyes wandered around the room for a moment before coming to rest on me once more. "You know, you're right. It's the same old game, a process of elimination that will lead us to the truth." He actually seemed buoyed by my suggestion, and so I made another.

"Come along, then. We've discussed Crump already. What do you think of the other players?" Under normal circumstances, I objected to the way he framed our investigations as games. If it helped him catch the killer before anyone else died, though, I was all for it.

"Well, they are interesting characters. And as I've already mentioned, we've been exposed to any amount of misdirection and mendacity today."

"Perhaps we could start by ruling out the people that couldn't possibly be involved. Ogilby has left, and you doubt he's even alive, so it seems a safe bet he isn't involved."

He sniffed a little, and the lightness faded from his face once more. "Oh, I wouldn't say that."

"Fine, then Miss Viner couldn't possibly have anything to do with the murder."

He raised his prickly eyebrows and waited for me to explain myself.

"Well, she's such an innocent sort of person for a start." He tilted his head at this and I spoke faster to circumvent any criticism he might have had. "And she's rather slight of frame. The man I saw in the woods was definitely… Well, I thought he was…" I cut myself short as I was no longer certain what I'd seen. "I suppose a tall enough woman in such a loose-fitting cloak might have been responsible. And now that I think of it, I'm not entirely sure how tall the figure was. Perhaps it was the snow playing a trick. Or perhaps the billowing fabric lent the impression of breadth."

The ends of Grandfather's lips pointed to the floor as he considered my point. He made no other response as I blathered on.

"The important thing, though, is that everything we've seen of Sophy Viner suggests that she is a sweet, humble person who has been caught up in this wicked scheme through no fault of her own."

"I must interrupt there, Chrissy." His eyes locked onto me now, and I could barely move under the strength of his concrete gaze. "Whether she is a 'sweet' individual, as you so generously put it, is far from the point. The one thing I have learnt today, with even an ounce of certainty, is that Sophy Viner is not the woman she says she is."

CHAPTER FIFTEEN

I can tell you this for a song; I did not sleep well that night. My dreams were filled with softly spoken young ladies in Japanese warrior masks shooting people through the heart and making off with their teaspoons. Giant Christmas trees in bronze casseroles pursued me down endless corridors, and a snowman with no face wandered out into the blizzard, never to be seen again.

Perhaps inevitably, considering the nerves I'd felt on leaving our cosy salon, I'd suggested to Grandfather that I sleep in his bedroom for our combined safety. He looked rather bemused by the proposition and said, "What good would that do? The killer would simply have to visit fewer rooms to finish us off."

I'd laughed as though he'd said something terribly funny, but still followed him into his room and made a bed for myself on a large leather chair beside the smouldering fire. I spent the night sliding off it and woke the next morning with terrible back ache (and joy in my heart that my head was still attached to my body). I felt like a young tyke on Christmas morning – which, incidentally, was now only a day away.

Thanks to the faint light penetrating the blue velvet curtains, I was no longer so frightened of that strange old place. Without disturbing my sleeping grandfather, I searched for my slippers and dressing gown, then descended the stairs in the hope that my fellow guests had already risen for breakfast. The positivity inside me led to a reawakened appreciation of my surroundings; I once more noticed every pretty bow and sparkling silver bell in the house.

I couldn't decide whether to head down to the kitchen to chinwag with Cook and the other servants or act like a lord and take my place at the breakfast table to be waited on hand and foot. I was growing up and my childhood adventures now seemed inappropriate for a man of seventeen. Though I loved the familiarity that I shared with Cranley Hall's staff, I could see that they were beginning to treat me differently.

Halfpenny, who'd always been a touch on the stuffy side, had taken to calling me "sir" all of a sudden. And I must admit that, whenever I took a trip to the kitchens, the maids would stop whatever they were talking about and curtsy to me. I wasn't convinced I wanted to grow up if it meant people treating me like an intruder.

In the end, I didn't go to the kitchen, and I didn't go to the breakfast room. I dared myself to do something terribly brave instead. I returned to the room with all those Japanese Samurai costumes and – with my hand on the handle for a good twenty seconds to build up courage – I flung the door open and marched inside.

I took one look at those terrifying characters and continued walking straight through the draughty ballroom and into the adjoining corridor. Facing your fears isn't always the best idea after all, and I was awfully glad to get away from those lifeless monsters.

The door I'd walked through (which I locked behind me, just in case) led to the oldest part of the house. Grandfather had mentioned something on our journey about the place being built and re-built several times over the centuries, with certain rooms remaining from way back in the middle-ages. It had apparently been a monastery at one point, but the dark spaces I walked through were more like the antechambers of an ancient castle, with swords, shields and helmets hanging wherever I went. Each room I passed had a name upon it. I spotted *Thrones*, *Hawthorn*, *Greenman* and *Chimera*, the last of which I ducked into with a spring in my step.

I had evidently walked in a circle, as I recognised this room as one that I'd poked about in when we arrived the day before. It looked like it might once have been a kitchen, as there was quite the biggest fireplace I'd seen outside of Hampton Court Palace. The top of it was carved in ornate alabaster. A scene of angels fighting demons dominated the central mantel and I would have happily studied that strange, apocalyptic image for hours if I hadn't encountered something even more frightening lying on the hearthstone.

Hilarious Harry Crump was still smiling after death. The comedian had told his last joke, delivered his last punchline, cracked his last... you get the idea.

He was lying in a pool of his own blood with a medieval spear sticking out of him. I didn't like to imagine which organs it would have popped, but there was a growing pool of blood and no sign of a struggle, so I had to hope he hadn't suffered long. I walked a little closer to consider the oddly cheerful look on his face when there was a crash in the far corner of the room and a suit of armour fell forward onto the tiled floor.

Perhaps I was still a little dozy after waking up, but it took me a moment to realise that there was someone there with me. Dressed in a thick black dressing gown and a silver helmet with the visor closed, a figure ran towards me with a gigantic broadsword over his head.

Not being the daintiest on my feet, I took a step backwards, slipped in poor Harry Crump's blood, and quite possibly saved my life. My assailant wasn't giving up, though, and jumped over the body, raised his weapon once more and was about to send me off to the land in the clouds where the angels live, when the door to the main part of the house swung open and Horatio Adelaide ran into the room, yelling something ferocious.

Crump's killer didn't like this and backed away – thank goodness!

"Not likely," Horatio yelled as he saw the chap calculating the best route past him. He held his immense arms out at his side and clearly had no fear whatsoever of that awfully long and terribly sharp sword that the fellow was wielding. "Where are you going to go now, eh, matey?"

Horatio snatched a pewter jug from the table he stood beside and threw it as hard as he could. It narrowly missed his target, and it felt as though Horatio had the upper hand. I'm obviously no fan of killers, but wouldn't have wanted to be in his place just then. The chap seemed quite harrowed by the experience and turned to escape, with Horatio hot on his heels.

"Are you all right, boy?" the onetime kingpin of London's criminal underclass thought to ask before giving chase.

"Fine, thank you," came my inappropriate response.

Horatio disappeared from the room in the direction I'd come from, and I attempted to stand up without getting any more blood on my pyjamas. I rolled over onto my side, away from the body. I thought this rather smart of me to consider my impact on the scene of the crime, though I did bang my head on the arch of the fireplace.

Standing over a recently slain body, with a killer nearby and my hands both sooty and bloody from my fortuitous escape, isn't a position in which I find myself every day. It was a real struggle to decide what to do next. In the end, my concern for my school chum's father won out, and I ran after the pair of them.

I followed the corridor along to the end, where the figure in the tin helmet had been trapped by the slowly advancing Horatio Adelaide.

It was a spot of luck that I'd thought to lock the door and, while I had only done so to stop those horrid Samurai chaps from chasing after me, I was rather proud of myself.

"What are you going to do now, eh? Your seconds are numbered, let alone your days!" Dressed in his shirtsleeves and waistcoat, Horatio dominated the full width of that corridor, and I wouldn't have liked to be standing in front of him just then.

Seeing the predicament in which he now found himself, the masked murderer slipped through the closest door before Horatio could box him in entirely. The big chap gave chase, of course, and would no doubt have caught him if the killer hadn't had some brains of his own.

I ran ahead to see what had happened and, peering through a crack in the door, was surprised to find Horatio down on the floor with his arms raised. I don't how he'd achieved the reversal, but the killer had a sword pressed right to the poor man's throat. They didn't see me looking in, and, to my surprise, the assailant nodded to Horatio and pulled his weapon back before retreating through the far door. I heard the key turn and the lock click three times, which put paid to any ideas I might have had of giving pursuit.

I dashed into the room to check on Horatio instead.

"Are you all right?" I asked, unsure what to think of the man whose life had clearly just been spared.

"Of course," he replied in a sullen tone, his eyes still on the locked door. "He was hiding as I came into the room and knocked me over." A note of anger entered his voice then, as though he considered this a great personal failure. "I'm sure I would have caught the blighter otherwise. Did you get a good look at him?"

I had to think, as everything had happened so quickly and I'd spent a good part of it on the floor. "Not really. I had the same sense as the first time I saw him. He was somehow broader than most people, but that doesn't really fit with anyone here."

"It was the clothes." He put his hand out for me to pull him up and I almost fell down on top of him. I gathered my strength and heaved a second time. "Thick pyjamas, open gown. It gave the sense he was larger than he was. The helmet didn't help of course. We couldn't see his face, and he couldn't see exactly where he was going, which is why he nearly got trapped."

There was a significant point that neither of us had addressed up to now, and I wondered if the pace and ferocity of Horatio's words were designed to distract me from asking the obvious question.

"Mr Adelaide," I began with great hesitation as, to be perfectly frank, I was just as frightened of Marmaduke's father as I was of the crazed killer who was stalking the ancient halls of our home for the holiday. "Don't you think it was a little odd?"

"What are you talking about, boy?" He didn't look at me but brushed his clothes off irritably. "Come along. Spit it out."

"Merely that… well, he had the sword to your throat. He could have killed you, but chose to let you live."

CHAPTER SIXTEEN

"Take me through what happened once more. And don't rush this time." My grandfather was wide awake the moment that I entered his bedroom, but still needed time to think through what I'd told him. "In fact, close your eyes and try to picture exactly what happened."

I was still shaken from the experience and unsure what more I could tell him. "Horatio may know better than I do, perhaps you should–"

"Never mind about Horatio. I'll talk to him forthwith." He was pacing up and down in front of the fireplace as Todd constructed a pyramid of logs in the grate. "Go back to the beginning."

"Honestly, Grandfather, there's very little to it. I found Crump's body, and the killer was still there. He ran at me with the sword from the suit of armour but I slipped over on the blood–"

"You said before that it was Crump's body that felled you, can't you be sure?"

Sat in an ornate French Rococo chair with my legs hanging over one arm, I felt quite unnerved by his questioning. "No, that's just it. I can't be sure of anything. Horatio came in, and the killer ran off. But he couldn't escape through the Japanese room because I'd locked it."

He stopped walking and looked puzzled. "Why on earth did you do that?"

"Because those warrior people give me the willies, of course! And I'm sure I'll never look at a suit of armour in the same way after what I've just lived through. Walking around Cranley Hall will be a living nightmare from this day forth."

"Concentrate, boy. What were his clothes like?"

"They were black and hard to describe."

"Black clothes that were hard to describe?" His voice went up at the end like he was singing a song.

"Precisely." I had become rather defensive. "That's why people wear black, isn't it? To blend in and be unremarkable. He wore a dressing gown. An elaborate silk one like Sherlock Holmes has. It swished around him when he moved. He seemed both bulky and thin at the same time."

"Very well, continue."

I had to think for a moment to remember how far we'd got in the story. "The killer entered one of the rooms that led off the corridor; one of Lord Mountfalcon's museum spaces. It's filled from floor to ceiling with crockery. I didn't dare enter, but when I got closer, I could see the two of them inside."

Grandfather confirmed his understanding with a *hmmm*. "So Horatio pursued our culprit?"

"That's right, but on entering the room, the killer had hidden behind the door. He knocked Horatio to the ground and held the sword over him. He could have cut his throat, but he clearly decided otherwise. Instead, he nodded to your old rival and shot from the room." I realised as I said this that the phrase "old rival" really didn't narrow things down in Grandfather's case.

"Very well." He started his pacing again and then immediately stopped. "And you're sure the killer nodded at Horatio? It couldn't have been the helmet slipping down on his head?"

I closed my eyes as he'd previously suggested and tried to remember exactly what I'd seen. "I'm certain."

I opened them again and noticed a change in him as he walked over and knelt down to talk to me. "Now, listen, Christopher. I'm going to make a supposition and I don't want you to become upset. We know that Horatio was one of the eight people invited here by the killer and we also know about his murky past." He spoke more slowly than normal, which was good as it meant I could just about keep up with him. "Finally, we have discovered that the killer passed up an opportunity to harm the man. So we must ask ourselves, who would do such–"

"No, I don't believe that Marmaduke is the killer." I surprised myself with the resolve I had summoned. Just six months earlier – after he'd given me a rather shiny black eye at school – I would have told anyone who cared to listen what a brute my fellow Oaktonian Marmaduke Adelaide was. In the time since, I'd discovered hidden qualities to the boy. Perhaps it was naïve, but I could no longer imagine that he would have indulged in such savagery. "Besides, he wasn't even in the county at the time of the first murder."

Grandfather's voice fell to a whisper. "I only said we should consider it."

For a moment, I did just that. In truth, I'd restricted our list of suspects to the five unknown commodities in the group; the cricketer, the teacher, the speed demon socialite, the comedian (who it now seemed safe to exclude from our enquiries) and the singer who had left us behind. I had never considered that my schoolmate or a member of my family could have been caught up in the carnage that had unfolded.

"What possible reason would Marmaduke have for murdering Harry Crump?"

Grandfather leaned backwards, breathing in through his nostrils as he went. "To impress his father, maybe? You know as well as I do that the pair have a strange relationship, through no fault of Marmaduke's, I might add. The very fact that Horatio would bring him here at this time of year – without the boy's mother or sisters – strikes me as odd."

"You took me away from my father!" I was quick to retort.

He shook his head in an impatient figure of eight. "That's different and you know it. And besides, weather permitting, we'll be home before long. My point is that Marmaduke could have staged all this for his father's benefit. We both know that he feels completely ignored in that family, so what better way of getting some attention than by showing Horatio he can be even more dangerous than his criminal forebear once was?"

This was a long sentence, and it took me a good few seconds to make sense of it. "Because… Because he…" I gave up as, at that rate, it would have taken me a good day to complete my response. I suppose that my grandfather accepted this as a concession of his superior judgement, but it was nothing of the sort.

"Come along," he said, and assumed a reconciliatory expression. "We'll get dressed, have some breakfast and then take a look at the body."

I'd like to have snapped at him that his priorities were muddled, but I was too hungry to distract from the possibility of eating. In the end, though, he couldn't resist a peek at the crime scene, so I left him to it. Cook had baked fresh muffins that morning and they were begging to be covered in butter and marmalade. I was the only one in the breakfast room until Grandfather joined me. Taking his usual place at the end of the table, with his face pointing straight at the door as always, he eyed each of our suspects as they arrived.

"I find you can learn a lot from the selections a person makes at breakfast," the eternal detective claimed, once everyone was there.

Well, Albert was still asleep and Delilah was presumably keeping warm in the kitchen, but the main figures had assembled, at least.

I didn't believe what my grandfather was saying for one moment. Like many of his games that weekend, this was another way to pluck at our already strained emotions. Former Superintendent Edgington was a great believer in not only stirring the honey pot, but shaking the beehive at the same time. It was as though he wanted to poke the killer into murdering every last one of us. I'm sure if I'd raised the issue, he would have given a jolly long speech about the necessity of climbing inside a culprit's head and forcing him to make a mistake, but it wouldn't have made me feel any better about it.

"Oh yes," Inspector Blunt responded. "And what do my bacon and eggs say about me?"

"They say you should think more carefully about your diet." My grandfather's pithy response drew a laugh from Idris Levitt, who was dressed in an elegant gown as though she were about to be photographed for one of the many newspapers that detailed her every move.

"Eh, watch it, Edgington!" Blunt grumbled and helped himself to more rashers of bacon with a rebellious grin.

"What fun," little Sophy Viner said, a rare note of positivity in her voice. "Why don't you try mine next?"

She had just collected a plate of plain toast cut into triangles, half an orange and a single stick of celery. If I'd been called upon to analyse her choice, I would have conjectured that she was resolutely mad. Who would choose any of that over a hot muffin?

Grandfather took his time studying first her breakfast plate, then her eager expression, before delivering his verdict. "Well, Miss Viner, your breakfast suggests that you have a secret to hide."

"Oh, Sophy. You dark horse!" Idris Levitt sounded quite impressed.

"But… we all have secrets, don't we?" The young teacher looked around the table as if she expected us to agree.

I saw that my grandfather was still looking at her intently, as though he couldn't decide whether the time was right to reveal what he had deduced about her. The moment soon passed and Marmaduke walked in with a pair of questions.

"Why do you all look so serious?"

Nobody answered.

"Where's Harry Crump when we need a joke?"

He helped himself to a croissant into which he inserted more or less every other ingredient on the buffet table. I couldn't imagine what the great Lord Edgington would have read into this, though I worried he might consider it further proof of my friend's guilt.

"He's dead," Grandfather replied once the mood in the room simply couldn't have grown any frostier. He spoke in that strangely nonchalant tone of his. I always struggled to understand whether it was callousness on his part or he was hoping to provoke a revealing response from one of our suspects.

"You're joking, aren't you?" Prowse asked, his voice almost breaking in disbelief.

When Grandfather wouldn't answer, I put them all out of their misery. "It's true. I found him this morning in the old wing of the house. He'd been cut right through with a spear."

Horatio straightened his posture. "If I hadn't heard the commotion, Christopher might well have been next." There was a touch of pride in his voice, but it was his son that my grandfather and I were still watching. He didn't show any fear or hesitation, as I believe a killer would have. In fact, he seemed perfectly happy, cramming as much food into his mouth as would fit.

"What I don't understand," I said, thinking out loud. "Is what the killer was still doing there, hanging around after his victim was dead."

Grandfather was quick to answer. "And that, my boy, is because you didn't return to the scene of the crime to examine what our culprit left behind."

"Ooh, what did you find?" Idris Levitt showed the most hunger for salacious details and did not seem the slightest bit scared of the danger in which we found ourselves. I certainly couldn't cross her off our list of suspects.

"I found a short poem and eight small paper dolls. They were stationed around the old table, as though waiting for a feast." He did not need any prompting and pulling his reading glasses from his pocket – which I'm certain was as much for dramatic effect as any particular ocular debility – began to read from a scrap of thick parchment.

"The minstrel boy has long since gone,
The speedy girl keeps driving on,
The clown's laughter has turned to tears,
While teacher's busy counting fears.
The pig inspects nothing but the bottom of his plate,
The delinquent's in a right old state,
The sportsman's not the man he said,
And the king's about to lose his head."

He allowed a few breaths of silence as one of the four green candles on the advent wreath reached the end of its wick and the flame turned to smoke. I had expected the assembled guests to object to the aspersions, but they all remained silent, waiting for Lord Edgington's judgement on the matter.

"I learnt two things about our culprit from the clues he left behind." He paused to make us run through the possibilities in our head before revealing his findings. "First, the killer is a truly abysmal poet. The metre is all wrong. Most of the rhymes are far too obvious and, had it been me, I would have shaved the odd syllable here and there. But more importantly, this poem confirms a theory that I formed the moment we found Ollie dead."

"You know who the killer is?" Prowse asked with his usual economy.

"No, not at all. But I know why he's killing. Think about the last line of that verse. He called me the king. I don't wish to sound arrogant—"

"Too late for that," Blunt interrupted. "Who's to say that you're the king and not the pig, eh? What exactly are you implying about me?" He rather undermined his point by licking runny egg from his fingers between the last few words.

"A fair point, old friend," Grandfather said most benevolently. "But as I am the only person who could connect you, Lord Mountfalcon and Horatio Adelaide, I have to assume that I am the thread that ties this unusual case together. As I told my grandson last night, I believe the killer is testing me."

"What about us?" Miss Viner asked, with plenty of reticence. "What links me to all this? Or Crump for that matter? I'd never heard of any of you before I arrived here."

"I think I might be able to provide something of an answer." I wasn't the only one who was surprised to hear my mother speak up at that moment. She was a discreet sort of person but, as her father's daughter, knew full well how to speak her mind when required. "Christopher mentioned that he saw Harry Crump at the theatre for his fourteenth birthday. Well, I'm the one who took him. My son may not remember what Crump joked about in his act, but I certainly do. The man's whole routine was about coming from the wrong part of town, rubbing shoulders with nefarious characters and never being mistaken for the gentleman he dreamed of becoming."

She was right, of course. The only thing I'd remembered about Hilarious Harry was how good he was at falling over.

"What are you suggesting?" Prowse had that same look of concentration on his face; a steely determination to make sense of the world before him.

Mother seemed a little cowed by the attention now directed towards her, and so her father answered on her behalf. "My extremely astute daughter is saying that Crump might well have crossed paths with Commissioner Mountfalcon when he ran the Metropolitan Police. Idris, you told us that you met Ollie once. Dicky, you became his close friend over the years. It's impossible to say whether my dear old friend ever met Ogilby, but I know for a fact that he loved music. It's hardly implausible."

"Which still leaves me!" Sophy Viner's statement was a short, sharp shout. The more questions she had to ask, the more desperate she sounded. "I told you, I've never had anything to do with any of these people."

Grandfather had barely moved a muscle throughout this exchange, but now sat forward in his seat. "Remind me, Sophy. What exactly do you teach?"

She stared down at her plate and her gaze would not budge, even as she replied. "I don't know why people keep asking me that. I already said, I specialise in languages. French and Italian most commonly."

Grandfather did not wait one moment before replying and practically spoke over the poor girl. "Not literature then?"

"No… well, on occasion perhaps. A woman in my position teaches what is required."

"Yes, jolly good." The old man smiled with all his grandfatherly charm. At such moments, I was awfully fond of him, even if I knew it was all an act. "I only ask because I do so admire writers. I find no greater pleasure than getting lost in a novel." I'd never once seen him open a work of fiction, and I had a sneaking suspicion that he was quoting something I'd once told him. "I do adore the classics, of course. Elizabethan drama has always been a favourite of mine, but I have been known to read more modern works from time to time. You know the sort of thing – George Eliot, Henry James, Edith Wharton. Have you read anything by Wharton? She really is the most marvellous commentator of the human condition."

Personally, I had read quite a number of books by the aforementioned authors. I still hadn't the faintest idea what he was suggesting, but Miss Viner clearly did. Her nerves had taken hold of her entirely, and she was shaking with fear.

"It doesn't prove anything," she managed to exclaim, but the effort was too much, and she allowed her head to sink to the table in front of her.

My mother was inevitably spurred into action, but before she could pull her chair back to comfort the poor girl, my grandfather had beaten her to it. Placing a warning hand on his daughter's shoulder as he went past, he reached Sophy and knelt to whisper something in her ear. I couldn't make out what was said, but it was almost like a bottle of smelling salts had been placed beneath the patient's nose and she immediately came back to life.

"What's happening now?" Horatio asked, perhaps afraid of whatever stratagem my grandfather had concocted and whom it would most disadvantage.

"You needn't worry." Grandfather was back on his feet and Sophy copied him. "I'm going to have a word with Miss Viner in private. Chrissy, come with me."

I didn't like it when he issued orders as though I were his pet. In an act of rebellion, I waited a good five seconds before doing as I'd been told.

CHAPTER SEVENTEEN

I was honestly relieved that the room my grandfather took us to did not feature disembodied warriors from either side of the globe. Instead, we entered another salon opposite the samurais' hangout, which was filled with artefacts from the far east. One wall was covered with papier mâché Chinese masks, with wide painted smiles and demonic red eyes. I had to wonder if the clever old fox had chosen that room to underline Miss Viner's duplicity.

The young lady sat down on the only chair in the room. It was wide and black with impressive hand-painted gold designs all over the wood. I made out a blossoming tree and songbirds, though I won't hazard a guess at what kind of bird they were. I'm bad enough at identifying British species and would be as likely to name a bird from some distant land as I am to pronounce it correctly.

"Sophy," Grandfather began warmly enough, but then looked uncomfortable with what he had to say. "You have no reason to be frightened of me." His voice did not achieve its usual smoothness, and he made it sound as though, in truth, she had every reason in the world.

She would not meet his gaze, but peered out of the window. The room we were in was at the side of the house and so sheltered from the worst of the wind, but there was still snow coating the panes of glass. We could see little outside bar a few bare beech trees. The thought of all that snow lying out there reminded me of previous Christmases when I'd longed for a few precious flakes to fall and made do with grey skies and plenty of rain.

It was Christmas Eve, and I hadn't even built a snowman. Did that mean I was now an adult?

"Really," Grandfather tried once more. "I will not expose your identity to the others, if that's what you're thinking. I am only interested in finding the killer and stopping anyone else from getting hurt. Now, why don't you tell me the truth."

She shook her head dejectedly – it was as though she knew that her every attempt at bluster would fail, but she forced herself to try one last time. "I don't know what you mean. I haven't lied. I'm nothing; just a teacher. I'm not like the rest of you, and I don't know why you're tormenting me like this. My name is—"

"I know… your name is Sophy Viner, but if that's the case, why did you get so upset when I mentioned Edith Wharton?"

I still didn't know what a contemporary American novelist had to do with anything, but a note of resilience entered her voice as she replied. "I've been dragged across the country at Christmastime for a job that doesn't exist, and people around me keep getting murdered. How do you expect me to act?"

My grandfather saw through her protests and continued as though she hadn't spoken. "Sophy Viner is a character in Wharton's 1912 novel 'The Reef'. A minor work by her standards, but not without literary merit. The Sophy in the book is a conflicted character who is searching for a sense of identity. Oh and, if I remember correctly, she's also a governess."

The Sophy before me, the fake Sophy if you like, kept her pale blue eyes fixed on her interrogator, even as tears poured from them. "It's no crime to take a pseudonym. Perhaps I was tired of being plain old Milly Brown."

"Ah, there we have it. Milly…" Grandfather is a wizard with words and knows just when to employ them and when to hold them in reserve. He made not a sound for ten ticks of the ornate Japanese clock on the mantel and, when he finally spoke again, the sound roared out of him. "Ollie Mountfalcon's niece was a Milly. I believe her family name was Bowen, not Brown. But then, when constructing a lie, it's a good idea to hew close to the truth. Such minor adaptations are easier to sell. Don't you think, Miss Bowen?"

I felt really rather sorry for the poor girl, no matter who she was. Her cheeks were blotchy and red even through her makeup, which was beginning to run with the incessant flow of salt water. "I didn't kill him," was all she could manage in reply, and she tipped her head back against the high wooden chair.

Grandfather finally took pity on her. "Dear child, why won't you believe that I am merely trying to help?" He went forward to her and took her dainty hand in his own weathered paw. "Tell me everything you've been through and we'll find the best solution. You were born in South Africa, correct? I thought your family was still over there."

Her accent suddenly made more sense to me. She didn't possess the fully fledged Afrikaner twang that some of my cousins had brought back with them after long stays in that distant country. But, now that I could place it, I realised that her accent was not continental, but trans-continental and, try as she might, she could not pass herself off as an out-and-out Britisher.

I witnessed the moment that she accepted defeat. Something seemed to crumple inside her and in a low, pained voice, she told us her tale. "My father ran into trouble in his work back home in Johannesburg. Things quickly went from bad to worse." She had to pause almost as soon as she'd started, and it was clear how difficult her task would be. "I decided I couldn't stay there any longer and came to Britain as soon as I'd finished my schooling. I'd only been here on summer holidays a few times as a child; arriving on a wet Wednesday in November, with little money and no friends, was like a plunge into an icy bath."

I could see that there was a question on my grandfather's lips, but he held it in and Sophy – or Milly or whatever her name might be – continued speaking.

"I took a job in a school and found I had quite the aptitude for teaching. I'd studied languages at university and could speak French, Italian and most of the romance languages proficiently. Brits aren't generally the best at second tongues, and so there was plenty of work for me."

The old man could resist no longer. "So you didn't come to see your uncle? You had no contact with Lord Mountfalcon?"

She shook her head, and I was happy to see that her flood of tears had been stemmed. "No, I couldn't. I'd already changed my name when I arrived and didn't feel I could go begging to him when times were hard. I read about him in the paper on occasion, but made no attempt to visit. I lived on the south coast for the first year I was in the country. I suppose it was the closest I could get to the warm weather in Jo'burg."

"So you didn't struggle for employment..." Grandfather prompted her.

She had drifted off with a memory, and his voice jogged her back to the present. "That's right. Things changed though when I met a young man who lived in London. We were engaged to be married and so I moved to the capital. It was wonderful... at first. I was young and in love, and nothing else seemed to matter. But then I lost my job without notice and I discovered that my fiancé wasn't the person I'd taken him to be. It all got too much for me and I didn't see a way out until the letter from my uncle arrived."

"Did the letter suggest he knew who you were?" I heard myself asking, and she responded just as though my grandfather had been the one to ask.

"I don't believe so. I thought it was blind luck. The heavens smiling down on me or some such nonsense."

"But surely you knew that your uncle had no children for you to teach?" Grandfather's voice became rather fragile as he tried to understand her thinking. "Didn't you think the circumstances rather unlikely?"

She gave a cold, sad laugh. "All I saw was the pound sign and the number alongside it. It's not easy to find work in the middle of a school term and I didn't know how I was going to pay this month's rent. I did find it unusual that my own uncle would have chanced across my name. There must be a thousand other young women in Britain he could have contracted, and the odds of him picking me seemed staggering, but I was desperate. That's all I can say on the matter."

Grandfather opened his mouth to deliver another question but hesitated and had to try a second time. "I have something to ask you, but I'm afraid I can find no delicate way of phrasing it." He waited for her assent and she delivered it with a silent nod of the head. "When we arrived here at Mistletoe Hall, we found letters written to the staff, granting them leave for the Christmas holiday. They included a small premium and... well... they were written in your name."

A look of shock passed over her pretty visage, but it soon faded away again, to be replaced by the same defeated expression she'd previously worn. "Where would I get any money to pay someone?" she asked, most pathetically, but held my grandfather's gaze as she answered more decisively. "And, no, I did not write any letters before arriving at Mistletoe Hall, except the one I sent to accept my position here."

I truly wanted to believe her; I swear that I did. Perhaps it was my grandfather's training, but a cynical thought had entered my mind and I couldn't dismiss it. I remembered that, when she'd arrived the night before, she'd been unable to show us the job offer she claimed to have received. If she were the killer, she might well have overlooked writing a letter to herself, and I couldn't help wondering whether she had fabricated this whole scheme.

There was the sound of scratching at the door just then, and Sophy stared at it in pure fear.

"Don't worry, I think I know who that is." Grandfather marched over to the entrance we'd come through and opened it to allow his golden retriever into the room. Delilah was carrying a short wooden pole in her mouth. It was intricately painted in purples and golds and I could only conclude that she had extracted it from some priceless artefact. Her master, however, had more pressing matters with which to take umbrage.

"Delilah, I'm interviewing a witness. You know not to interrupt me at such times. Your desire to play fetch does not take precedence over the pursuit of justice."

The loveable creature let out a whimper in reply and came to sit on my feet.

Grandfather clearly understood this mournful sound as he replied, saying, "And I should think so too!" before returning to our suspect. "I'm terribly sorry about that. I'm afraid that it's too cold for the old girl to go outside, and she gets terribly vexed trapped in the house all day. Now, where were we?"

Miss Bowen, or rather... Do you know what? I think I'm going to stick to the name she chose for herself. Sophy Viner considered the question for a moment before replying. "I've told you the whole story, except for the fact that I only hid my relationship to Uncle Oliver as I was sure you'd think me responsible for his murder."

"Why ever would you have imagined such a thing?" I asked, with more than a touch of naivety.

She looked back and forth between my grandfather and me. "Well, because my father was his closest relative. I might be wrong, of course, but there's a good chance my family will benefit from Lord Mountfalcon's death."

"You can't know that." I'd taken up her cause and wasn't going to be dissuaded now. I never could stand to see a young lady suffering. "He might just as easily have left the lot to Dicky Prowse or some other waif he's adopted over the years. Who knows, he might have had a fancy woman."

As I was ranting, Grandfather had faded out of the conversation and was staring at a case on the wall which contained weapons from all over the world. There were scimitars and katana, jian and dao – I should point out that I don't actually know anything about swords and the like and only recognised them thanks to the nameplates under each one.

Without turning to look at our suspect directly, the more experienced detective spoke. "There's one thing you haven't told us."

Miss Viner swallowed loudly, perhaps imagining any number of devilish questions that my grandfather might put to her.

"Why did you feel the need to change your name in the first place?" His eyes shot back to her to put a resolute dot on the question mark in his voice.

She glanced down at her delicate hands. I doubted for a moment that she'd find the words she needed, but they came in time. "I read 'The Reef' on the crossing from Cape Town. I had never felt so sad in my entire life, and the fate of Sophy Viner in the novel seemed tied up with my own. There were times, in fact, when I was convinced we were one and the same person. When I stepped off the Union-Castle ship at Southampton, I felt that I really was her and I never went back."

A note of aggression entered my grandfather's voice. "But that's not the whole story, is it?" he waited and when no answer came, he poked her once more with his words. "There must have been a reason you were so eager to get away from South Africa and so desperate to distance yourself from your family that you would change your name."

Miss Viner looked as though she might burst into tears once more, but she raised her chin and, with no shame in her voice, delivered the final piece of the puzzle. "My father's reputation was in ruins. He was a shell of the man he'd once been. You see, he'd moved our family halfway across the earth to take advantage of the diamond boom. He ended up working for Cecil Rhodes."

"The founder of De Beers diamonds?" I'm awfully glad that my grandfather asked this question, as I hadn't a clue to whom she was referring.

"That's right. Despite falling out with uncle Ollie, my father had some money of his own to invest. He became a scout for De Beers, searching out mines that were ripe for purchase. Things were fine until his beloved boss died at the turn of the century. He never had the same influence after that and…" She couldn't finish that sentence, but she'd said enough to tell my whip-smart grandfather what he needed to know.

"And through some indiscretion, your father was disgraced."

Miss Viner's reply came shooting towards us like a steam train. "My father has never committed a crime in his life, but those vultures he worked with made him the scapegoat for their wrongdoing. I changed my name to leave behind the iniquity of what those men did to him."

"Well, that may be, but it does put a different complexion on things, don't you think? With Lord Mountfalcon deceased and your family's fortunes restored, you can save your father from scandal. And that's the real reason you hid your identity, isn't it, Millicent? You've known all along that you are the most likely suspect."

CHAPTER EIGHTEEN

Miss Viner left that pretty room just as she'd entered it; with her nerves racked and on the point of tears. At least she had a nice breakfast to comfort her. I'd barely had a single muffin when all that drama had commenced, and I was still starving.

"Do you really think she could have killed her uncle?" I had to ask once she'd left.

"I don't know what to believe," Grandfather responded. "I honestly don't. Every hour dredges up a new possibility for who killed whom and why. The one thing I can say for certain is that no one must be ruled out entirely."

I thought about this for a moment. In fact, I closed my eyes and imagined that it had been Miss Viner in the visored helmet, running at me with that sword. Horatio was right in that the killer was clearly wearing several layers of clothing, though it was hard to say whether this was merely to fight against the elements or better conceal his frame. Now that I thought more carefully, I realised that it wasn't just the helmet the killer had been wearing, but chain-mail gloves too. So I couldn't say whether it was Miss Viner's dainty hand that had attempted to murder me, or one of the gentlemen's big meaty blocks.

She wasn't as tall as Idris Levitt or Dicky Prowse, but she was no Napoleon either. Perhaps from down on the floor – as both Horatio and I had best regarded our assailant – she would have appeared taller than she really was. Perhaps she simply had thick soles on her shoes. The bigger question, I felt, was whether she would have had the strength to knock Horatio over with one push.

"Boy, what are you doing?" Grandfather asked when I'd been standing in the middle of the room for more than a minute with his dog still warming my feet and my eyes firmly closed.

"Oh, I… I was just trying to remember something."

"Did it work?"

I gave a nervous laugh. "I'm afraid not. Everything is as hazy in my mind as it's ever been. To tell the truth, if you suggested that Delilah was the killer, I'd end up finding the evidence to make it seem possible. That's just how my mind works."

He regarded me for a moment with his head turned to the side. "Well, jolly good. That shows that your mental capacities are really starting to expand. Flights of fancy – whether correct or off the mark – are a key tool in a detective's arsenal. You should be proud of what you've already achieved."

This was unusually complimentary of him and made me feel rather chipper. "All right then; I will!"

"Fabulous. Now let's have a look around outside, shall we?"

Delilah immediately dived behind the chair where Miss Viner had been sitting, so you can imagine how I felt. "I'd rather not, if you don't mind. It's awfully cold out there and I'm really not dressed for the snow."

"We'll soon change that. There's nothing like a walk in the fresh air to help one think." He didn't show much sympathy as he spun on his heel to march off towards the front door.

Once I'd put my boots, scarf, hat, gloves, an extra scarf and my thickest coat on, I was ready for the outside world. I must say, it felt rather wonderful to open the front door and escape from that large, luxurious, though strangely claustrophobic house. The air did indeed feel fresh, and England was as bright as any time in my memory. The snow on the ground was nearly blinding and beams of light broke through the clouds to illuminate it, like candles on a Christmas tree.

While it had stopped snowing for the moment, and Todd was doing his best to clear the front steps, we would not be setting off in search of help anytime soon.

"It must be up to our waists in some places." Grandfather took an experimental step off the front porch. "I don't remember seeing snow like this since eighteen… Well, I don't recall what year it was, but it was a long time ago."

I noticed that such fallibilities had been creeping into his speech over the last few months. While it was tempting to believe that they were the first signs of his brilliant mind finally diminishing, I thought it just as likely that he was doing it on purpose to make all of his grand discoveries seem that little bit more impressive.

I followed him into the cold white pool of snow and was soon up to my middle, just like Doctor Foster.

"Are you sure this is a good idea?" I asked, wading after him. The old chap was a good foot taller than me and, to be perfectly honest, I was worried I might get lost and never be seen again.

"Quite sure." He turned left and left again to take us around the outside of the house.

I didn't have much more to say on the matter, but I noticed that wise old Delilah had remained inside. It was high time she gave me some lessons on how to say no to her master.

As soon as were a good distance from the house, he stopped and took a look over his shoulder, as though he wanted to make sure we weren't being followed. He did this three times before finally leading us through an arch in a gigantic ring-shaped holly bush. Poking his head back out to confirm that I was following, he waved me inside.

"I didn't just bring you here for the exercise, you know. I wanted to talk to you."

"We could have done that inside. There are hot drinks inside and not everything is covered in wetness."

"Oh, do stop fussing, boy. Back at the house, I couldn't be certain whether someone was listening to our conversation. The killer clearly knows the house rather well, and there's something I need to ask you that I don't want anyone overhearing."

I could think of at least one issue with his logic. "Then why didn't we go down to the kitchen? We might not be able to trust the other guests, but we can rely on the staff from Cranley Hall not to say anything."

"That's a wonderful idea! Why didn't you suggest it before?" His whole face was transformed by a sparkling smile. "Ah, well. Too late now."

If I hadn't been so cold, I might have taken one glove off and slapped him with it. Instead, I sat down on a circular bench, which ran around the interior of the cave-like bush we'd entered. Little snow had penetrated its prickly boughs, but it was just as cold as if we'd been under the open sky.

"I rather like it in here." He let out another brief laugh, which I thought rather inappropriate in the midst of a murder investigation. I suppose that, after a forty-year career in the police, dealing with dead bodies and murderers, he had to maintain his sense of humour somehow. "When your grandmother and I were younger, we used to come to visit Ollie with the children and spend hours exploring these gardens. Your mother often hid in this very bush when she was a tiny thing."

I must admit, it was a pretty spot, and his mischievous enthusiasm was infectious. I looked up at the living shelter we were sitting within and had a pang of longing for the simpler Christmases of my childhood. Seeing all those bright red berries against the waxy green leaves made it feel as though we'd climbed into a giant decoration.

"Is that what you brought me here to tell me?" I asked him, and he shook his head and fell to a more conspiratorial whisper.

"No, my boy. I wanted to ask you about the poem."

"The one you found with the body?"

"That's right. It certainly suggests that a creative mind is at play and I was wondering whether you were able to draw any significant conclusions from it."

"I…" I tried to remember the words he'd read. There was definitely something about a pig and…

"The minstrel boy has long since gone," he recited from memory. "That will be Wentworth Ogilby, of course, and the wording made me wonder whether the killer has already done away with him. There's certainly no sign of him today."

"What was the next line?" I asked, as I felt jolly dreadful about poor Ogilby, who had apparently sacrificed himself for no good reason at all.

Grandfather cleared his throat to move onto the next line. "'The speedy girl keeps driving on'. That will be Idris Levitt, of course. She's a unique woman, don't you think?"

"Yes, unique indeed."

Idris Levitt was the kind of woman over whom men seemed to lose their minds. She was the sort of person who was always in newspapers being interviewed for one reason or another, but, truthfully, I couldn't understand the appeal.

He continued to share his thoughts on our suspect. "She certainly made a big noise, demanding to know what had happened to Ollie when she arrived. And I don't know if you've noticed, but she's fallen rather silent ever since."

"Yes, she's an odd one, but we've yet to find anything that would suggest her motive for resorting to such violence. So let's move on to someone else."

He nodded. "Very well. 'The clown's laughter has turned to tears,' that one's self-explanatory. Poor Crump must have been lured downstairs by someone who then ran him through with the spear. To add insult to injury, the killer lingered at the scene of the crime to compose a poem on their wicked deeds."

"You know that it was Dicky Prowse who bunked up with him last night?"

He considered this fact. "Yes, you're right, but that doesn't mean he was awake when Crump left the room. I'm more inclined to believe that Sophy Viner had a hand in things. The poem explains that 'teacher's busy counting fears', which fits with the picture she's painted for us. But what if she wrote the verse herself? In my mind, if she's innocent and was invited here by the killer, he must know her connection to Lord Mountfalcon. In which case, it puzzles me that he didn't mention her duplicity. Alternatively, if she's guilty, she would have left out such a detail from the poem that was clearly written to taunt me."

I was quick to respond to his unfounded assertion. "But what could she have against you? Her uncle I can understand – and she clearly didn't think much of Crump from their interaction last night – but why would she have gone to all this trouble to bring you here?"

"An excellent question," he replied. "And one to which I'm not yet ready to reveal the answer." I believe that this was my ever-so-humble grandfather's way of saying he didn't know. "On we go to Inspector Blunt. 'The pig inspects nothing but the bottom of his plate'. What do you make of that?"

"I think it's cruel. Blunt never means any harm and, just because he likes to fill his belly, it's no reason to mock him."

He chuckled once more. "And I think you're too generous, my boy. Though I accept that Blunt is an experienced officer, that wouldn't stop a criminal getting around him with a jug of gravy and a joint of meat."

Leaning forward to support his head on his fist, his gaze intensified. "What I'm most interested in, though, are the last three lines of the poem. 'The delinquent's in a right old state,' surely that's Horatio Adelaide – former criminal and eternally dubious businessman. I hate to think that his own kin could be responsible, but who, other than a son, is more likely to say such a thing?"

"An enemy!" I countered, but he remained unconvinced.

"The fact is that the killer spared Horatio's life. You saw it with your own eyes. Though I may have defended Marmaduke Adelaide in the past, we cannot rule him out as a suspect – at least in Crump's murder."

"Fine, if Marmaduke killed Harry Crump, who murdered your friend?" I reached down to push together what little snow there was on the ground. "There's surely another explanation for it. Perhaps the killer is knocking off his enemies in a special order and didn't want to deal with Horatio yet."

"What 'special order'?"

"How about… alphabetical?" I proposed without thinking it through. "First Lord Oliver Mountfalcon and then… no, that doesn't work. Numerical then?" I couldn't begin to tell you what the numerical order of a group of people would be, so I was happy when he interrupted.

"All right, Christopher. You've made your point. I'm not about to lock the boy up, but we must at least consider his involvement. Besides, the part of the poem that interested me most was the penultimate line."

I thought this rather big of him, considering that the last line informed everyone that he was the king.

"Was it about Dicky Prowse?"

He extended one long finger in my direction. "That's correct. Our heroic cricketer, captain of Hampshire and the Players' team, with an average strike rate of… Well, I don't precisely know, as I don't follow the sport. But I'm sure Albert would only be too happy to inform you."

"Prowse isn't the man he says he is; that's what the poem revealed about him," I remembered, just in time to stop Grandfather waffling. "I wondered what it could mean when I first heard it. He certainly seems to be a frank sort of chap. He was honest about his father's ignominious brushes with the law, and he was clearly fond of Lord Mountfalcon."

"Hmmm," was all my grandfather would say in return. He could make such a sound mean any number of things. *Hmmm* could mean that he agreed, or indeed disagreed. It could mean I'd made a good point, or, in fact, a terrible one. It could mean that he was paying the utmost attention, or that he wasn't listening at all. The one thing I could say for certain at such moments was that he always knew exactly what he wished to imply and, for my part, I occasionally worked it out.

"You mean to say you don't believe his story about Lord Mountfalcon becoming his patron? Or you doubt their friendship ever existed?"

"No, it's not that exactly." He came to a stop again and kicked the frozen ground in something approaching frustration. "He was perfectly believable and communicated just the right level of emotion to relay his feelings."

"So?" I knew my economy of language would rattle him.

"Please speak in full sentences, Christopher. How many times do I have to ask you? You are not a dog and have no excuse."

"So please explain, O wise Lord Edgington, what was wrong with Dicky's story." There was an ever so subtle edge of irritation to my voice.

"That's much better." He straightened his back and his whiskery cheeks perked up a little. "You see, it really isn't so difficult to observe the correct rules of speech. In fact–"

"Grandfather!"

He looked a little chastened himself then and finally got to the point. "The problem is that Oliver Mountfalcon has been a close friend of mine for the majority of my adult life. I knew him to be a generous individual, but he never mentioned a young boy he was supporting. Nor did he tell the story of a debtor over whose imprisonment he suffered any guilt."

"But, Grandfather, you locked yourself away from the world for a decade and barely communicated with the man. Isn't it possible that you've forgotten?"

He looked at me as though I'd told him we'd be eating hay and oats for Christmas dinner and that the horses would be having roast turkey in our place. "That's ridiculous. I would never forget such a thing. And besides, we maintained a regular correspondence."

I wasn't looking for an argument, if only because I knew any such discussion could take hours, I was bound to lose, and I was eager to get back to the warmth of Mistletoe Hall.

"Fine, then what do you think the killer hoped to imply? If Prowse isn't the man he says he is, who is he?"

He thought for a few moments, his eyes scanning the bumpy ground where roots were showing through the mud and snow. "That may not be the most important consideration. What we must ask ourselves is why the killer decided to reveal such a fact. And, even more vitally, how has the killer used the poem to disguise his own identity?"

I tried to look very serious on the matter, but finally gave up and admitted, "No, I'm sorry. I've no idea what you mean."

He stretched out one leg, as though it had been giving him bother; I was certain it was all part of his innocent-old-geezer act. I've known seven-year-olds who were less spritely than my grandfather.

"Well, if we exclude the possibility that your young friend is involved, one of the lines must refer to the killer." He had illuminated a really very obvious fact that I'd failed to consider. "In which case, he wouldn't want to reveal too much about himself. So what is he hiding?"

I went through the poem again in my head. *The musician's gone, Idris drives on, something about a pig...*

It didn't help a great deal, and I struggled to answer. "I haven't a clue. But do you really think it will help us find the link that connects our suspects?"

"That's just it." He clicked his fingers in irritation. "I keep going over everything in my head; the answer is just within reach, yet out of my grasp. I'm convinced there must be a common thread that runs between our group of apparent strangers. But I can only find connections between six or seven of us, and not the whole lot. It's maddening."

"Perhaps you'll be able to think more clearly beside a roaring fire." I stood to leave then, as I was afraid the hint I'd dropped was too subtle. "I'm inclined to believe that the killer is just playing games. It might seem clever of him to have constructed this elaborate enigma for us to solve, but what if it's a trick? What if he's merely showing off and there's no connection after all?"

I ducked out from under the holly and was once more impressed by the amount of snow on the ground. As my grandfather was clearly intent on sitting there a while longer, I took the opportunity to plough into the frosty white flakes. It was quite taxing, like pushing my way through compacted sand. I tried standing on top of the stuff but my feet kept sinking in and, when I shifted my legs back and forth to push through as my grandfather had, I was soon exhausted.

I made it to the top of a large bank, overlooking the gardens at the rear of the house, only to notice something in the distance. There were more footprints running from the side door to the elaborate network of outbuildings. The killer had been busy.

CHAPTER NINETEEN

"'And the king's about to lose his head,'" my grandfather muttered as he finally emerged from the cluster of holly bushes. He looked about for me and shouted over. "Chrissy, how's your history?"

"That's a silly question, Grandfather. You've met my teachers."

"Oh yes, good point. But I've got a better one for you." He followed my tracks through the snow and made surprisingly easy going of it. "Which British king lost his head?"

He was right; this was an easy one. We'd spent months studying the English Civil Wars, and I knew with great certainty that it was… well, one of the Charleses. "Charles… the… First?"

"That's right. And the last line of the poem made me wonder whether there might be a historical reference hidden within the killer's–"

"I'm sorry to interrupt, but I think you had better look at this." I gave him a hand up to the highest point, where the snow had gathered against the garden wall. It was surprisingly dense there. I could stand on the top and see all the way around two sides of the manor.

"What of it?" he asked.

"You don't think it's suspicious that there are footprints going back and forth to the house? It was still snowing when I woke up. They must be quite recent."

He narrowed his eyes in that typically suspicious manner of his. "I suppose it's worth investigating, though it might well be one of the staff."

"Why would they be out here? They're just as averse to the cold weather as I am."

He gave a belligerent sniff before conceding my point – to an extent. "There's only one way to find out."

With something of a running start, he descended once more into the snow. I was impressed by his strength as he pushed on through the drifts. Even with his determination and successful technique, though, we moved slowly. I had to wonder whether even a strapping young fellow like Todd or Dicky Prowse would have the stamina to make it all the way back to Snowshill village.

We met the trail of footprints halfway to the formal gardens that I'd visited the day before. I'd been hoping that there might be some unique pattern to the tread, or that they'd be remarkably large or remarkably small to help us in our task. Sadly, we'd have no such luck. All I could make out were deep holes in the snow that looked like they'd been walked over a number of times.

"Perhaps you could take the lead for a while, dear boy." Grandfather was puffing away from the exertion. Obviously, I heeded his request.

This made our progress slower, but in time, we left the open spaces around the house and entered the corridor of carefully demarcated squares that functioned as miniature gardens. With the frozen blanket now descended entirely, there was even less to see than the day before. The only remaining sign of the peculiarity of Lord Mountfalcon's landscaping was an occasional stone sculpture which poked through the snow. They looked like desperate arms reaching out from the grave. The sight of them certainly didn't fill me with Christmas cheer.

We eventually came to a fork in the path where the footprints led off in different directions.

"That clever devil." This wasn't the first time I'd heard my grandfather sound impressed by a killer's stratagems. "He would have known we could find him, and so he covered his tracks."

"Literally!" I added, as though such a thing needed saying.

"Which path should we take?"

There were four to choose from and so I took my time deciding. "Ip dip, sky's blue, which path should I choose? Between you and—"

"Christopher, what are you doing?"

I sent a sheepish look back to him. I hadn't realised I'd been reciting the rhyme out loud. "Oh… it's nothing. Just a poem which helps me to make decisions."

"You're seventeen years old." He spoke as if I'd been sucking my thumb and crying for my mummy – two things I hadn't done in quite some time. "But more to the point, you're a detective investigating a murder, not a schoolboy choosing between boiled sweets."

"I don't often use it," I said in my defence. "Just when I'm feeling uncertain about something."

Grandfather had the most expressive eyebrows and, with one slight inflection, he reminded me that I was one of the least decisive people in Britain.

"As detectives, we must use scientific fact, reason and, above all, the evidence in front of us to come to the right conclusion." He sounded so full of pomp at that moment, I thought he might start singing the national anthem.

"All right, then," I replied. "Which way do you think we should go?"

That got him! He peered around the four routes, which sprang off between hedgerows like the start of a labyrinth. "Evidently, when faced with such an impossible choice, the only solution is to go with the simplest option."

"Which means?"

He rolled his eyes. "Which means we continue onwards."

He nodded confidently to himself and set off along the most central path. There was little greenery on display on the neatly cut thickets on either side of us. It was as though some meddlesome spirit had come along with a can of extremely thick paint and turned the living world white.

After some strenuous rambling through the snow, we came out on a small, enclosed terrace which had little of interest except a few well-hidden wooden benches and an empty dovecote. The footprints we were following took a turn around the square and came straight back upon themselves.

"Science and rational thinking triumph again!" I said to bait the old genius.

"No one likes a gloater, Christopher." He looked at me through the side of one eye, as hurried past me, back the way we'd come.

"I say we should take the second from left," I told him before we reached the crossing once more.

"And why would we do that?"

"I don't know, I suppose it's a feeling I have."

"You have 'a feeling'?" He let out a scoff. "Well, lead on, my boy. If you have 'a feeling', it must be investigated at once."

"You can call it intuition if it makes you more comfortable."

He had nothing to say to that, but waited for me to follow my chosen path.

"Well, I never!" he exclaimed, when we reached the end of the curling route. Draped over a topiary figure, were the same black clothes I'd seen the killer wearing earlier that day. "I'll have to listen to your intuition more often."

He fell quiet as he inspected the silky dressing gown. It was draped over the outstretched branch like a tea towel hanging from a waiter's arm. The fabric had an exotic pattern upon it, in a black gloss on matte. I hadn't noticed it that morning, but it clearly meant something to my grandfather.

"I believe this belonged to my friend."

"To Lord Mountfalcon?"

"That's right." He reached his hand out as if to take the item of clothing, but he couldn't bring himself to touch it. "The killer must have left it here to mock us for even trying to find him."

I looked around the scene and spotted more clothes strewn about the place. There were two woollen jumpers and a pair of thick trousers with long underwear inside them.

"I thought that the killer had worn all those clothes in order to disguise himself, but perhaps he only did it to keep warm outside."

Grandfather didn't respond. He was staring at a piece of shrapnel in the snow. That was all I could see of the medieval helmet; a triangle of metal sticking up out of the raised white ground.

"We should take it for when the police get here. We can make sure no one else will interfere with it at least."

He let out a defeated sigh. "I have to assume that would be pointless. No one would go to this amount of trouble and not wear gloves."

I feared he was right, but hated to see him so utterly bereft. Until now, he'd maintained his good humour in the face of great adversity, but this was the moment that his friend's death came home to him.

"I've been arrogant, Christopher. I thought I could solve this case just like any other, but at least two people are already dead. I only wish I knew why the psychopathic character doesn't kill me and get it over with. The poem says that 'the king's about to lose his head', but it's not happening fast enough if you ask me."

I walked back over to him. It wasn't really in my family's nature to do anything so affectionate as putting a hand on a shoulder, but that's what I decided to do. "We'll stop him, Grandfather. Well, you will. It would take me a century to puzzle out what's been happening here. I'd be surprised if you require more than a day."

He laughed, but there was no joy in it. It was a sad, uncertain sound. "I've already missed that milestone, my boy. I believe it has been noted that a pessimist is never disappointed. And, with that in mind, we might just as well return to the house and wait for the killer to make the next move."

He turned to tramp back to Mistletoe Hall. I wasn't sure whether I should keep looking for evidence of what the killer had been doing out there or follow him. In the end, I remembered how cold my feet were and did the sensible thing.

CHAPTER TWENTY

My grandfather rushed ahead with his thoughts, and I took my time. As I approached the door at the side of the house, the sound of singing drew me forward. It was a high, clear voice that I didn't recognise.

"The angel Gabriel from heaven came,
His wings as drifted snow, his eyes as flame,"
All hail, said he, thou lowly maiden Mary!
Most highly favoured Lady, Glor-or-or-or-ria!"

I had never heard the carol sung quite so exquisitely before. I knew it from school assemblies, of course – though, I must admit, I had always thought the lyric was "most highly flavoured gravy" as that's what most boys sang.

"Of her, Emmanuel, the Christ, was born,
In Bethlehem, all on a Christmas morn,
And Christian folk throughout the world will ever say,
Most highly favoured Lady, Glor-or-or-or-ria!"

I followed the sound, the way a dog would trace a scent, and ended up in a small room in one corner of the house. It was filled with musical instruments of every kind. And there, sitting at a piano, quite consumed by the performance, was not Sophy Viner or Idris Levitt as I had imagined, but my friend Marmaduke Adelaide.

"That was beautiful!" I told him, without announcing myself, and he quite nearly jumped out of his skin.

"Chrissy…" he stopped and sought some explanation for why he would be sitting alone singing Christmas carols. "I was just killing time before lunch." He heard his own words and apologised. "Sorry, I didn't mean to be indelicate. It isn't the moment to be talking of killing, I suppose. I just…. You see… Father's on the warpath. He's forever shouting at me about who knows what, and I decided to get away for a while."

I ignored his anxious look and returned to cheerier topics. "Honestly, Marmaduke, old pal. That was some tip-top warbling. Truly five-star stuff. If the choir master at Oakton ever finds out you've got pipes like that, he'll never let you shut your mouth."

He glanced down at the piano as though he didn't know what it was or how he had got there. "Don't go overboard. I can hold a tune, but I'm hardly going to make my living on the stage. Father wouldn't allow it for one thing."

It's hard to put into words the schism between the picture of the boy who every student at Oakton academy had feared at the beginning of that year and the shy, humble cur sitting before me. I wasn't the one who'd mentioned the stage and yet he spoke as if this was exactly what he wanted.

"I'm sure if he heard you sing, he'd support you all the way." I couldn't stop smiling. "Here, how did you learn to play the piano like that in the first place?"

Even when he wasn't playing, he continued pressing the keys lightly – silently practicing another piece. "My sisters didn't want anything to do with me when I was little. Mother never had time for me, and Father was barely around. We had a piano in our nursery, though, and I started bashing away one day and never stopped."

This cheered me up even more. "You taught yourself? That's incredible. I wish I had any talent. The best I can do is an impersonation of my grandfather, and very few people outside of my family would know who it was supposed to be."

He still looked glum, so I decided to do my impression. *"Really, Christopher, must you insist on breathing at the specific pitch at this time on a Tuesday? How is one supposed to solve a murder when one cannot think?"*

He glanced up at me, his expression quite transformed. "Hey, you know that's jolly good too. I bet that, if you can do that, with a bit of practice you could do anyone. We would make a decent double act."

I had to slow him down then, as this certainly wasn't the conversation I'd been expecting. "Ummm, sorry, old chap. But I get the most dreadful stage fright. It would take an awful lot of cream cakes to get me up in front of an audience."

We both fell silent, and he played a few mournful notes on the piano to cover the awkward hush. I looked around the room, which was yet another of Lord Mountfalcon's exhibition spaces. One wall was given over to brass instruments. There were a hundred horns, pipes and trumpets pinned in place. The biggest tuba I'd ever set eyes on hung from the ceiling like a lamp, and I was rather tempted to take something down from the percussion wall and accompany my friend. Bashing a simple drum is almost certainly the zenith of my musical ability.

I thought of something to break through the gloom and, in a cheery voice, told him, "By the way, grandfather was wondering whether you're the killer."

His face dropped.

"No, don't worry, I set him straight. I told him that you'd never hurt anyone… well, except for that time you gave me a black eye. Oh, and the run in you had with Derek McGeorge – you broke his wrist if I remember correctly. I'm sure it was a mistake." The silence returned for three long seconds. "It was a mistake, wasn't it?"

He threw his hands down on the keys and it sounded like he'd dropped the piano from a great height. "No, of course it wasn't. I was after his pocket money. He wouldn't give it to me, so I bent his hand back the wrong way until he changed his mind."

"Oh…" was all I could say in response, as I couldn't think of any explanation for such behaviour.

He turned on his stool to look at me. "That's the problem, you see?"

I didn't, but he kept talking so that I didn't have to look silly.

"People have only ever seen me as a bully and a vandal. That's why, now that I'm trying to be a tad nicer – a touch more mature – no one believes it's true."

I put myself in his shoes for the briefest of moments, but it was long enough to feel sorry for him. "*I* do. I think you're a jolly good chap. And I'm sure that if Grandfather heard you sing a rendition of 'The Holly and the Ivy' he'd never doubt you again."

He did not look convinced by my suggestion. "To be honest, Chrissy, I'm not certain that my singing voice is enough of an alibi. Otherwise, choir boys across the country would get away with murder."

"Hmmm. You're probably right." I had to hand it to him; this was sound logic. Several of the nastiest boys I'd ever met had served behind the altar and could sing like angels. "But I'll tell you what… Shove up on that stool and I'll join you for a song."

He smiled at last, and I nudged him over a smidgen. "I'm a dreadful singer, but I make up in enthusiasm what I lack in talent." I had to consider which song we could sing together. "Do you know how to play that new one, 'Ding Dong Merrily on High?'"

He didn't reply in so many words, but began tinkling on the ivories and, all of a sudden, the room was full of his sweet voice once more. He played in a slow, maudlin manner and I felt dreadful to interrupt, but it wasn't my idea of Christmas spirit.

"No, no, no. Put a bit of life into it. Play it faster so that we can really scream out the words. That's when singing's most fun. You know, like in assembly at school."

"Like this…?"

He played the introduction again at twice the speed and, when he got to the first verse, I joined in with the song.

> **"Ding dong! merrily on high,**
> **In heav'n the bells are ringing:**
> **Ding dong! verily the sky,**
> **Is riv'n with Angel singing."**

It probably sounded quite abysmal – my caterwauling mixed with Marmaduke's melodious tones – but we didn't mind. We were having a wizard time and made it right through the dipping chorus before I heard a sound at the door, and in marched Horatio Adelaide.

"Marmaduke, why are you wasting your time?" His broad frame seemed to fill the small room and, as though he'd pulled the needle off a gramophone record, our song came to an abrupt conclusion.

"I was just…" His voice transformed by melancholy, Marmaduke wouldn't finish the sentence. He couldn't even glance up at his scornful father.

"Well, don't. Close the fallboard and come with me." He wrapped one gigantic hand around his son's arm and pulled him up to standing with a violent tug.

I thought that Marmaduke might shout out in complaint, but he kept his trembling lips shut. With his head down, he stalked from the room.

"Excuse us, Christopher." Horatio nodded and walked after his son, still looking as though someone had insulted him.

I thought about staying behind to try out some of the instruments, but want to be alone – what with the crazed murderer on the prowl and all that. Leaving the music room, I caught sight of Marmaduke and his father through a window. They were outside in the snow, really screaming at one another.

"I'm asking you a question, boy."

"Why even bother when you clearly won't believe me?" Marmaduke's face was bright red and, for once, he found the courage to look his father in the eye.

"I want to hear you say it. Did you kill that man this morning?"

The boy's eyes widened, and he shook his head in horror at what he was hearing. "How could you think that of me? You know we weren't here when Lord Mountfalcon was killed."

The former-criminal took a step closer, every muscle in his body rippling with the potential for violence. "I'm not interested in Mountfalcon. I'm asking about this morning. Harry Crump, or whatever his name was. Did you kill him?"

Marmaduke could produce no sound for a whole five seconds. "No, of course I didn't."

His father seemed to relax just a fraction. "Don't you think it's a little odd that the killer could have cut my head off, but decided otherwise? Christopher Prentiss was there with me. If he tells his grandfather what he saw, you'll be in a world of trouble."

Marmaduke breathed out a disbelieving puff that materialised in a small cloud of hot air. "Funnily enough, he did tell his grandfather, and Chrissy was loyal enough to know that I would never do such a thing."

"Don't ever rely on your friends, Marmaduke. I've made that mistake too often in my life." He turned to look up at the house. Luckily, I was hidden at the side of the large sash window and he couldn't see me.

Marmaduke moved to go, but had second thoughts. "Actually, Father, I have a question for you. Why did you even bring me here if you think I'm such a terribly evil person?"

Horatio pulled his shoulders back and, taking his time, secured the buttons on his morning jacket. "Never mind that, boy. The important thing is that you're not to blame." He nodded, as though as to reassure himself before walking in the direction of the house.

His son immediately stepped into his path, and I could see how hard it was for him to stand up to the notorious fellow. "You're not getting away so easily this time. You dragged me up here without a word of explanation, and, just for once, I'd like to know what you were thinking."

Horatio stared straight back at him. "Be careful what you say, boy. You might regret it."

Even as his father pushed past him, Marmaduke hadn't finished. "Tell me," he screamed, the despair plain in his voice. "Tell me why you brought me here!"

CHAPTER TWENTY-ONE

I'd had a number of doubts brewing in my head that day, and this was another to add to the list. If everything Marmaduke had said about his father on the last night of the school term was true, why did Horatio bring him along to Lord Mountfalcon's imaginary party?

It was difficult enough to think up reasons for why the main guests had received the phantom invitations. If I had to imagine why their companions were brought along too, what chance did I stand?

In my own case, it made sense. Grandfather had spent most of that year ferrying me about to new places. It was his way of providing his unique form of education and, as far as I could tell, a good opportunity to show off his superior mind as often as possible. He'd brought my mother and Albert to Mistletoe Hall to keep me company at Christmas, and the ridiculous number of staff came because… well, I still wasn't certain why he insisted on travelling with so many servants, but he must have had his reasons.

I wandered back to the main part of the house with these mysteries occupying a large part of my small brain. Grandfather was keen to teach me the tricks and techniques of the best detectives, but I was yet to solve one of our murders for myself and didn't feel as though I'd have much luck this time either.

I thought it might be a good idea to pick a suspect and stick with them throughout. That way I wouldn't be swayed by red herrings. With the killer helpfully bumping off suspects, there was now a one in five chance that I'd get it right. Of course, knowing my luck, Harry Crump had probably faked his own death and would end up being the real culprit.

I was puzzling this over in my head when I spotted Idris Levitt, 'The fastest girl on Earth', acting suspiciously a way along the hall from me. I thought, *fine, she'll do,* and chose her as my designated suspect. In one sense, she was the obvious culprit, if only because she'd been so invisible since the night before. Having stormed into the house demanding attention, she'd fallen terribly quiet. And though I'd seen countless mentions of her in the papers, her roots were a mystery to me.

As I trailed along after her through the endless gloomy corridors of Mistletoe Hall, she glanced furtively into each room we passed. She carried a burlap sack and there was a nervousness about her that I hadn't witnessed before. The longer this went on, the more I believed I was really on to something. She led us right through the house to the sitting room where we'd spent the previous afternoon. I'd kept my distance until now, but hovered just outside the room to spy on her.

Looking around once more, she went over to my less than sparkling Christmas tree and knelt down before it.

"I've got you!" I yelled, pushing the door open with a bang and scanning about for a weapon, in case she should give me any trouble.

Shocked by my ever-so-dramatic entrance, she dropped what she'd been holding and shot up to standing. "Christopher, I…" She couldn't find the words she needed. She obviously hadn't thought up a credible excuse for whatever frightful misdeed was underway.

"How thoughtful, Miss Levitt," a voice came from the corner behind the door. Both my suspect and I had failed to spot my grandfather, who was sitting in an armchair, apparently doing nothing. "Christmas wouldn't be Christmas without a few presents."

I saw now that, with the empty sack in her hand at her side, she'd deposited a number of small items wrapped in green tissue paper.

It would take more than a few trinkets to throw me off the scent. "Presents, eh?"

She emitted a nervous laugh. It was high-pitched, lilting and decidedly different from her usual no-nonsense tone. "They're nothing special, just a few things I brought as a concession to the season."

I looked at Grandfather, expecting him to deliver the key piece of information that would undermine her story. Instead, he mumbled, "That's very kind of you," and went back to his thinking.

I would not give up so easily. "Is there one for each of us? Or rather, one for each of those who received an invitation to Mistletoe Hall?"

She glanced back down at the floor. "You know, I believe there's just enough."

"Wonderful." I walked over to inspect her handiwork. "But, out of interest, how did you know who was going to be here?"

Clearly not at ease with my questioning, she looked over at my oblivious grandfather as though he would be the one to furnish her with an answer.

"I didn't, of course. But knowing it was a Christmas party, I thought I should probably make an effort. They're all rather generic; ties for the gents and perfume for the ladies, that sort of thing."

I thought this a likely story and gave the presents a good poke. Each had a name tag on and there were two clearly distinct shapes, so her explanation appeared accurate.

"I brought far too many perfumes and not nearly enough ties," she explained. "Don't get too excited by yours, Christopher. It's a tie."

I suppose that Grandfather had been listening to the interrogation, though his eyes were closed. "As I said, that's really very thoughtful of you."

Idris Levitt looked at me as though she knew what I'd been thinking. "Sorry to interrupt. I'll leave you in peace. Perhaps Miss Viner is nearby and we can explore the house together."

Grandfather raised one hand and finally opened his eyes. "There's no need to apologise, my child." He had his assumed his old fogey voice again, and I could tell he was about to charm or disarm her. "Why don't you sit down by the fire next to me?" Though he was attempting to sound innocent and loveable, he reminded me of the wolf in 'Little Red Riding Hood', dressed up in her grandmother's clothing.

"I really don't wish to disturb you." Idris Levitt dithered between the two options and remained suspended in space.

"I know; we'll call for some more mulled wine. Christopher, ring the bell for a member of staff to come up from the kitchen."

She couldn't resist such a festive libation and I couldn't resist my grandfather's order. She sat down in the arm-chair opposite Lord Edgington and I pressed the button beside the door that would ring a bell below stairs. With my job done, I went to make a fuss of Delilah, who was laid out on a lion-skin rug in front of the fire.

My two companions sat in tongue-tied silence while they waited for a footman to arrive. This was no accident on my grandfather's part. He knew that this uneasy peace would unsettle our suspect; he was setting the poor woman off guard before his interrogation even began. The pair occasionally looked back and forth at one another, as though to say, *hmmm where could all the servants have got to,* before (mercifully for everyone in that room) Todd finally appeared.

"You rang, M'Lord?"

"Yes, thank you, Todd. We'd like a carafe of mulled wine for the three of us and a bowl of water for Delilah." With eyebrows raised, he looked at Idris and me to see whether we might fancy anything else.

"Mince pies!" I said, a little desperately.

"Yes, of course, Christopher. A splendid idea."

"Very good, M'Lord." Todd bowed, ready to leave, but his master interrupted him with another thought.

"I was also wondering whether you'd made any progress with the snow? It would be nice to get away today. It's not much fun around here with a killer on the loose." It was another skilful piece of understatement from my grandfather, and our chauffeur-cum-butler-cum-just-about-everything-else gave a wry smile.

"I did my best, M'Lord, but once I got as far as the main path, the snow got deeper and I didn't like my chances of making it to the village without catching hypothermia. I could give it another go if you think it's sensible, but I believe we'll have to wait for a thaw."

"No, no. If that's the way of things, then that's how they'll have to be." Grandfather sounded perturbed, but shook his head and soon recovered.

"I did have one idea, M'Lord. If you'd give me permission to look through the house and outbuildings, I was wondering if I might discover some device to make leaving the grounds a simpler task."

"You mean a sledge of some description?"

Todd gave an efficient nod. "Something along those lines, M'Lord."

"Perhaps Delilah here could pull us all to safety!" This idea flashed through my mind and I haven't the faintest idea why I repeated it *à voix haute*.

Grandfather gave me a troubled look. "Permission granted, Todd, and may I compliment you on a fine idea indeed."

Showing no excessive pride in the compliment, our capable servant bowed once more and retreated from the room. Idris Levitt looked quite bemused by this exchange, and I had to wonder whether she was as comfortable around toffs and their domestics as the papers would have us believe.

"I'm sorry about all that," Grandfather began, his gaze now directed squarely at the young lady in front of him. "I promise that, from now on, you'll have my undivided attention."

CHAPTER TWENTY-TWO

Idris Levitt was an odd sort of person to encounter. She was not exactly beautiful by traditional standards – with her thin, angular face and severe manner – but the papers adored her and she was considered the height of fashion by many women her age. She was forever dressed in gauzy fabrics which would whip through the air as she accelerated around a racing circuit or across some dry plane on a speed trial.

"It's nice to have something to distract me," she said with a wave of her hand, and I was reminded of her extreme confidence the night before. "I don't have anything urgent to be getting on with, except doing all I can to stay alive."

Grandfather inhaled a sharp breath. "Yes, it is quite unnerving, I agree. In my experience – and I'm sorry to say this is not the first time I've been in such a situation – the best thing to do is simply pretend it isn't happening."

I thought this quite the silliest piece of advice I'd ever heard and was quick to respond. "How on earth are we to pretend that our lives aren't in danger from a spear and pistol-wielding madman?"

My grandfather was the picture of serenity, even in the face of my impertinent question. "One must imagine a happier milieu. I, for example, like to picture myself at the seaside. Brighton, maybe, or even St Ives. I close my eyes for a moment, breathe in the fresh sea air and all my worries disappear."

I considered pointing out the fact that, were we to close our eyes for any length of time, we would make the killer's task a simpler one. He was already unhappy with me for talking out of turn, though, and I decided to keep my thoughts to myself.

"I believe you must love the coast, Miss Levitt?" the old fellow hypothesised. "I'm forever spotting you in the paper about to break some new speed record on one English beach or another."

I don't think she enjoyed having the attention directed back to her and cleared a tickle from her throat before responding. "That's largely to drum up an audience. We could probably find flat places inland for the challenges, but who would watch them?"

Grandfather's moustache wiggled a touch, as though his nose was itchy and he couldn't scratch it. I could tell he was about to change the topic to something far more relevant to his investigation.

"I hope it's not too forward to say it, but you've always struck me as something of a mystery, Miss Levitt."

"Please," she replied, and I thought that the pressure on her was already telling. "Call me Idris. I simply cannot stand the formality of surnames."

"Very well, Idris." Grandfather cracked his knuckles combatively. "And you may call me Lord Edgington."

She laughed at this and seemed to relax into the conversation. "I've met a lot of knights of the realm, but none quite like you, sir."

Grandfather jerked his head, as though he'd just remembered something important. "Of course, I keep forgetting that you knew Ollie. Well, I can tell you this, there is no other person on earth quite like former Oliver Mountfalcon."

"Yes, he was a card, I'll give you that." Her face softened as she cast her mind back to happier moments she'd shared with the dead lord.

"How long had you known him exactly?" Grandfather's innocent tone rose to a high point.

"Oh, you know," she said, still grinning broadly before noticing the trap into which she'd fallen. "I… I think I told you yesterday, I only met him once. Barely knew the fellow, in fact." I saw that she dug the toe of one shoe into the back of her leg as she said this, as though angry with herself for making such a simple mistake.

"That's surprising, in a way." The old man was a terrible tease and let this assertion hang in the balmy air between them. Delilah had fallen asleep and appeared to be fighting something in her dreams. She kept tapping her paw aggressively onto the rug and must have seen off a good few foes by the time that Idris finally responded.

"I'm sorry, what's surprising?" She arched her eyebrows in confusion. "Lord Edgington, to speak plainly, I don't understand what you want of me. I–"

As a happy quirk of the speed at which the cogs of the universe were turning, it was at this exact moment that Halfpenny came in with a tray of drinks, mince pies and a bowl of water. He was such a fragile old chap that he looked forever on the precipice of a great fall; he was truly the Humpty Dumpty of Cranley Hall's staff. I jumped up from the floor to take the bowl and prevent any spillage.

Grandfather continued as though nothing had happened. "I just thought it surprising that you seem to know your way around the house so well if you've never been here before."

When it came, her reply was most acerbic. "Good spatial awareness, that's what it is. I see a house and some part of my brain must be able to analyse its structure. I swear I don't know that I'm doing it, but I always know which way is up and how to reach the drinks cabinet." As she said this, Halfpenny poured her a steaming measure of wine in a metal tankard, which she raised to us in turn.

"So you've never been to Mistletoe Hall before?" Grandfather confirmed. "That is quite remarkable."

"Must be my career." Her sentences were often short releases like bullets. "In motor racing, it's essential to know where your opponent is. It's the only way to win."

"Ah, yes, you must tell me about your career." He was like a seasoned journalist, rooting out an angle to a story that only he could see. "Or rather, tell me how you got started. It appeared as though you popped up overnight. Before Idris Levitt, young ladies didn't drive fast cars, but then you appeared from the ether and everything changed."

She shuffled about in her seat. "It might have seemed that way, but I can assure you I didn't appear from thin air. I worked for a long time to become the person I am."

My grandfather looked at me for a brief moment, as though to say, *did you hear that, boy?*

"What an interesting turn of phrase you have, Idris. So you built yourself, much as you would one of your cars?"

"Well, I meant to say that I learnt my trade. I worked as a secretary for Marshall motors. Mr Marshall himself picked me out and sponsored me to travel to Paris to study engineering and work with some of the best drivers on the planet. But I was the one who had to do the hard work to learn what I needed."

A note of anger transformed her voice. "I was the one risking my life on the track every day in training. People act as though I'm a fraud, just because I had a hand up through the industry. Men have such luck all the time, and no one complains about that."

"Quite!" Grandfather gave a stern nod and then returned to his more placid expression. For all his attempts to unnerve her, she was no fool. In fact, he was yet to land a clean blow. "Which is why I said that you're a mystery. I wouldn't wish to diminish your myriad achievements for a second, but the one thing I have never seen explained in the press is, why you?"

Her gaze had drifted to the sleepy golden retriever, who was now running a somnambulistic marathon. "A foolish question if ever there was one. You'd be wiser to ask, why not me?"

Grandfather hit straight back. "All I mean is, why were you chosen? Out of all the women who were working at the end of the war, why were you the one whom first your boss and then the press plucked from obscurity to turn into a celebrity?"

Her eyes shifted about like the second hand on a clock. "I told you, I worked harder than anyone else. I might have had training, but I also have the instincts to drive faster than near any man I've met."

"Ahhh…" This soft exclamation faded out and Grandfather ran a pensive finger over his lips. I thought he might have met his match and would give up on his attempt to extract the woman's hidden secrets, but he wasn't one for surrendering. "Idris is a Welsh name, is it not?"

She released a snort of amusement. "That's right. I'm named after my father. He always wanted a boy but had to make do with me."

"His name was also Idris Levitt?"

She was beginning to lose her temper. "No. Levitt was my mother's name. The papers suggested I adopt it because Idris Jones didn't have the same ring to it."

"Oh, you're a Jones!" Grandfather gave no sense of what he was thinking, but suddenly looked more focused, more intense. "I knew plenty of Joneses when I was in the police. You grew up in London, is that correct?"

"Yes." She stretched the word out to show her irritation at the banality of the conversation.

"The London-Welsh community was strong at the turn of the century. Small communities would spring up around the Welsh chapels there. Who knows… I may have met your parents at some point."

"Who knows indeed! And I didn't say my mother was Welsh. Levitt is a Jewish name, or the anglicised version of one at least." She had lost interest entirely by now and got up from her seat. "If

150

you don't mind, I think I'd prefer something a little stronger." She stomped off across the room in that strangely confident manner of hers and, pulling a book down from the wall, the whole shelf came with it. She had uncovered a previously concealed bar, with bottles of every spirit one could desire.

Personally, I didn't want any of them. I wasn't much of a drinker and the mulled wine was already too strong for me. I helped myself to a third mince pie to soak up the alcohol.

"This will do the trick!" She'd selected a bottle of cognac and proceeded to pour half of it into her tankard.

"Do you still wish to deny that you've ever set foot in Mistletoe Hall before?" Grandfather was quick to enquire.

Far from being horrified by such a question, she had a good laugh and shook her head, clearly feeling foolish for giving away her secret so easily. "You've got me, guvnor. It's a fair cop, and you've got me."

Grandfather didn't look surprised and had presumably been waiting for just such a breakthrough. "I don't know if Oliver ever spoke to you about me, but of all the close acquaintances I've had in the last fifty years, he may well be the most important. Not just professionally, but personally. I considered him a good friend and, though I have been proven wrong in such instances before, I would like to believe that I knew him rather well."

"Your point being?"

"My point being that you remind me of every woman I saw him show an interest in since we first joined the police. I knew that the two of you were photographed together in the newspaper. I could tell that you were familiar with the layout of the house from the moment you arrived, and the rest was simple enough to put together."

"I wasn't his lover, if that's what you're suggesting!" She sounded quite scandalised by the idea.

"What went on between you is no business of mine. Still, I'm sure you will have benefitted from your relationship with Ollie, just as many of the women before you did. You see, he was a supremely intelligent man in all but two respects. He was the best commissioner the Met has ever had; he could have led the Charge of the Light Brigade and ended up with more soldiers than he began. But he was useless with money and a fool with women. Whenever the two came together, it spelt disaster. So forgive me for imagining that he would have done all he could to spoil you rotten and, as he was a good forty years older than you, not expected an awful lot in return."

"Ah, I see…" She took her time before elaborating on this response.

As the conversation had progressed, and I fell deeper into the trance of their voices, I'd started to stroke Delilah increasingly fast. She took advantage of this quiet moment to wake up and look at me like I'd been very naughty indeed. Then, after a quick, maternal nip on my hand, she closed her eyes and went back to sleep.

"You think I killed him." Idris's voice remained as flat as a fresh sheet of paper.

Slowly and purposefully, Grandfather crossed his arms. "It had crossed my mind."

"Naturally." She tipped her drink down her throat and went in search of another. "But tell me this. Why the song and dance? If I wanted the old fool dead, why would I draw so much attention to the crime? I could have come here and quietly done away with him. Why the theatrics? And why would I have murdered that clown Harry Crump?"

A silence fell between them, but grandfather broke it with a slow, steady clap of his hands. "That's quite a battery of questions, including several that I have already asked myself any number of times. However, if you consider this to be evidence of your innocence, I could make the same argument for anyone else here. Perhaps you sought to complicate the enquiry in order to cover your real intention. Perhaps you murdered our host in order to steal some rare and valuable artefact that you've already smuggled off the property."

"I didn't kill him."

Grandfather abruptly changed tack. "How did you know Lord Mountfalcon?"

For every new question he served, she knocked it away just as easily. "I met him through my racing, as you well know."

"Who was your father?"

"He was no one. Why would you even ask such petty questions?"

Grandfather's voice rose then, and I had to wonder what had got into him. "Tell me who your father was."

"His name was Idris Jones, and he was nothing, nobody. He left my family when I was ten years old." She was becoming more perplexed by his questioning.

"So he was not the Idris Jones who distinguished himself during the Battle of St Quentin Canal?"

She searched for her words, before finally repeating in a lupine growl, "He was nobody."

This was enough to kill off my grandfather's interrogation entirely. I had no idea why he'd asked that specific set of questions, but it was plain how much the poor woman was suffering. I didn't like it when he was so forceful in his technique. Acclaimed detective or not, he didn't have to be pushy.

Standing in front of the secret drinks cabinet, Idris Levitt directed a pointed glare in my grandfather's direction. "Thank you for entertaining me, Lord Edgington. I do so enjoy games at Christmas."

She selected a bottle of gin, tucked it under her arm, and left the room. I very much expected my grandfather to be aggrieved by this defeat, but instead, he sat in his armchair and grinned.

154

CHAPTER TWENTY-THREE

"I'm sorry to tell you, Grandfather, but I'm quite lost. I'm not certain I can explain a single question you put to her. What was all that about the war?"

He had poured himself another mug of mulled wine, which he brought to his lips but would not drink. "The war?" he asked absentmindedly, before answering the question himself. "Oh, that. It was just a ruse. I have no idea if there was an Idris Jones who fought at the Battle of St Quentin Canal. I was hoping she might take exception to the compliment I paid her father and tell me who he really was."

He slumped lower in his chair and chewed on the rim of the metal tankard.

His answer simply conjured up further questions in my mind. "But why were you interested in her father in the first place?"

"Because, Christopher… Because none of it makes sense. We're supposed to believe she was some ordinary assistant in a factory which produced automobiles. A woman who appeared from nowhere to become the world's foremost female motorist. An apparently ordinary woman who has been featured in every newspaper for the last decade. It's frankly beyond my comprehension."

I realised he hadn't quite answered my question, so I tried once more. "That doesn't explain what her father has to do with anything."

"Think about it, Christopher. Can you tell me a single detail of her life before she started driving? One day she didn't exist and the next she was famous. That tells me she has a past to hide. I get the definite impression that she does not enjoy talking about her family –and her father in particular."

"But what has all this got to do with Lord Mountfalcon and the murders?"

His voice flared up again. "Haven't you realised yet? I don't care about the murders." His eyes bore into me like… well… drills, I suppose. What else can bore? "The snow has done a good job of hiding too much evidence. I found little except for the poem at the second murder scene, and our killer is far too clever to give himself away. In order to catch our culprit, I have one task and one task only.

I must work out why we were invited to Mistletoe Hall."

"I've been thinking about that," I began, then remembered that I hadn't got very far. "I was thinking that our suspects are all quite young – except for Horatio and, if we're including him on our list, Inspector Blunt, of course. Ogilby, Prowse, Miss Viner and Miss Levitt are of a similar age. Don't you think that might tell us something?"

He looked a little hopeful, but then his enthusiasm faded. "It's worth noting, but I can't say it's the vital clue we require."

"Then what about crime?"

His response was as dry as a rich tea biscuit. "Well, yes, that is something we tend to consider in a murder investigation."

"No. I mean that there are several criminal connections. As Dicky Prowse has already pointed out, his father was in prison. You, Lord Mountfalcon and Inspector Blunt are all police officers. Idris has been in the courts a number of times for speeding. Couldn't that be it?"

He finally took a sip of his drink. "It's too vague. Why would a killer play on something so tangential? Evidently, with three policemen involved, there would be connections to the world of crime, but that's hardly an explanation."

"Yes, but–"

"I'm sorry, Christopher, we're no closer to solving the puzzle now than we were when we arrived." He had lost his positivity, and his voice was little more than a feeble croak. "We'll just have to hope the killer further reduces our suspect list and we can eliminate all the innocent names."

"You've returned to your pessimism, I see."

A flood of emotions washed over him then and he raised his free hand skywards. Well… ceiling-wards, at least. "Oh my goodness! I've got it!" He crashed his mug down on the table next to him and stood up from his chair. "Chrissy, we've been eliminating the innocent names, but what if they're not so innocent?" He seemed most energised by this. As ever, I hadn't a clue why he was getting so agitated. "You're a genius, my boy. An absolute genius."

"But you're the one who said that, not me."

He was alive with excitement and danced across the room. "Then I'm the genius; an absolute genius!"

I wasn't about to encourage such vanity and put another question to him. "So what do we do now?"

"Now…" he said, his powerful voice more mysterious than ever. "Now we must dress for the feast."

With his piece said, he strode from the room, and I tailed after him somewhat apathetically. While I was starving hungry and very much looking forward to whatever Cook had prepared, I wasn't sure how I felt about sharing such a special dinner with a murderer.

In my family, it's a tradition to eat just two meals on Christmas Eve. To make up for this, our early dinner lasts half the day and feels like four to five banquets combined. Normally I would have been at home with just my brother and parents in our house at Kilston Down. Thanks to my grandfather's re-engagement with the world after ten years of solitude, our regular routine had flown clean out of the window. I very much doubted things would ever go back to normal.

I was about to head upstairs to do as instructed when my mother and brother came along the corridor. Their arms were loaded with an unusual collection of objects and there was a smile on both their faces. I really couldn't remember my brother looking less hard done by in years. He was always crying his heart out over some girl or other, and I could only conclude that the magic of Christmas had brought him back to his old (marginally more cheerful) self.

"What on earth are you doing?" I asked as they disappeared into the dining room to heap their exotic finds onto a chair.

"Come along, Chrissy," Albert said. "There's no time for gawping. It will be dinner soon and we've work to do."

"We looked all over the house," Mother explained, not a great deal more helpfully than her firstborn. "Help your brother in the sitting room and I'll start organising here."

In a daze, I wandered back to the comfortable salon where Delilah was still snoring away. Albert bumbled along ahead of me, whistling 'Silent Night' as he went. He knelt down beside my rather sad-looking Christmas tree and glanced up at me with great expectation in his eyes.

"Well, come on then."

I finally comprehended what we were doing and so I crouched down to take the other handle of the brass cauldron and transport the poor spruce into the dining room.

"I love decorating Christmas trees," Albert was positively…

well…positive. "It might well be my favourite part of the holiday."

This begged the question of why he hadn't helped me out the night before, or back home at Cranley, or for the last five Christmases when he was being sullen, for that matter.

I had no desire to put him in a bad mood again and so I crouched down to help. "Me too. I truly adore it."

As we sidestepped through the house, the tree swayed a little but did not fall, and we made it all the way to the dining room without incident. There was another suit of armour in the corner, which I was only too happy to obscure with our arboreal guest.

Mother was busy separating their haul up into three piles that were spread out over several dining chairs. There was a chair which held long pieces of fabric that they had extracted from various wardrobes upstairs. Though they may have started life as dressing gown belts and curtain ties, I could see that they would make perfect decorations for our tree.

The second chair displayed any number of shiny trinkets, which had already been threaded with red cotton to hang on the tree like baubles – the sparkling glass and polished metals made my bent spoon from the night before look rather shabby. The final chair was covered with a selection of jewellery. There were chains of pearls so long that they could wrap right around the tree, garnet earrings, golden rings, and silver hoops.

"There's a whole room given over to jewels and gems," Albert explained as I took in this last treasure trove. "I don't suppose the old lord would have minded, and we can we put everything back before we leave."

As Halfpenny and Dorie were busy setting the table, my family decorated the tree. We didn't speak a great deal, but worked away in unison like the mice in 'The Tailor of Gloucester'. Before long, my personally selected spruce had gone from looking drab and a touch lonely to being the resplendent showpiece of the room.

"Sirs, madam, if I may be so bold as to say something," our footman began in his usual hesitant yet formal manner, as we stood back to appreciate the fruits of our labour. "That is truly the handsomest Christmas tree I've seen in many a year."

"Thank you, Halfpenny." Mother was all smiles. She had a singular capacity for finding positivity in even the darkest times. "I think we've done a respectable job."

It was more than just respectable; it was a work of art. I imagined that William Morris and all his creative friends couldn't have done a better job. There was only one thing missing, but it wasn't quite the time yet.

Halfpenny's expression turned grave. "I'm terribly sorry to interrupt your diversion, but the Christmas Eve dinner will be served in fifteen minutes."

He, not too subtly, looked us up and down, and I had to laugh a little. Albert was covered in dust and black greasy marks from his trek around Mistletoe Hall. Mother's dress was creased and unkempt, and my thick woollen jumper was covered in pine needles.

It was the twenty-fourth of December, a feast was on its way, and we'd most definitely worked up an appetite.

CHAPTER TWENTY-FOUR

By the time I went upstairs to change, Grandfather was already dressed and waiting.

"Will you please hurry up, Christopher. I do detest tardiness in all its forms. You wouldn't appear at a dinner party back at Cranley Hall five minutes late, and you shouldn't here either."

I wasn't fully paying attention, as I was trying to comprehend how there could be more than one form of tardiness. "Yes, Grandfather."

Bustling about in that uppity manner he occasionally adopts, he went to knock on the door next to ours. I'd hardly seen Dicky Prowse since breakfast and was about to discover why.

"Have you spotted anything?" Grandfather asked as soon as the door was cracked open.

"Nothing, M'Lord." The cricketer had good manners, and I wondered if he'd learnt a thing or two from Lord Mountfalcon. He stepped out of the room and I noticed a small pair of binoculars in his hand, as though he had been watching birds from the heights of his bedroom windows. As his room faced the forest at the front of the house, this would have been a prime spot for it but, with the snow falling intermittently throughout the day, the visibility would have been dreadful. I doubt I could have told a wigeon from a pigeon in such weather.

"Well, I appreciate you trying." Grandfather let out a faint cluck with his tongue and continued in a weary tone. "It's almost time for the meal, but I really do appreciate it."

Prowse nodded, then withdrew, and I was once more puzzled by events. "Grandfather, what was the task you set our fearless sportsman?"

He was a little distracted and didn't look at me as he strolled up and back down the long corridor, which was lined with ancient paintings of classical scenes. "Hmmm?" He seemed very distant at that moment, but finally came back to the present. "Oh... I'd asked Prowse in there to keep an eye on the path in case the horses returned or the police arrived. Though what I was really hoping for was a sighting of the killer."

"How clever of you!" I never failed to be surprised by his schemes, especially as he often set them into motion without my having the slightest clue what he was doing. "Of course, if Prowse is the killer, he's hardly a reliable witness."

The austere and upright Marquess of Cranley Hall couldn't hold in a chortle at this. "Yes, I suppose you're right." The chortle became a chuckle, which soon transformed into a hearty guffaw. "Still, if he is our man, I kept him busy up here instead of giving him the chance to kill someone else, eh?"

I joined in with his laughter and he patted me on the back jovially before remembering the state I was in and repeating his command. "Now will you please get dressed?"

I went back to my room and sought out my very best dinner suit. I'd been given it for my birthday – it was as personal a present as my father had ever bought me – but I was yet to have an opportunity to wear it. As I may have mentioned before, I know nothing about clothes, but I felt truly majestic in that neatly tailored number. It was as black as onyx and fitted me like a sock. I combed my hair into a perfect side parting – the line just so. Then, as the cherry on the cake, I secured my white gold, mother-of-pearl cufflinks.

I must say, I took a moment to admire the effect in my mirror, and I didn't look half bad.

As I stepped from the room, the two young ladies were just coming out of theirs and we looked at one another, clearly excited about the evening's festivities. Christmas Eve doesn't come around every week and we were determined to enjoy it, come what may.

Idris Levitt was dressed in one of her typically wispy outfits. It was long and purple and rather made her look like a stalk of hyacinths, blowing in the breeze. Lord Mountfalcon's niece, Miss Viner, was dressed far more to my traditional tastes. She wore a deep green gown with simple stitched adornments on the sleeves and bodice. She looked like a rather attractive Christmas wreath.

I considered offering them an arm each to escort them down to the party, but thought it a little presumptuous. Instead, I stood out of their way and said, "After you, ladies." In a very squeaky voice, which I immediately regretted.

Blunt didn't quite manage the same level of style as the rest of us, but at least he'd made an effort. The fresh jumper he'd put on didn't have any stains on it. His black trousers looked as though they might have been pressed in the not so distant past, and he even had a tie on, though it was fairly well hidden.

"I'm going to stuff my face!" he said, less than delicately. "The only reason I came here was because I knew they'd put on a good spread. I love Christmas dinner. I absolutely love it." He'd already pushed past me down the stairs and looked as though he was trying to work out how to get around the young ladies when they moved aside to let him sprint towards the food.

Grandfather was waiting at the bottom of the stairs, though, apparently, not for me. "Miss Viner, if I may have a word…"

They stepped into the smallest salon for a moment and, when they reappeared, poor Sophy looked quite shocked.

"Are you sure you're all right?" Grandfather whispered. And she nodded without any further response.

"M'Lord," Todd said, stepping in from outside just in time to catch us. "I found some skis."

He was wrapped up like one of those northern tribesmen who have all those words for snow. I could barely make him out beyond his fur-trimmed hood and I had to wonder whether he'd found the costume somewhere in Lord Mountfalcon's collection.

"Oh, jolly good, Todd!" Grandfather was cheered by the news. "Have you ever skied before?"

He propped them up on the floor so that they were almost as tall as he was. "Never, but I've spent the last half an hour trying them out and I think I've got the hang of them."

When I was a child, I'd spent a week in the French Alps, falling over in the snow. I swore never to go skiing again after that. In contrast, it had taken Todd half an hour, but he'd apparently mastered the art.

"That's marvellous." Grandfather gave his chauffeur a paternal squeeze of the shoulder. If Todd weren't such a thoroughly good chap in every respect, I'd have been terribly jealous of him. "But be careful out there. It doesn't look as though Ogilby made it. Keep your eyes open for trouble at all times and, if you run into problems, come straight back."

"Yes, M'Lord." Todd was clearly ecstatic to be heading off on a dangerous mission. For my part, I was glad to be inside in the warmth. "Let's hope that Ogilby got to Snowshill and found that the police were unable to get through at the other end. I'll raise merry hell if they drag their feet, I can tell you."

"Oh, and one more thing." Grandfather glanced over his shoulder in the direction of the room where the guests were congregating. "I'm going to have Dorie lock up the house for the night. If you need to come in, give a musical knock and we'll know it's you."

"Musical, M'Lord?"

"Yes, you know." He walked over to the wood panelling on the wall to drum out a rhythm, but said the words at the same time. "Rat a tat tat, tat a tat tat tat; that sort of thing."

"I'll do my best, M'Lord."

Grandfather nodded solemnly. "I know you will, lad. I know you will."

The two men exchanged one last appreciative glance and turned to head off in different directions. I followed my grandfather to the dining room, but he stopped me before we entered.

"Are you ready for this, Christopher?"

As I wasn't clear whether he was referring to the hearty meal or whatever wild plan he had hatched, I played it safe. "I can't say for certain, but my stomach most definitely is."

"That's the spirit, Chrissy. In we go."

CHAPTER TWENTY-FIVE

As I'd been hoping, Halfpenny and Dorie had lit the candles on the Christmas tree. Though I couldn't help worrying that the house would go up in flames, it was a sight to behold. There must have been fifty of the things burning brightly, and they lent the room an almost indescribable warmth. I just wished my father and the rest of the family could have been there to celebrate.

Miss Viner was still a little pale after whatever my grandfather had said to her, and Marmaduke couldn't look up from his empty plate, but the rest of the guests were in good spirits.

"This is just like the Christmases of my childhood," Dicky Prowse announced, his face blossoming with a smile that was all the more charming for being so rare. "Before my father was in prison, of course."

"This ain't nothing like any childhood I ever had," Blunt compared. "We were lucky if we had a scrap of chicken for Christmas when I were a boy." It was easy to read a touch of bitterness into the inspector's words, but he was soon distracted by the healthy measure of wine that our footman poured him.

Perhaps the biggest surprise of the day was that our devoted cook, Henrietta, had kept the dinner simple. We started the evening with an oxtail pottage – or, "pottage de queues de boeuf," as Halfpenny insisted on calling it. To my amazement, there were no chunks of ginger in it. No pilchards or surprise balls of cheese. It was in every way imaginable a simple (though thick and richly flavoursome) beef soup. It filled me with excitement over what the menu might offer.

"I once spent Christmas Eve on a boat on the Nile," Idris Levitt exclaimed with some excitement. "I can say with great sincerity that the food was nothing like this."

"What do they eat in Egypt?" I just had to ask. "Is it all snake and camel?"

My grandfather shook his head at me censoriously. "What a very odd assumption to make."

Miss Levitt laughed and waved away the comment. "Not on the boat I took, at least. As I recall, all we ate were stews and heavy rice dishes. Nice for a meal or two, but not a whole week."

"I've always dreamed of travelling to Africa." My mother finds some new way to surprise me at least once a day. "Perhaps I would have if my husband, Walter, weren't so unadventurous. He says that he can see no reason to travel when Britain has all we could desire, but I've never spotted a pyramid in the home counties, nor a sphinx on the south coast." She sighed then, and I could tell she was missing my stuck-in-the-mud father quite as much as I was.

"I'd like to go to the Far East," Miss Viner said, her voice lighter than I might have expected, considering the distressed phizog she'd previously displayed. "China, Mongolia, Japan and the like. I'm sure there are any number of marvels to discover over there."

"I'm more comfortable at home," Horatio stated. "Much like your husband, Mrs Prentiss."

Mother nodded her appreciation for his courtesy, and the room fell silent. It was clearly expected that the senior member of our party should have his say.

My grandfather had a talent for blending into the background in conversations. I'd become accustomed to it during our investigations that year, and I knew why he behaved in such a way. He was listening, always listening. Even when he made a pretence of being distracted, or not quite hearing, I was certain he knew just what was taking place around him.

But now the spotlight had been turned upon him, and it was his turn to speak. "Ollie once told me that travelling the globe is like exploring the tunnels of someone's mind. He said that he never quite knew what he would find and that he'd encountered any number of things which defied explanation. When I retired, he encouraged me to take a trip to the Andes with him and I was sorely tempted. You know, if my wife hadn't died when she did, I suppose I…"

His words grew gradually quieter, so that we had to strain to hear him before they finally vanished altogether. He never finished the sentence and so, to smooth over this noticeable crack, I raised my glass.

"A toast then. Though I never met him, Lord Mountfalcon sounds like a man who had to be seen to be believed. If his house is anything to go by, he is a wonder that the world will long miss."

Prowse sucked in his lip at this moment, and I genuinely thought the poor chap might cry. "To my uncle Ollie. Long may he be remembered."

166

"And to Harry Crump," my brother spoke up far too earnestly. "Who... ummm... also died."

"And Wentworth Ogilby," I added. "Though, no... perhaps we should hold off on that until we're sure. To Ollie and Harry!"

I watched our suspects as they raised their glasses. Sophy Viner had gone back to her mournful expression, while Idris looked to be having a wonderful time. I still found her the greatest enigma in the group. Though my grandfather had interrogated her, I didn't feel we'd got any closer to the secrets she was clearly hiding. At the very least, her frivolity felt ill matched to the events of those last two days.

"Halfpenny, please ask Dorie to lock the main doors to the house before she brings the next course." Grandfather spoke in a hushed voice, but there was a lull in the conversation and several faces turned to look at him.

"What are you thinking, you old schemer?" Blunt immediately asked. I'd hoped that, with the amount of time the two men had spent together, they could have moved beyond bickering and past jealousies, but Blunt was often quick to take offence where none was meant.

"Didn't I see your driver heading off just now?" Prowse asked. "Do you really think it's a good idea to lock him out in this weather?"

"Oh my good grief." Idris Levitt raised her glass to her lips, then put it back down on the table once more. "You know something, don't you?"

Grandfather didn't reply, but crossed his arms across his chest. I was seated a few places away from him and viewed that cunning fox through the light of a dancing flame. He looked mysterious and perhaps a little diabolical as the heat haze obscured my vision and his expression seemed to transform.

"Yes, I believe I do." He said nothing more and kept his eyes fixed on Idris Levitt at the far end of the table.

Blunt clearly doubted this outcome. "How could you possibly know who the killer is? Did one of this lot cough up to the murders? Or were you eavesdropping and chanced upon the right name?"

Prowse spoke in his soft, plaintive voice. "Lord Edgington, please tell us what you know."

Always willing to put on a show, the great detective should have been a circus magician. He knew just how long a pause to leave before putting us out of our misery. "I have developed several theories on the matter as our stay here at Mistletoe Hall has continued." He also knew when to avoid a question completely, and that this would only make us want to know the answer more.

His eyes shifted to look at Sophy Viner for a moment, before turning upwards to study the ceiling "The poem which the killer left near Harry Crump's body this morning said that the captain of Hampshire Cricket Club, Dicky Prowse, is not who he says he is. I found this phrasing odd as several of you have clearly been lying to me. Isn't that right, Miss Viner?"

"I haven't the faintest idea to what you could be referring." Her tone was as lifeless as the Cranley Hall rose garden in winter, but she didn't hesitate to fire a frosty look down the table at him.

"That's funny, because I think you know exactly what I mean. You've been lying to everyone since you got here. You're not really Sophy Viner, your name is Millicent Bowen."

I couldn't make any sense of what was happening, as I'd already seen this conversation play out once that day. Sophy Viner was really Lord Mountfalcon's niece. I knew this, as did my grandfather, but, most importantly, Miss Viner had already admitted the truth. So why was she now denying it?

I noticed that, when she spoke again, her tone had become just a tad less refined, a touch more working class. "You're persecuting me, hounding me until you get what you want. Some toff picking on the poorest among us – that's typical, that is."

Dicky Prowse had been watching the scene unfold with some trepidation, clearly unsure whom to believe in the matter. His desire to protect the underdog had been sparked, though, and he flew in to rescue the innocent creature.

"Now, steady on, Lord Edgington. If the lady says her name is Sophy Viner, we should take her word on the matter. There's no need to go casting aspersions. Unless you're suggesting that she herself is the killer." He was most heroic in his defence, if entirely mistaken in his reasoning.

"No, we're not there yet. There's no need to worry about who the killer is before we attempt to understand why we were all invited here." My grandfather's booming voice faded out and he gave us the time to process his words. "So you deny it, *Miss Viner*? You deny who your parents were and from where you have come?"

"My folks were just shopkeepers. I don't know what you're suggesting."

"There you are then," Prowse spoke up once more. "You've heard what she has to say, and I think it's best if we consider the issue settled."

While Grandfather might have let the matter rest, Blunt was less inclined to do so. "Always thought there was something fishy about that one. Who's this Millicent Bowen when she's at home anyway?"

Miss Viner stuck with her original defence. "I couldn't possibly tell you. This is the very first time I've heard of her."

Blunt clicked his tongue. "Oh yeah? Then where'd your funny accent come from if your parents were only shopkeepers?"

It was my grandfather himself to whom the poor girl now turned for help. Without giving anything away, he smiled, and she knew she should answer the Inspector's question.

"I told you, I've lived abroad in France and Italy. Holland too for some time. I'm just one of those people who absorbs accents wherever I go. I've quite lost my own."

"Yeah?" The ever-blunt inspector wasn't giving up. "And where did you get the money for trips to fancy places?"

Perhaps it was in response to his cynical tone, but Miss Viner found some confidence and replied with a good, clear answer of her own. "I won a grant for my education when I was at school and then took jobs as a governess abroad. There was plenty of work after the war as people rebuilt their lives. Our country was lucky to be left relatively unscarred compared to many places on the continent."

Her assertion changed the atmosphere in the room, and we no longer considered her such a helpless victim. Her strength appeared to spread to the suspects on either side of her. Prowse gave her a fraternal smile. Idris sat up a little straighter in her chair, with a knowing expression, and even Marmaduke appeared buoyed by the development.

I should probably have worked out a good few minutes earlier that my grandfather had engineered this scene for the benefit of his audience. He'd evidently told Miss Viner to deny her roots and her connection to Lord Mountfalcon when they'd spoken before the meal. Of course, this belated understanding did little to help me determine why either one of them would perpetuate such subterfuge. In my defence, I'd only had a bowl of soup and was still very hungry.

I can't tell you how relieved I was when Halfpenny returned and my grandfather said, "Ahhh, time for the second course."

CHAPTER TWENTY-SIX

"Les esperlans frits et saumon fumé," Halfpenny explained as he whipped the silver cloche off the serving tray. At least, I think that's what he said. I very much doubted that our footman had studied French in his life, and his pronunciation was decidedly provincial.

A few of the guests were looking a little nonplussed by the announcement, and so, in a polite mumble, my mother added a translation. "That's fried smelts and smoked salmon."

"And toasted bread," I added unnecessarily, as they could all see the third, unmentioned, ingredient on the table.

Halfpenny got to work serving, Dorie made a rare appearance in the dining room to pour (or rather spill) drinks, and our conversation resumed.

"I'm sorry, but I don't feel that we're any closer to learning the killer's name." Idris Levitt sounded quite aggrieved by the matter. "Are you going to come out with the truth now?"

Grandfather said nothing. He was such a ham when he wanted to be.

Marmaduke's father was the next to prod him onwards. "Sorry to break ranks, Edgington, but I'm with Miss Levitt on this one. If our lives are in danger, you must tell us what's happening."

The old lord smiled and adjusted his fish knife just a fraction so that it was perfectly straight. "I think what you mean to say, Horatio, is that you're still worried that your son could be the culprit."

As was usually the case when in his father's presence, Marmaduke had remained muted and restrained throughout the meal. He only risked a brief twitch of the eyes towards my grandfather before looking back at his plate.

Horatio tugged at one shirt cuff. "Well, yes. I confess that may be part of it."

Though he hadn't eaten any of the fish course at this point, my grandfather took a moment to dab at the side of his mouth with his napkin. "In which case, I should remind you what I said the last time you suspected your son of some diabolical deed, and the time before that, too. You must learn to trust one another. Marmaduke is not the killer. For one thing, he was most likely still at school one hundred miles away when Lord Mountfalcon was murdered."

Horatio was not backing down from his suspicions. "I'm not worried about Mountfalcon. It's Crump he could have killed. I was there, don't forget. I saw what I saw."

There was a serenity to my grandfather just then that was usually absent at such moments. "You mean to say that the killer spared your life. Our culprit had a sword to your throat as you lay on the floor, and yet he did you no harm. So, let me ask you a question. Have you considered any other possible reason for why you are still breathing than the idea that your son was the one standing over you?"

"It's the logical conclusion," Horatio retorted and inserted a small chunk of toast and salmon into his mouth.

"No, it is one hypothetical possibility. As far as I can tell, your son had no connection to Harry Crump. And, despite your regular insistence to the contrary, he has never killed before. While I accept that Crump's comedy was an acquired taste, I very much doubt it would have turned Marmaduke here into a bloodthirsty maniac."

Horatio was becoming increasingly angry at the humiliation he was receiving at the hands of my grandfather. "I've told you before, Edgington. The boy has violence in him. He attacked Christopher and countless other boys in that school of theirs."

Grandfather sighed and shook his head. "You're quite right. We *have* had this exact same discussion on a number of occasions, and yet you still fail to realise whence that violence originates. But let us not argue. I merely wish to reassure you that your son is no killer and, from everything I've seen of the boy since he and my grandson became friends, he has the makings of a fine individual."

Far from being appeased by these words, Horatio muttered to himself and appeared to fade out of the conversation. I had to wonder whether he was more concerned with the question of who his son really was than who the killer might be.

"Marvellous," Idris Levitt put in. "So that's another suspect crossed off the list. I wonder who will be next."

Grandfather made us wait before providing each answer, this time taking a sip of the cool white wine that Dorie had served. "What about you, Miss Levitt? You're not the killer, are you?"

She was all bravery and bluster now; the same huge personality that the papers had filled columns with week after week. "If I was, you would never pin it on me."

"And why's that?"

She laughed as she picked at the tiny white fish on her plate with a silver fork. "Well, I wouldn't be so stupid as to get caught, would I?"

Grandfather gave a short, soft round of applause. "I believe those are the words of every would-be assassin in history. Tell me, why exactly do you believe you would break the mould of so many men who have swung from the hangman's noose?"

Idris looked into the faces of her fellow diners. We were all just as curious to hear her answer as my grandfather.

"Because I wouldn't go about killing people in such a very foolish fashion, of course." There was great intensity to her words and no one there doubted how serious she was. "I cannot begin to comprehend what the fellow was thinking. Bringing us all here with no chance of escape? Inviting along two policemen to boot? He's guaranteed to get caught, don't you think?"

Lord Edgington looked mildly impressed by her reasoning. "And you wouldn't commit such a basic mistake?"

"No, I would not." Her voice rose in feigned horror. "If I wanted to murder someone, I would get him on his own and do the deed when no one could link me to the crime."

"I concede that would be a wise plan." Grandfather allowed his eyes to narrow, as though deep in thought. "And after all, you must know something about crime… considering your background."

I wondered where my grandfather's sly aside might lead us, but Idris Levitt showed no sign of having heard and Prowse, the apparent spokesperson for the group, made another comment.

"She has a point, Lord Edgington. Why on earth would anyone go to all this trouble? Surely Lord Mountfalcon was the main target, and he was already dead when we arrived."

"No, I'm afraid I have to disagree with you. Lord Mountfalcon's death was merely the means to an end. I believe he was murdered in order to give the killer the time and freedom he needed to set a trap for us. And while the grand affair to which we have all borne witness may seem an overly elaborate piece of theatre, the killer was secure in the knowledge he could get away with it in spite of my presence here.

You see, I believe that I was his real target all along. The only thing I don't understand is why I'm still breathing."

There was an intake of breath from several around the table just then, though Blunt was chomping his way through the last of the fish and somewhat drowned out the noise.

My grandfather was quick to set minds at ease. "I can assure you that there will be no more bodies here this week. The killer's threat has been eliminated." He paused once more to observe his listeners' reactions. "I have no plans to become the next victim and I will do everything in my power to ensure that we all leave this house in one piece."

"Not that you're arrogant, or nothing," Blunt said with a laugh. "Why do you reckon you're the one he wants? And why would he have killed so many people before you?"

Grandfather had finished his food by this point and, to communicate this fact to our server, he pushed the plate forward half an inch. "Blunt, my dear old colleague, I am going to confess something now, and I think it will both amuse and appal you." He smiled over at his close rival. "I do not have all the answers to your questions at this time. Though I may know who the killer is. I have not yet landed upon the thread that links us together. I have found small clues as to the connection, but no perfect answer."

My grandfather's prediction was proven correct when Blunt let out a laugh like an artillery gun. "I knew it! I knew you were only faking. You probably think I don't notice what's going on around me, but you've been sitting there spouting *inanities* this whole time." This was quite a long word for the inspector and it came out with a syllable or two too many. "You haven't held up a scrap of evidence for our perusal. You haven't come across a single concrete fact. You don't know nothing about nothing. Just like I've always said."

The renowned Superintendent Edgington did not seem offended by the man's assertion. In fact, he laughed along with him and said, "That's right. I'm a fraud, a mountebank. I couldn't possibly know who the killer is."

Blunt's laughter came to a sudden halt as he realised that my grandfather didn't mean a word he'd said. The pair had maintained a rivalry for thirty years or more. Hearing such a confession from him was simply too good to be true.

"'And the king's about to lose his head,'" the king continued. "I have studied the poem carefully and, when considering the eight people who received invitations, I feel that this line could only apply to me. I do not like to make use of my title, but as Marquess of Edgington and two-hundredth or so in line to the throne, I believe I fit more closely with the description than anyone else."

I found myself wondering how far removed from the king I must be if my grandfather was number two-hundred. However, there were more pressing issues to address and he soon continued.

"This *murder note* told us everything and nothing. It revealed that Ogilby had left the house; we already knew that. Miss Levitt drives cars, ditto. Crump was dead, idem. Inspector Blunt likes his food, Horatio Adelaide has a criminal past, etcetera etcetera and on and on."

Blunt might well have taken exception to being referred to in such a manner, but, as he was busy licking his plate, there wasn't much he could do to complain.

"It is only in the final lines of the poem that we get a hint of the killer's real intentions. The whole thing was written as a threat to get my attention. 'The king's about to lose his head,' is all he really wished to communicate. Everything else was a garnish, a pretty bow, mere window dressing to lead us to the crux of the matter."

I think we were all surprised to hear my dreamy brother pipe up then. "So, are you saying that the murders played a similar role? Lord Mountfalcon and that clown chappy were killed to scare you, or perhaps disguise the real motivation for the crimes?" I hadn't imagined he'd even been listening. If I'm perfectly honest, I thought he only had room in his head for young ladies, cricket scores, and the odd game of tennis.

"That's a perceptive suggestion, Albert, but no. I believe the killer had a reason for his crimes, and that I was the one who could connect our disparate band together."

My grandfather was holding something back then and looked at me in the hope I might work it out. To my genuine astonishment, I actually managed it.

"You missed out a line of the poem. You talked about all of our suspects, except for Dicky Prowse." I tried my darnedest to recall the line about our dashing cricketer, but drew a blank. Fair play, though, I'd done well getting us this far.

"Precisely, Christopher." He slapped his hands together with glee. "The poem informed us that 'The sportsman's not the man he said' and yet, of all the guests this weekend, I would argue that Dicky has been the most open and honest about his past. Even I have some skeletons in my dressing room which I'd rather not release, but our cricketer was only too happy to divulge the details of his troubled youth."

"I'm not just happy to discuss it." Prowse sat up to his full height and looked at the former detective dead on. "I'm proud of what I've achieved in spite of my humble beginnings."

"As you should be." The old man closed his eyes deferentially as he spoke. "But that left me wondering what the killer knew about you. I was forced to question whether the public persona you have cultivated over the last decade – which you displayed to us here this weekend – could be a sham."

There was no fear in the young man's voice as he responded. "With all due respect, Lord Edgington, I can promise that it is not. My father's fall from grace is well documented, and I have nothing to hide."

"Yes, it's quite the conundrum." Grandfather let these words mark a pause in the conversation as he signalled to Halfpenny to clear the plates and bring the main course.

There was a faint rumble of discussion as we puzzled over the enigma that the esteemed former superintendent had set before us. The two young ladies chattered between themselves, clearly intrigued by the unusual case. Mother complimented Albert on his own contribution to the discussion, and Albert did the same to our mother in return. Horatio Adelaide still hadn't recovered from the dressing down that my grandfather had given him, though his son looked really quite chipper. Marmaduke popped the last crumb of toast into his mouth and winked at me down the table.

It was Dicky Prowse whom I struggled to read, though. His face oddly expressionless, he had barely moved a muscle since my grandfather stopped talking. He remained just so until our footman reappeared, pushing a small trolley that bore a roast turkey big enough to feed the whole of Snowshill village.

"Now that's more like it." Inspector Blunt, who had gone two minutes without eating anything, had eyes bigger than his stomach and a stomach bigger than a hydrogen balloon.

"Hear hear." Grandfather smiled at his former colleague and raised his recently refilled wine glass. "We shouldn't focus on the negative when we have so much to be thankful for. We should feast and be merry."

I raised my glass to agree with him, though I could tell there were some in the room who did not feel the same way.

CHAPTER TWENTY-SEVEN

I'd be derelict in my duties if I didn't give you the full picture of what went on that night. I don't just mean the details of who killed whom and why, but, perhaps more importantly, exactly what we ate.

As Halfpenny produced a frighteningly large serrated knife and very pointy carving fork, Dorie appeared, pushing a trolley loaded with crunchy roast potatoes, parsnips and carrots. She had several jugs of piping hot gravy, enough peas to fill Cheddar Gorge, and a selection of homemade sauces. Cook had even prepared a type of fruit which had been imported from the Americas. While they were all the rage in the Colonies – and I had no doubt that Fortnum & Mason were charging a pretty penny for them – to me at least, they tasted rather like sour cherries. I couldn't imagine these *cranberries* catching on in Britain.

The only other elaboration in which our cook indulged was her choice to serve savoury scones to accompany the turkey, much as we normally eat Yorkshire puddings with beef. This was much more to my taste, and the cheese and rosemary in the small, bready bites went perfectly with the thick gravy into which I dunked them. It was a real shame that anyone had been murdered. I would much rather we had all kept quiet and gorged ourselves than rehashing the debate of why we were there in the first place.

Sadly, there came a moment when good old Dicky Prowse could take it no more. As though an important cog in his brain had suddenly sprung loose, he made a noise like an injured wolf and banged his fist down on the table. The cutlery before him jumped into the air and the dining room fell silent.

"I'm sorry to be dramatic, but I must insist you finish what you were saying, Lord Edgington. I have the terrible feeling that every person here now suspects me of murder."

My grandfather's eyes opened wider, and he adopted that wonderfully innocent tone of his. "And why should anyone think such a thing?"

Prowse looked at my mother – who is usually the most sympathetic person in any room. I don't know what he was hoping for, but he received a compassionate frown in return.

"I… Well, you see…" He stumbled over his words and perhaps his thoughts. "Not only did the killer imply that I'm not the honest man I make every attempt to be, you yourself made it sound as though I could be involved in the killings."

This had all the smackings of a guilty conscience to me, and my mind suddenly ran with the idea that it was Prowse whom my grandfather had identified as our culprit. This resolutely went against my plan to stick with Idris Levitt as my likely culprit, but there was no time to worry about such minor concerns.

"Oh, I wouldn't say that," Grandfather responded. "Though there were certain factors that made me consider your involvement. As I've already said, you stood out for your honesty."

"My apologies for telling the truth," Prowse replied in a prickly tone that I had not expected from him. "Next time, I'll know to lie like everyone else."

There were a few laughs at this, but Grandfather was not distracted and continued on the same path. "The poem suggested you are not who you say you are, but it was also the only line that implied that a falsehood was at play. My suspicions were aroused."

We all leaned back from the table then. The turkey had been carved and serving had begun.

"I'm sorry," Prowse peered around Halfpenny to be heard. "But you're speaking in riddles. The fact that I was honest suggests I must be guilty. The fact that the killer said I was a liar proves the case. Is that right?

"Not quite." Grandfather kept his eyes locked on the cricketer, even as the two servants moved around the table and in and out of his view. "That the killer would suggest only one person's duplicity is, to me, a red flag."

"Because that devil wanted to throw us off the scent but would assume that we wouldn't believe what he'd written." My mother was energised by her quick-witted response. In my defence, I was probably only a few minutes behind her. "If Dicky were the killer, by incriminating himself he appears less likely to have committed the crime."

"That's just it." With the food now apportioned, Grandfather took his fork and skewered a juicy morsel of turkey breast. "Fiendishly complex logic but sound enough."

"Except, of course, I'm not guilty." Dicky did not sound any cheerier on the matter.

"But neither are you lying, so why would the killer have made such a claim?"

I must concede that I was lost in the fog of my grandfather's words by this point. I was a lone explorer in a blizzard, a man overboard in a vast, lonely ocean.

"My dear man," he continued, "You must admit that the circumstances are remarkable. The poem can quite easily be read as evidence against you."

Prowse clicked his fingers and pointed across the table most decisively. "And that is exactly what the killer would want everyone to think."

Grandfather's moustache trembled as he breathed out an audibly amused puff of air. "Excellent work, Prowse. That's it in a nutshell."

"Really, Grandfather. You're terribly cruel," I felt it necessary to inform him, before turning to Dicky. "He does the same thing to me all the time."

The cricketer scoffed at my explanation. "He accuses you of murder?"

"No, not that... Well, not yet anyway. But he's always trying to teach me new lessons without explaining what he really means."

Grandfather's eyes wiggled up to the ceiling like balloons escaping from a child's hand. "I merely believe that those around me should make the best use of their gifts. A brain is a terrible thing to waste."

Dicky Prowse found some relief at last. "So you didn't suspect me of murder after all?"

"No, I did. I have considered the guilt of every single person in this room, including my daughter and grandchildren – if only to dismiss them from the list of potential suspects."

"How kind of you, Grandfather." Albert sounded like himself again; he was chagrined and morose. "You've just made me feel an awful lot better about leaving your Christmas present at home in Kilston Down."

Grandfather was enjoying himself and gazed lovingly at the second of his four grandsons. (The other two didn't even get a mention in this story, just so you know.) "Your presence is enough, dear boy."

"This is all just a game then," Idris Levitt concluded. "I suppose it is Christmas after all. Tricks and traps come as part and parcel of the festivities. I've always been fond of-"

"Wait," Prowse interrupted. "I'd like to hear what evidence you dredged up on me." He hadn't taken his eyes off Lord Edgington and the old fellow soon relented.

"Very well. As I have already suggested, your innocence was almost too perfect. Perhaps not for nefarious reasons, but, when everyone else had gone to their rooms last night, you remained to talk to Christopher and me. You were clearly desperate to share just how much you missed the man you called 'Uncle Ollie'. Yet, though I have no reason to doubt you knew Lord Mountfalcon, he never mentioned your name to me in all the years we were friends."

Grandfather's eyes caught the light of the candles as he laid out his suspicions. "All of which led me to consider two distinct possibilities. Either you were playing up to your image as a good, solid sort of chap, who missed an old acquaintance, or you were trying to distance yourself from the crime."

"No, that isn't it at all." Prowse lost his composure once again.

"You must admit that, of everyone here, you would have found it easiest to kill Harry Crump."

"Why would you suspect such a thing? I admit nothing."

"You shared a room with him, didn't you? You could have woken him and persuaded the poor man to explore the house with you before breakfast. It would have been quite simple to run that spear through him as he admired one of Lord Mountfalcon's curious collections."

"I've never heard such nonsense." He immediately dropped his gaze to the spitting candle in front of him.

I, meanwhile, was treating this as a dinner-spectacular. I gobbled my plate clean as the entertainment swirled around me. I wasn't the only one. Blunt was licking the gravy from his fingers and everyone else had made a good start on the delicious third course.

"It's all just hypothetical," his relentless inquisitor put to him. Grandfather managed to sound both combative and reassuring at the very same time. "But you are also the person who would have known this house best, if you were as close to *Uncle Ollie* as you claim."

He looked as though he really didn't know how to respond and started several sentences without finding a verb to continue them. "If I… Should you… When… Oh, I give up." Rather than losing his temper entirely, he sat back in his chair and an unexpected smile took possession of his face. "You can say what you like, Lord Edgington, but I didn't kill my dear friend Oliver Mountfalcon, and I didn't kill Harry Crump. I also have a sneaking suspicion that you already knew that."

His expression was suddenly mirrored in my grandfather's. "Very well. You've got me. We'll say for now that you're not the killer and leave it at that. I'm sorry to be such a bully, but you must allow an old man his eccentricities."

"So he's not the stinkard who killed off the toff?" Apparently as confused as I was, Blunt flared his nostrils, while Miss Viner literally turned her nose up at his coarse choice of phrase.

"Perhaps we could enjoy a hand of rummy after dinner, rather than continuing with such macabre pastimes." Idris rolled her eyes in exasperation, while Albert's ears perked up at the mention of a card game – much like Delilah's whenever anyone mentions lunch.

"Wait just a moment, the show can't be over," I said, as I'd witnessed such scenes several times before. "Grandfather, now that we've been through all of the people who aren't killers, are you going to tell us who actually committed the crimes?"

"No," my grandfather responded, and the word was like an arrow from a bow. "You are." He was very excited by his plan, and his good cheer spread around the other faces. Even old Halfpenny, who was standing to attention in the corner, looked most taken with the idea.

"Me?" I felt it necessary to confirm. "Or rather; I am?"

"That's right Christopher." He looked at his neighbours for support. "As the remarkable Miss Levitt just informed us, Christmas is a time for games and challenges. When I was a child, it was always the youngest member of the family whom my parents singled out for such fun. In my day, that responsibility fell to me, but this evening, my dear grandson, it is your turn."

"How splendid!" my friend Marmaduke declared, and he was lucky I didn't point out that he was only a few months older than me.

"Oh and, Christopher, to make it more sporting, you won't be allowed to eat anything else until you've given me the name of the man who killed Lord Mountfalcon and Hilarious Harry Crump."

CHAPTER TWENTY-EIGHT

This was serious.

No more food meant no dessert. No dessert meant no Christmas pudding, and I'd been looking forward to Cook's most celebrated creation since she'd started preparing it several weeks earlier. I immediately fell silent and put my brain in gear.

My grandfather must have believed I was capable of solving the strange case or he wouldn't have set me such a task in the first place. He could be demanding, perfectionistic and often bordered on arrogance, but he would never intentionally embarrass me in front of so many people. I had to conclude, therefore, that he'd given me the tools I needed to complete the task.

Perhaps the whole evening had been designed to prepare me for this very moment. Perhaps I didn't need to consider everything that had happened at Mistletoe Hall since we'd arrived and could concentrate on the brief summary that he'd given us. This was probably a good thing as, while on previous investigations we'd stumbled across a veritable glut of evidence, it seemed in short supply this time around.

There were the footprints we'd examined beside the house which told us... well, nothing much whatsoever. The clothes we found in the snow had belonged to Lord Mountfalcon. I'd seen glimpses of the killer himself, which would normally have been helpful but did little for us, as far as I could tell. In Grandfather's own words, the poem told us everything and nothing. There was no obvious connection to draw between Lord Mountfalcon, the dearly departed (at least in a literal sense) Wentworth Ogilby, and Crump, the comedian who'd been run through with a particularly savage medieval spear.

As my grandfather had seen fit to ignore such details, I'd have to forget all that and focus on the facts as he'd presented them. The first curious thing was the deal he'd entered into with Miss Viner née Bowen. They'd clearly hatched a plan together in the moments before we entered the dining room. Sophy had denied the truth of her upbringing and it seemed to me that this was at my grandfather's bidding. What I couldn't grasp, however, was why he'd devised such a scheme.

After that, he'd moved through the group, discussing the potential guilt of our suspects. Despite his reservations over Idris Levitt's secrecy and, in the case of her claim that she'd never set foot in Mistletoe Hall before, her outright prevarication, I felt that Lord Edgington respected the adventurous motorist. He'd presented no clear evidence of her guilt in the case, or an incentive for her bumping off relative strangers here and there. The only conclusion I could draw was that she was not the murderer.

While we were at it, I felt I could cross off all my existing acquaintances from the list too. My mother was the saintliest person in nineteen hundred years of human history and Albert rarely had the energy to get out of bed before ten o'clock, let alone plot a murder. Inspector Blunt had spent his whole time there stuffing his face and would surely have developed a stitch if he'd had to run about the place killing people, and the Adelaides, though a far more complex pair, had already been eliminated from the enquiry – unless, of course, they were in it together. Perhaps Horatio had come to murder Lord Mountfalcon in advance, and then Marmaduke had killed Crump!

This seemed improbable. For one thing, I trusted my friend and had yet to see any evidence that he got on well enough with his father to plan a picnic, let alone a string of complex killings. As far as I was concerned, the Adelaides were innocent…ish.

I took a break in my thinking to soak up the last of the gravy with one of those delicious scones. I hadn't noticed that the room had fallen quiet and a few eyes had drifted towards me. I spotted Miss Viner casting a surreptitious glance my way when she thought I wasn't looking. I liked to think that my fellow diners were considering the details of the murders, much as I was, and that they were curious what cunning solution I would reveal. The truth is, they were probably just hoping I'd hurry up so that we could eat the next course.

I tried not to ignore the pressure as I returned to my mental exertions. It occurred to me that it would be foolish not to consider the role of our staff in the preceding events. Might our creaking footman have slain two poor souls? And who was to say that our dear cook, Henrietta, hadn't grown tired of her culinary endeavours and escaped from the kitchen for a quick murder or two? Even our beloved chauffeur, who was known to wear a number of different hats in the household, could have taken on the role of assassin for some gruesome reason.

I had to snicker at this dastardly solution and I wondered if any author of murder mysteries had ever struck upon such an ingenious solution. *The chauffeur did it* certainly had a ring to it.

I moved on to my final suspect. Dicky Prowse was definitely an enigma. He was a friendly sort of chap. A man of humble origins who had emerged as a national star, captaining several important cricket teams to success in their field (and fielding). What marked him out from most of the others, though, was his long association with Lord Mountfalcon. Despite my grandfather's claims that he himself was the glue that held the group together, I couldn't help wondering whether our deceased host fulfilled a similar function.

And yet, Prowse was the only person who hadn't concealed the truth and, from the beginning, had attempted to solve the mystery of why we had been summoned to his benefactor's house. He wasn't the killer. He couldn't be, but whom did that leave?

A pang of sadness ran through me as I realised that I would have to wait until Christmas 1926 in order to enjoy Cook's Christmas pudding. There was no chance in the whole of Great Britain that I was going to land upon the right name.

Grandfather was watching me expectantly, and it was apparent that the moment had arrived to admit defeat. Almost as much as missing out on a delicious dessert, the disappointment I was about to cause him stung me deeply. I had ruled out all the possible suspects. There was no one left… except…

"Wentworth Ogilby!" I shouted, rising to my feet in delight. "He's the killer."

My mentor showed no sign of what he thought of my assertion but calmly uttered, "Go on."

"He's not dead. It's the only thing that makes sense."

"I don't understand," Idris Levitt raised one hand to say. "Surely he went out into the snow and no one's seen him since. He either froze to death out there or got knocked off by the real killer."

"No, that's what we all assumed." I'd found my confidence now. "But what if he's been out in the gardens this whole time and popped back inside this morning to kill Harry Crump, plant the poem and set us all wondering what would come next?"

"This is just conjecture, boy," Grandfather adopted a pompous tone to rile me. I knew what he was doing and it wouldn't work. "Show us the evidence."

I thought for a moment. "We know that someone was walking around in the gardens this morning. We found the footprints, and they didn't look so different from the ones we'd already spotted when the killer chanced upon me near Lord Mountfalcon's body."

"That's right. Keep going." His words were encouraging, but his tone remained calm and detached.

"We found the abandoned togs that the killer had worn to disguise his own clothes on a hedge near the folly. We assumed he'd led us on a wild goose chase and had simply gone out in the snow and returned to the house. But what if he was still there? What if he left last night and doubled back through the forest? What if he's been hiding in one of the outbuildings this whole time?"

"You know, that's pretty clever," Blunt said. Everyone else had finished eating by now and yet he'd managed to find an extra portion of potatoes from somewhere and popped them in his mouth one at a time. "I would never have thought of that."

"And that's why you locked the doors, Lord Edgington," Miss Viner concluded, sounding rather impressed by my grandfather's bright idea. "To keep us safe, and the blighter outside."

The real detective in our midst still wouldn't be drawn on the matter. He sat impassively, his eyes fixed on mine, and it was a good ten seconds before he reached forward, seized his champagne flute and said, "Halfpenny, you'd better open the jeroboam of Moët et Chandon. Chrissy here has just solved his first murder."

What joy there was in the room at that moment. Every last face was painted with a smile. Inspector Blunt stood up to shake my hand. My mother gazed proudly at her youngest son, and even my silly brother gave me a fraternal punch on the arm. I really can't remember another moment in my life when I felt so thoroughly exhilarated. It must be what having your birthday on Christmas Day feels like. As the young ladies clapped my performance and Grandfather looked on approvingly, I thought, just perhaps, I could get used to the life of a detective.

"I do hope Todd will be all right out there," my mother declared once the jubilation had died down.

"He'll be fine." Grandfather leaned across the table to place a hand on his daughter's. "I told him of my suspicions before he left and he'll be much faster on skis than Ogilby is on foot."

"I do hope so."

The old fellow took his daughter's hand in his own. "He'll be at Snowshill by now. Trust me. He'll be there at the police station, convincing them to call in the army to clear the snow."

She looked a little reassured, but Idris Levitt had another issue to raise. Oh, and I sat back down again as my grand moment had clearly passed.

"But who was Ogilby and why did he invite us all here?"

I certainly didn't know how to answer her question, and everyone turned to Lord Edgington to discover what secrets he had unravelled.

"I'm ashamed to admit that I simply don't know. I very much doubt he's a professional musician, for one thing. Anyone could have a visiting card printed, and we took it for granted that he was telling the truth. All I can conclude is that he was someone that Commissioner Mountfalcon, Inspector Blunt and I crossed paths with in the police. I don't see what else could make sense."

"Why did he ever show his face here in the first place?" Prowse enquired. "He might just as easily have remained lurking in the wilderness and picked us off as we ventured outside."

Halfpenny had returned from the wine cellar with an absurdly large double-magnum of champagne. It looked old and dusty, so I had to assume it was another prize pick from Grandfather's collection back at Cranley. The footman worked his way around the table, pouring a little in each of our glasses and waiting for the fizzing substance to bubble upwards and back down before dispensing more.

Grandfather took his time to consider the question. "Well, I suppose he needed access to the house to kill his later victims. Had he been spotted, he could have said that he'd come back from the village without any help. From what I can tell, he must have arrived at Mistletoe Hall before us, murdered poor Ollie and set up camp in one of the buildings in the gardens as my grandson conjectured."

"So that's it?" Albert asked, a little snootily considering how little he'd contributed to the investigation. "We don't know why Ogilby killed anyone, and we don't know who he is. Seems a bit of a swiz if you ask me."

Grandfather looked philosophical then. "I've long since learnt to be grateful for what we do have, my boy. The important thing is that the doors are bolted, the shutters closed and, as the night of Christmas Eve sets in, we are safe."

"I couldn't agree more," Idris added.

The old man's face hardened then, and a touch of the devil came about him. "Besides, when the police get here, we will hunt down Wentworth Ogilby and make him pay for his crimes. By this time tomorrow, I can guarantee, we will know exactly why he executed such a despicable plan."

CHAPTER TWENTY-NINE

Any misgivings we might have had were forgotten as the festive cheer overwhelmed us. At long last, it really felt like Christmas and the party could begin in earnest.

Cook herself came up from the kitchen with her flaming Christmas pudding and Grandfather took the opportunity to deliver their Christmas envelopes to his staff. Sadly, Todd wasn't there to celebrate with us, but, knowing just how capable our chauffeur was, I had no doubt he'd be in fine fettle. He'd be back at Mistletoe Hall in the shake of a reindeer's tail.

Hang on… do reindeer actually have tails?

Halfpenny did the honours, cutting up the large pudding that every last member of the Cranley household had helped stir a month before. It had been maturing in flavour ever since. The smell wafted about the room and I breathed it in, trying to recall the many ingredients that had gone into its production. There was the flambeed brandy, of course, deep brown sugar, cinnamon, cloves and nutmeg. I could make out the black indentations of raisins in the pudding's crust and hidden underneath were currants, sultanas and minced apple, all blended in with porter stout and rum.

Best of all was the moment I sank my teeth into that Yuletide indulgence and was rewarded, not just with a mouthful of heaven, but a silver sixpence. I held it up to the light and my companions cheered me once more. It truly was a wonderful evening.

And when dinner was over, the parlour games began. To begin with, we each took a brightly coloured cracker from a box beside the secret drinks cabinet. We formed a circle in the middle of the sitting room, linked our arms together and pulled. I didn't win either of the prizes I had a chance at, but Grandfather won both of his and shared his bounty with me. We spent the rest of the evening wearing the silver paper crowns which had flown across the room when the snapper went crack! I hadn't laughed so much in days.

After that, we played *blind man's buff*, *squeak piggy squeak* and *pass the slipper*. Marmaduke tried to persuade everyone to join in with a round of *snapdragon*, but it turned out that we preferred our fingers, tongues and mouths unscorched by flaming raisins. It wasn't just these traditional festivities that I found uplifting. It melted my heart to see the way in which a group of perfect strangers could form such a bond so quickly, and a fine time was had by all present.

Dicky sought out some records for the gramophone and, having wound the handle to the maximum, took a turn around the sitting room with Idris – I was glad they didn't suggest a trip to the ballroom as I had no wish to see those Japanese warriors again for as long as I lived. My brother was a little shy at first, but finally found the courage to ask Miss Viner to join him for a brief, jaunty foxtrot. I must say, they went rather well together. By the end of their first dance, I could tell that Albert was in love all over again. I doubt he thought about Evie, Izzy, Bessie, Jessie, Billy, Lizzy or any of his past loves for the rest of the evening.

My mother talked to the Adelaides, Delilah enjoyed an awful lot of attention (when she wasn't chasing after my dancing brother) and I sat in an armchair beside the two police officers, admiring the scene.

"I have a confession to make, Blunt," my grandfather announced as Halfpenny turned over the record. "I never took the time to get to know you when we were working together, and I take full responsibility for your bad opinion of me."

Blunt looked flustered, but remained unbowed. "Oh yeah?"

"Sincerely, my man. Our rivalry has gone on long enough. You're a good copper, and I am deeply sorry for the troubled waters that have passed between us."

The inspector snuffled into a handkerchief before replying. "Well, that's decent of you, Edgington. And perhaps you're right. At this time of year and all that, it's only right to bury the hatchet."

"Quite. And, I must say, it is long overdue." My grandfather smiled, as though waiting for something to happen. When nothing did, he gave Blunt an affectionate pat on the shoulder. "Well, go on then. Tell me about yourself."

The fellow really did look bemused by the change in the man he'd considered an enemy for several decades, but he summoned up a response. "I'm not sure there's much to say, really. I'm from the East End, as you probably know. My mother were a maid in a big old house, much like this one, and my Daddy did what he could. No doubt you ran into him a few times in your early days on the force. He were a jack the lad, like I say, but never meant any harm. It was my mother I felt sorry for, mind. There never was a better woman. She only died a few months back now, but she were the kindest…"

Blunt's sad (though really rather dull) tale continued on like this for some time and I was relieved when my mother spotted my eyes glassing over and pulled me up for a dance.

"You were wonderful, Chrissy," she told me as I tried to remember how to waltz and mainly tripped over my own feet. "Really, everyone was so impressed. I don't know how you produced the name like that. I never could have guessed."

I knew she was just being modest; she was her father's daughter. The much-celebrated Superintendent Edgington – the grasping hand of the long arm of the law – had taken her along on his cases when she was young, and I could state with some confidence that she was a better detective than I would ever be.

"It was probably luck," I said. "Nothing more than a process of elimination really."

The smile on her kind face stretched wider. "Don't sell yourself short, Chrissy. You've improved in leaps and bounds this year and your father and I are so proud of all you've achieved."

I could tell that we were both fighting not to think of our absent family members, but the warmth and wonders of that evening won out and I resisted a maudlin frown.

"May I cut in?" Marmaduke asked with a cheeky look on his face. The great lanky ginger-top hadn't been himself all holiday, and it was good to see him smiling once more.

"Why, of course." My mother put on a courtly voice and bowed foppishly, like some Italian count. "Far be it from me to stand in the way of two young people cutting loose."

I was a little relieved that it was not a dance that my school chum was after, but my companionship.

"It's time we had a proper poke about the place, Chrissy," he informed me. "Let's leave the old fellows to their stuffy pastimes and set off for adventure. Are you with me?"

The thought of that creepy old house in the dark on Christmas Eve scared me rotten, but I wasn't about to let Marmaduke know that.

"Lead on, my good man." I tried to sound confident and failed.

He took one look at his father, who had fallen into conversation with my brother and Miss Viner of all people, and we scuttled from the room. Much as I feared, the passageways of Mistletoe Hall were dark, with only the odd oil lamp about the place to light our way. This twilit atmosphere made even the most innocent shape in the shadows turn grotesque and violent in my mind. Chests of drawers became winged demons, a hat stand transformed into a lurking assassin, and my heart beat as fast as the clicking of a stock ticker.

"To be honest, I didn't have the courage to explore this place with a madman on the loose," Marmaduke eventually confessed. "But if your grandfather's confident we're safe in here, that's good enough for me."

"I'd feel safer back with the adults, old chap. Why don't we–"

I knew he wouldn't listen, and, sure enough, he immediately changed the topic.

"You know, the Victorians used to tell ghost stories on Christmas Eve," he kindly informed me, and I remembered the time I'd read M. R. James's 'Lost Hearts' and not slept for a week. Even Dickens's 'The Signal-Man' was too frightening for me, and I searched for something less bloodcurdling to discuss.

"Look at that lovely vase on the bureau there." It wasn't the subtlest attempt, but I couldn't think of anything else to say. "I'd imagine that must be Vietnamese or German or something of the sort."

"Yes, very nice," my friend said without turning his head. Instead, he grabbed me by the arm and yanked me through an unlocked door. "Now, this is more interesting."

He would have to take me to see the samurais, wouldn't he? The whole lot of them were in there waiting for us, and they looked more lethal than ever. There was a floor lamp on either side of them that cast its faint light up to their faces to make them look devilish. Well... more devilish.

Marmaduke went up close to the most dangerous of the lot and stood mere inches away from the hideous mask.

"I really think we should go back now," I said, but he kept staring into the figure's hollow eyes.

I don't know how he had the courage to stand there like that. I was terrified that the warrior's blade would crash down on his skull at any moment. The silence in that airy space was deafening. I was just about to run back out to the hall to calm my nerves when Marmaduke released a piercing scream, like a fox at night, and it sent me sprawling backwards across the dance floor.

He immediately burst out in hysterics. "You jellyfish, Chrissy. It was just a joke."

"Well, it's not funny!" Not only had the rum fellow scared me witless, I'd hurt my bottom falling over. I was not amused. "Can we please return to the sitting room?"

He looked rather forlorn at my rebuke, and I felt awfully guilty until an enormous grin broke out across his face. "Of course, old boy. Of course we can. Follow me."

He raced across the room to the door in the corner, which led to the oldest part of the house. As I got to my feet, I had to pray that it was still locked from the last time I'd been there, but I would have no such luck. With a perfectly bone-shaking creak, the door opened and my classmate disappeared into the pitch-black corridor.

"Marmaduke, this is silly," I said, taking a few steps after him. I couldn't clear the image from my mind of Ogilby raising his sword to stab me when last I'd been there. "Let's go back, old bean. They'll be bringing Christmas cake soon."

I could see no sight of him in the corridor, but a faint light emanated from the room where I'd found Harry Crump's dead body. I don't know what had come over me, but I was drawn towards the light like an… ummm… fly. I paused on the threshold, as I really didn't think I was brave enough to go inside, but I forced myself forward.

I don't know what I imagined finding in there – Ghouls and ghosts and living dead, almost certainly – but the reality was equally unsettling. The room was filled with dancing shadows. Marmaduke had lit a lantern and placed it on the table where my grandfather had found the poem. I couldn't bring myself to look at Harry Crump at that moment. I hadn't known the man well, but I thought him jolly unlucky to have been the second to die. Just being in that ice-cold room again made me sorry for him.

"Chrissy!" Marmaduke bellowed, and I flew several feet in the air.

"Would you stop doing that?" My reply emerged in a rasping yell.

"Oh, I am sorry." His voice lacked a certain sincerity. "I didn't mean to scare you – this time. Come and look at these."

He was examining the paper dolls of which my grandfather had spoken. There was one for each of the invitees and they were actually rather nicely made. I had to imagine that Ogilby had prepared them in advance of our arrival, as he'd clearly taken his time over them. They were propped up around the table, as though partaking of a formal dinner. My paper grandfather was at the head of the feast, of course, and was recognisable by his grey morning suit with its long coat and neatly drawn watch chain. Idris Levitt also stood out in her signature dress and I could identify Miss Viner, as she was the only other woman, but the remaining characters were harder to recognise.

The figures of Ogilby and Prowse really didn't have much to tell them apart. You would have thought that the killer might have possessed the good sense to draw the cricketer in his sporting whites, instead of a smart brown suit. Blunt was suitably unkempt, but the doll of Horatio Adelaide, which his son was now holding, looked nothing like him. In fact it looked far more like–

"Chrissy, I think this is supposed to be me." Marmaduke sounded just as confused by the revelation as I felt.

"That doesn't make a jot of sense. What have you got to do with anything?"

"I really don't know." He looked quite amused by the turn of events. "The fact is, though, that the line of the poem might just as easily apply to me as it does to my father."

"'The delinquent's in a right old state'," I said, and felt rather pleased with myself for finally remembering a whole line of the poem.

"That's right. And, now that I think about it, father never showed me the invitation. Perhaps I was the one whom the killer wanted here, not him. You know, that would explain why he brought me here in the first place."

"I think you must be right." I considered how this might help Grandfather determine the elusive connection between the eight guests. "Perhaps it's nothing. We know that Ogilby is the killer. I don't see how this changes anything. Whether it's you or your father that the madman invited, we still don't know who he really is or what links you all together."

"I suppose you're right." With a glum expression that did not hold possession of his face for very long, he put the paper man back where he'd found it. "Come on. Let's go down to the cellar next. I'm sure it's absolutely petrifying in the dark."

It was clear that what Marmaduke and I looked for in our Christmas entertainment differed somewhat. I chased after him nonetheless, if only so that I wouldn't be left alone with a dead body.

CHAPTER THIRTY

We eventually returned to the toasty salon where the rest of our party were still enjoying themselves. There was more food and plenty of drink. Marmaduke sang a truly beautiful version of 'God Rest Ye Merry Gentlemen', by which even his father appeared moved, and we finished the evening handing out the presents that Idris Levitt had brought. And, no, they were nothing more sinister than ties and perfume. Delilah looked most put out when there wasn't a bone for her, as was the habit at Christmas back at Cranley.

Once everyone else had gone to bed – in their own rooms this time, safe in the knowledge that no one was coming to murder them – I told my grandfather what Marmaduke and I had found.

He did not seem too concerned about the matter. "Oh, how foolish of me. I should have realised that, these days, Marmaduke is very much the delinquent in his family. I didn't pay enough attention to the dolls the killer left behind. I feel quite the dunce."

It was an evening of firsts; I'd certainly never heard my grandfather refer to himself as a fool before.

"Not to worry, old chap," I tried in a rare moment of sauciness. "In the future, if you find you're having trouble solving a case, you can always ask me for advice."

He did not take kindly to the joke. "Very droll, Christopher. Very droll indeed." He crossed his arms across his chest in disapproval. "By the way, I said that Miss Viner should take my room tonight. Hers was terribly draughty and I don't want her catching a cold. After spending her life in the tropics, this weather really can't agree with her."

There was a glint of something in his eyes just then, but I couldn't imagine what he was scheming. It half crossed my mind that, as the room we'd slept in the night before was next to Albert's, he could be playing matchmaker. I doubted he would have encouraged a nocturnal tête à tête between two young people, though, and pushed the idea clean away.

We bade the other guests goodnight and mounted the stairs to Bedfordshire. In previous years, I would have been alive with excitement when going to bed on Christmas Eve. My head would have been full of the possibilities of what the morning might bring, and I would have surely struggled to sleep. But something had changed. It was hard to say whether it was the fact I was now seventeen, or it was due to all that had gone on over the last two days, but I felt nary a tingle of expectation.

Even the strings of ivy threaded through the bannisters and the mistletoe hanging at the top of the stairs failed to put me in mind of Father Christmas and the presents he'd bring. Seventeen years old and I was already a stone-hearted cynic. How sad.

"Christopher," my grandfather whispered when we reached the door to his new room. "Once you're ready for bed, come in here so that we can talk for a while." His voice was quite serious, and I was afraid of what he might have to tell me. I nodded and did as instructed all the same.

Returning to my room, in which I was yet to sleep, I discovered that my mother had pinned a pair of red socks above the fireplace. I must say that I finally sensed an exhilarating jolt. Seeing them so limp and empty only served to remind me how they would look come the morning, filled with tangerines, chocolate, nuts and perhaps even a book or two if they were the stretchable kind. It was enough to make me think back on Christmases at my own home. It certainly put a smile on my face and I concluded that I might not be such a Scrooge after all.

I got changed into my silk pyjamas, wrapped myself up in a thick towelling gown and then added a scarf to counteract the draughtiness of Miss Viner's former room. By the time I was ready, the house was quiet, and it seemed that everyone was fast asleep.

"Grandfather?" I asked, tapping gently on the door. For some reason, I'd expected to find him sitting up in bed, but he was standing by the window, looking out at the clear sky. It looked as though the snow had stopped for the night and I had to hope that we'd be able to return to Surrey for our big family party the following day.

"It's beautiful," he said, that solemn tone still controlling his voice. "So bright and peaceful. It reminds me of when I was first sent away to boarding school and it snowed for a month. I'll never forget those days." He fell silent, and I had to wonder once again why he'd asked me there.

"Did you want to talk about something, Grandfather?"

Looking at me head on, he appeared to come back to himself and the present day. He smiled and pointed over to a chair on the other side of his bed. "Perhaps it's my friend's death or being here for Christmas, but my mind has been racing with thoughts this evening. I think, perhaps, that it's time that I told you a story."

I sat down, but he stayed on his feet. He wore his long, embroidered smoking jacket, a high sleeping cap on his head, and looked even more eccentric than normal.

"You're not going to tell me a ghost story, are you?" I asked, remembering what Marmaduke had told me a few hours earlier. "Only, I know that it was common when you were a boy, but… well… if I'm telling the truth, I prefer happy endings."

He laughed. "I didn't invite you here for a ghost story, my boy."

I let out the breath I'd been holding. "That's a relief. Anything more frightening than 'A Christmas Carol' and my heart starts beating like a military drummer. Actually… I must confess that even the Ghost of Christmas Yet to Come gives me quite the howling fantods."

"I swear that there won't be a ghoul anywhere in my tale."

"Jolly good." I didn't know what else to say, so I added. "I'm all ears."

It was his turn to hesitate and, glancing around the elegantly furnished room, he appeared to be searching for some spark to help him. Whether he found what he was looking for, I cannot say, but, in time, he started his story.

"I've been thinking about my life and what I've achieved." This was as much as he managed at first, and those pale grey eyes of his set off on a journey once more. "In my career, my family, and on the Cranley estate."

I could tell how hard it was for him to say even this much and so I did what I could to encourage him. "Grandfather, I think you've done things to which the rest of us can only aspire. You've had more impact on this country than most rich lords and ladies. And though I may not say it often enough, I think you're wonderful."

He smiled a patient smile, but it was clear that my words were not what he needed at that moment. He sighed and attempted to express his state of mind. "I joined the police to make a difference to Britain, but I'm not sure that's what I achieved. We still live in a world that is corrupt and divided. People still go starving every day in this country, and evil prevails."

This really wasn't the kind of story I'd have chosen at Christmas, but he rarely spoke about his past and I tried once more to egg him onwards.

"You can't take all the blame on yourself, Grandfather. No single police officer could wipe out criminality entirely." My voice had grown quieter, and so I tried to inject some enthusiasm into my speech. "I know, from the stories I've read and the way people talk about you, just how admired you are. But, most of all, I've seen your amazing abilities for myself. Let's not forget that, if I identified the killer this evening, it's only because you directed me to the right man."

His voice suddenly rose and I could see that my effort was in vain. "It's not about being right, Christopher. Anyone can arrive at the correct answer to a problem. What I'm talking about is doing things as they should be done. I have always tried to treat people fairly, but—"

"So there you have it!" I have no idea why I insisted on talking time and time again. I really should have learnt by this stage in my life when to speak and when to keep my lips sealed.

"You are not concentrating, Christopher." He was storming back and forth in front of the glowing embers of the fire. "You might be listening, but you've failed to decipher what I'm trying to say."

"Then say it more clearly." A hint of irritation had crept into my voice. "If you have something to tell me, come out with it. Not everything in this life has to be a riddle."

He stopped in the middle of the hearthrug and turned to look at me. "What I'm trying to explain is that…" His words came to a halt, and he breathed in deeply to steel himself for what came next. "This is a confession, Christopher. I'm not the saint that you imagine me to be. Try as I might, I haven't always kept to my own high standards."

Despite the understated politeness of his words, the passion with which he delivered them knocked the wind from me. I couldn't imagine what he was going to say, but he evidently believed that it would change the way I looked at him forever.

I must have been quite affected by his announcement, as I didn't utter a word in response. I simply stared at the man who, over the last six months since he'd emerged from his cocoon at Cranley Hall, had become a true mentor.

He turned his back to me and gazed into the fire. "Even if it was only once, I broke the rules; I allowed myself to be swayed from my better judgement."

This was when my imagination ran away from me. My head was filled with every potential dark deed he could have committed. The contrast between those lurid images and the respect I held for the genteel old chap standing before me was impossible to reconcile.

"What did you do?" My words emerged in a low, hollow susurration.

He placed his hands together in front of him, as though he were about to say a prayer. "Do you remember what I told you about John Fletcher Schoolcraft?"

I had to think for a moment to recall the name. "The man you arrested for murdering his lover? You said he had a grudge against you from your days on the force."

He gave one short, efficient nod and continued. "Perhaps there are more figures from my past to whom such a description would apply, but he's the one I best remember; he's the one I wronged."

"Do you mean to say he wasn't guilty?" My pitch rose to match a starling's high note.

"Oh, no, he was guilty. Guilty as the blackest sin you can imagine, but that isn't the whole story. This was almost fifty years ago, and I was still a sergeant at the time. I don't like to use such base language, but Schoolcraft was an out-and-out toe-rag. He positively flaunted his guilt, stepping out with a new girlfriend, even as his wife remained at home with their son, and his lover rested in her grave. The press took up the story, and he became the devil of his day.

"Oliver Mountfalcon was my district superintendent at the time and there was a lot of pressure on him to get a conviction. He'd been a military man and was drafted into a senior position, while I had worked my way up from constable, but we already knew one another through our families."

I thought this might be a riddle I could solve on my own after all, but he came to a stop and so I prodded him on. "What did you do, Grandfather?"

I'd rarely seen him so wild or impassioned before. His eyes were swollen and red – as though he'd been rubbing hot peppers in them

– and his skin was deathly pale. He sat down in a chair opposite and, far from maintaining his usual perfect posture, hunched forwards to speak. "Mountfalcon came to me in my lodgings one night and told me that Schoolcraft was making a fool of us. He said that, if we didn't do something to hold him to account for his crime, the Metropolitan Police would be a laughingstock."

He let out the contents of his lungs in one great push. "I don't blame my friend for what he made me do, but I've never forgiven myself for going along with it."

"So you lied or planted evidence? Of what exactly are you guilty?"

He peered despondently at the floor before replying. "I took the dead maid's scarf. She'd been wearing it when we found the body and it was covered in blood. I hid it in a desk in the office where Schoolcraft worked. Mountfalcon paid an informant to report the information, and our suspect's fate was sealed. My colleagues raided the office, they found what they were looking for, and the dead woman's sister identified the scarf."

I had more questions, but I couldn't speak. I was struggling to know what I made of any of it. If an evil man had been punished for an evil deed, surely it was the right outcome, but it was hard to say whether what my grandfather had done was in any way just. Perhaps that was the hardest thing for me to accept. Not the former officer's guilt, but the fact I couldn't immediately condemn it.

He continued without further prompting. "The problem was that Schoolcraft knew we'd conspired against him and would tell anyone willing to listen. From being a monster in the eyes of society, the press turned him into a martyr. The evidence was solid enough to get some form of conviction – we found letters that he'd exchanged with the victim, threatening her if she didn't keep their liaison a secret – but Schoolcraft used his influence to avoid a heavier sentence. It's rather ironical, but that may be my one saving grace. If I'd condemned a man to death on concocted evidence, I'm not sure I could have forgiven myself."

I couldn't bear to see him suffer and spoke softer words to reassure him. "You've told me before that such things happened all the time in the police. I imagine they still do. What you did wasn't really so terrible, was it?"

His eyes seemed to jump at me then and he growled out his

response. "That's irrelevant. I broke my own rules; I betrayed myself. When I became a policeman, I promised to do things differently from other officers. I swore a silent oath that I wouldn't break the law in order to uphold it. But, in the end, I was no better than anyone else."

There was no echo in that room. His words were absorbed by the thick carpet beneath our feet and it made the place seem unnaturally quiet. For a few minutes, as he endured the pain of his memories and I considered what his revelations truly meant, the only sound was the faint hiss and crackle from the remains of the fire. It took me that long to decide upon my next question.

"Why are you telling me this tonight?"

He looked up at me, his face still racked with sorrow and shame. "Perhaps… perhaps this is a time for forgiveness. This time of year has meant many things to many people, right back to the pagans of old. But if there's one thing that unites them all, it's the hope that Christmas brings. And I was rather hoping you might accept my explanation and forgive me for not being the model that I claimed to be."

He turned away before I could reply. The sky through the window was ablaze with stars, the glare of the snow still just as bright, and my love for my grandfather hadn't dimmed either.

"There's nothing to forgive," I told him, as if it had ever been in doubt. "But there's something you can do for me." I pulled a Welsh blanket from his bed and wrapped it around me on the chair. "You can tell me a happier tale from your days in the police. Tell me something of which you're proud."

He peered at me once more, and the fine lines around his eyes made it seem as though he were amused by my request. Something of his official bearing returned, and he sat up straight to regard me. "Very well. What sort of tale would you like to hear?"

"Something exciting… with a happy ending."

He actually smiled at this and crossed one leg over the other before selecting the right anecdote. "I'm sure I've mentioned the Bow Boys gang to you before. And I think I've told you about their leader, Tommy Bow."

"The human elephant who once ripped a rival's head clean off its shoulders?" I asked, knowing full well that was the chap.

"The very man! But I don't believe I've told you about his twin brother, Timothy. Well, this is a case of two halves of the same apple being quite unalike. Timothy was a strange character, but never cruel like his brother…"

He unfurled his story with all the art and grace of a master raconteur. I could have listened to him for hours like that – if my eyelids hadn't been quite so heavy at least. I think I made it to the point where Timothy Bow was about to shop his own gang to the police when Grandfather's words became strange and elongated and I finally fell asleep.

CHAPTER THIRTY-ONE

"Put it down, man," I heard him say, as I woke up in a haze. The room was dark except for a small electric lamp that had just been switched on in one corner. There was a shape beside the bed, a figure by the looks of things, but I was still waking up and nothing quite made sense.

"A pillow's not going to do you much good now," Grandfather continued, and I realised that his voice was not coming from the bed as I'd imagined, but over by the lamp.

I sat up in my chair – my neck in agony, my back stiff – and rubbed my eyes in an attempt to understand the scene in front of me. The dark shape by the bed was Inspector Blunt. My grandfather, meanwhile, was sitting almost out of sight behind the door. He was wide awake, still dressed in his smoking jacket, and had a short-snouted revolver pointed at the intruder.

"Don't be a fool, man. I'll shoot you if I have to," he promised, and I really didn't doubt it. "There's no way out of this. If you'd sneaked in here with a knife or a gun, you might have half a chance of getting away, but a pillow isn't going to save you."

"You knew?" Blunt said in a gruff, throaty voice.

"I had my suspicions, which were confirmed this evening when Chrissy and Marmaduke realised the mistake I had made with the paper dolls you'd left for us."

Blunt clearly didn't know what to do with himself. He glanced down at the bed, which I had to assume my grandfather had stuffed with cushions and clothes to make it look as though there was someone asleep there. He plumped up the pillow in his hand and, much like a parent would for a young child who couldn't sleep, placed it down softly on the bed.

"That's more like it." Grandfather's voice was clear, his words concise, and I had to assume he'd managed to fight off the urge to sleep in order to be alert for this very moment. "The only thing that surprises me is that you went after the others before me."

"Oh, you'd have got your turn, matey. Don't you worry about that. In fact, tonight would have been quite the little adventure if you hadn't decided to stick your oar in."

"Grandfather, I don't understand." I think they might have to engrave these words on my tombstone. "Are you saying that Blunt was working with Ogilby?"

He cast me a repentant look. "No, I'm sorry, dear boy. That was part of the ruse I enacted in order to entice the inspector here into Miss Viner's room tonight."

I was trying my best to work out what this all meant, but could only land upon, "Pardon?" in response.

"I wanted everyone to believe that Ogilby was the killer, as I knew for a fact that the real culprit would be most upset at having his limelight stolen. I can only imagine that, while the rest of us were getting changed last night, Blunt here followed our singer out into the snow and cut his throat. Am I right, old chap?"

Blunt's face was like a bulldog's then, all scrunched together and unnerved. "Oh, he's dead all right. I wasn't going to let him spoil the fun by calling the police, was I?"

As they spoke, I searched for the missing connections in the case. I looked for every last question mark I'd ignored when I happily accepted the idea that the mysterious Wentworth Ogilby was the killer. Blunt had his sword to Horatio's neck but didn't kill him. Grandfather had hatched some sort of plan with Miss Viner that would have been unnecessary if our killer was locked outside.

"The room," I yelped. "We changed rooms last night because you believed that Blunt was going to kill Sophy Viner, but how did you know?"

With his revolver still trained on his rival – well, more than a rival; Blunt was a fully fledged enemy by this stage – Grandfather rose from the chair. "I asked Sophy to deny her heritage in front of the whole group. That's something Blunt really isn't keen on, and why Crump and Ogilby had to die. Dicky Prowse, meanwhile, has been open about his past from the beginning and is still breathing as a result."

"Yeah," Blunt said rather thoughtfully, as he sat down on the edge of the bed. "I like that Prowse fella. Nice chap he is. Decent cricketer and all."

I thought back to the conversations when the guests had arrived the previous day, and it was true that Crump and Ogilby had been dismissive of their upbringings. But I still couldn't see how this fit together with Lord Mountfalcon and everything else that had occurred.

"Far be it from me to say so, Blunt, but you did too good a job choosing your guests. You sought out others just like you. Figures who had parents with a criminal past. I imagine you were curious whether they had denied their upbringings like Harry Crump and Sophy Viner. Or, like you, they could admit to what their fathers had done."

A picture was emerging from the fog. Grandfather had discovered the gossamer thread which might finally pull us all together. Blunt had mentioned his parents after dinner. We knew that Dicky Prowse's old man was a debtor. Miss Viner told us the story of how her father had been disgraced over that business with the diamonds and… the paper doll! If it was Marmaduke to whom the invitation was addressed, and not his father, it all fit rather neatly. What's more, Blunt knew the Adelaides from our previous cases and, as my friend, Marmaduke was an obvious choice to include in his sick scheme.

"That's why you didn't kill Horatio," I blurted out. "It wasn't the criminal fathers with whom you took umbrage, it was the children who denied their existence."

Blunt did not seem ashamed of his actions. "Well… to an extent. Though I mainly wanted to kill the men who fitted up my old dad. You should have heard old Mountfalcon begging for his life. He didn't remember me at the trial when my pa were sent down, but I remembered him."

"So it's true; you're Schoolcraft's boy."

To be perfectly frank, I had quite failed to make this connection. Grandfather had pieced everything together before I could, and his Christmas Eve storytelling suddenly made more sense.

Blunt was a wild animal now and howled out his complaint. "He were innocent, and you destroyed him. You destroyed me! My whole life was ruined because of the name you gave my dad. My mother left him, and when he got out of gaol, he weren't the same."

Grandfather replied with just as much fury and passion. "Anything bad that happened to you was down to your father's actions, not mine. The man was a killer, and it's hard to believe that, after a life spent dealing with criminals, you still fail to see that."

There were noises in the corridor and I saw my brother peek in through the crack in the door. I could only assume that the others had been woken by the shouting.

Blunt was back on his feet then, but, with his hands empty, it did little to balance the equation. "I joined the police to make sure such things never happened again, but people like you always win. The game's fixed from the start."

Grandfather raised the pistol a little higher to remind Blunt not to do anything foolish. His response, when it came, was not what I had expected. "You're right. I'm not going to contradict you. The world is unfair and the place you are born makes a far greater difference to a life than the brains in your head or the nature of your character. I'm sorry that's the way things are, but murdering innocent people won't solve the problem."

"They weren't innocent." Blunt's words seemed to echo up the chimney. "Mountfalcon was a killer for what he did, and Crump and Ogilby weren't much better. Harry Crump sold his father out to the police, but that musician chap was the biggest fraud of all. It was his own mother he turned his back on. No one else knew about it, but I chanced upon some old files at the station and it made for a very interesting read."

Grandfather lifted his chin a fraction so that it was perfectly parallel to the floor. It reminded me of the way he'd adjusted his cutlery at dinner the night before. He was ever the perfectionist, and he had Blunt's number.

"That's what I meant about you doing too good a job. Only someone with access to restricted information could have dug up all the facts on the people you invited. Prowse and Marmaduke were easy enough, but Ogilby, and especially Mountfalcon's niece, Millicent Bowen, would have taken a great deal of work to uncover. That's why I began to suspect you. You'd done a wonderful job leaving the crime scenes free of evidence, but I doubt anyone else here could have set such a plan in motion."

"Well ain't you just the master detective!" Blunt spat the words across the room, as I hesitantly walked around the bed to be out of the line of fire. "You must admit, it was a pretty good plan, though. And I never gave up. It might have taken me a lifetime to get even with Mountfalcon, but it was worth the wait." He seemed quite jolly for a moment until the darkness within him reared up once more. "I should have killed you when I had the chance last night. Or the very first time I met you forty years ago."

His opponent continued as though Blunt hadn't spoken. "Oh, and I mustn't forget your terrible poetry – though I really wish I could." Trust my grandfather to focus on such a point. "I doubt any of the other guests would have written such tripe. I'll admit, however, that it did have merit in one respect."

"You're really too kind, Your Highness." Every word that Blunt said came out in a mocking grunt.

Lord Edgington ignored the petty man and proceeded to lay out his case. "You made me suspect Dicky Prowse." He let the words settle before continuing, and I believe that he must have considered this fact damning in itself. "If anything, Prowse was too good. You should never have invited him here. He loved his father, despite the man's crimes, and has remained the honest and upright soul that he presented himself as."

My grandfather's stare was as sharp as any knife in that moment. "Thanks to the line you wrote about him in the poem, my cynical mind concluded that Prowse couldn't possibly be so saintly, and I hunted down the slightest scrap of evidence that might point to his guilt."

"I said I liked the chap." Blunt let out a cruel laugh. "Doesn't mean I would have wanted to take the blame ahead of him."

"Idris was another poor choice. You must have known I would connect her with the London-Welsh gangs of the nineties; after all the trouble we had back then with the Jones gang, of which, I can only assume, her father was a member. It would explain the funding she must have had for her racing career and her reticence to talk about her upbringing. Jones was too common a name for me to be certain, of course, but the very idea set me on a path to you."

"What a mind you must have! I don't know how you do it." Blunt adopted an awestruck expression before curling his lip once more. "But it clearly hasn't entered your skull that I set you a puzzle to test your mettle in the first place. You clearly never considered that I was putting you to the test."

"Well then, it looks like I passed." With the hint of a smile behind his substantial moustaches, Grandfather gave up on his didactic speech and decided to ask a question. "What I don't understand is, why now? Why did you wait all this time to seek revenge?"

For perhaps the first time since I'd known him, Blunt straightened his back, de-hunched his shoulders and stood at his full height. "You said it yourself, old man. I was a good copper. I worked hard, treated people fair and did my best. But then you reappeared and made me feel just as small as when I was a kid. How everyone marvelled at the great mind of Lord Edgington as he solved crime after unsolvable crime! And how they pitied me.

"But that wasn't everything. It took something bigger to break me." He breathed in aggressively through his nostrils and embarked on the final part of his explanation. "I've said it more than once, but my mother, Muriel Blunt, was the best of women. She passed away just before you came back from the dead and I looked at her life and saw how little reward she ever got. Her husband was stolen from her. She lived in abject poverty and died in pain. And there you and Mountfalcon still were, living large in your palaces. Injustice, that's what I'd call it. Pure injustice, and so I set out to make things right."

I still expected my grandfather to show his anger, but he maintained his peaceful disposition. "It's a sad tale, Blunt, and I truly am sorry for the part I played in it. But the saddest thing of all was that this could have been avoided. You might not like me, but I respected you as an officer. Perhaps if I'd done more to take you under my wing, you wouldn't have followed in Schoolcraft's footsteps."

The mention of his father's name was enough to ignite the killer's rage once more. "That's not an insult, Edgington. I'm proud to walk in his shoes." Perhaps it was unconscious at first, but he took a step towards his foe and then one more. "There are very few people on this earth who are worthy of following in–"

He never finished the sentence but lunged forward, his arms outstretched. The bang that followed echoed in my ears for hours after. Dicky Prowse burst into the room with Albert and my mother just behind him, but he was too late.

CHAPTER THIRTY-TWO.

Though still dark outside, it was already six in the morning when the scene concluded. Dorie and Halfpenny appeared and ran about like headless rabbits. No, wait, that simile doesn't work. Never mind.

Of the rest of us, no one looked desperate to go back to sleep and so, slowly – like ghosts on all hallows' eve – we floated off downstairs. I didn't feel like talking to anyone and went to sit with Delilah in her usual spot by the fire. She looked up at me as I entered the sitting room and gave my hand a lick when I lay down next to her. With my head resting against hers, the world didn't feel quite so lonely or perverse. Listening to her soft breathing, with my eyes closed, I didn't have to think about the secrets that had been revealed, or the gunshot, or the blood.

I suppose I must have drifted off for some time as, when I next opened my eyes, the room was full of people and two voices rose above the others.

"All I'm saying is that you didn't have to shoot me."

"You called us all here this weekend to murder us one by one. I hardly think you're in a position to be sanctimonious."

I looked up to see Blunt hobbling into the room with a bandage on his leg and my grandfather helping him into a large leather chair. This probably sounds a little generous after all the man had done. I should mention, though, that someone had found a pair of ancient looking shackles and that Blunt's hands were chained together.

"As my arresting officer," the swine continued in a bureaucratic tone, "you should have avoided discharging your weapon."

Grandfather was having none of this. "You ran straight at me. And, even then, I only gave you a flesh wound. If it hurts so much, run outside and stick your leg in the snow. That should numb the pain."

"A flesh wound?" He looked across at Dicky Prowse, who was sitting on a sofa with Idris Levitt. "A flesh wound he says! All wounds are flesh wounds, you nincompoop. I'll be lucky if I don't bleed to death."

Grandfather froze and attempted to make sense of the unusual character in front of him. "You really are a despicable man. You're lucky I don't get Dorie to put you away in the wine cellar until the police arrive." He smiled then and added, "Actually, Chrissy, lend me a hand."

I jumped up to help push Blunt, chair and all, back out of the sitting room and around to the closest of Lord Mountfalcon's museum rooms. I hadn't been in there before, and the four walls were lined with keys. There were examples of every shape, size and colour pinned in place from ceiling to floor.

"That should give you something to think about," Grandfather said as we stationed him in the middle of the room. "Who knows; one of them might even fit the lock."

He veritably shot back to the hall then, laughing a little as he went.

"No, don't leave me in here." Blunt clearly wasn't happy with the decision. "Please, Chrissy! You could at least bring me some mince pies or something!"

Grandfather turned the key and waited outside for a moment to listen. "Despicable man!"

We walked back towards the lounge and a question occurred to me. "Grandfather, where did you find the gun?"

"Ha ha." He was clearly rather impressed by his own performance. "I smuggled it up with me after dinner. It really is shocking how many dangerous weapons there are in this house. Boxes of ammunition too. It's like poor old Ollie was asking to be shot." He shook his head despairingly before delivering a question of his own. "Is there anything else you'd like to know?"

"Well, yes. There was one more thing." I considered how to phrase it. "As it turns out that Ogilby isn't the killer, does that mean I haven't solved a murder after all?"

He paused in front of the door to consider his answer. "Of course you have, Christopher. You solved the very tricky case that I put before you. The fact that I didn't present you with all the evidence I had at my disposal shouldn't take anything away from it. Besides, you and Marmaduke provided the final clue we needed. I might have known that Blunt was our killer, but the exact connection between our suspects remained elusive until then."

"Oh… right." There was something I felt a little guilty about, and so I forced myself to confess. "But it's my fault that we didn't spot Blunt's involvement from the beginning. I saw the killer in the gardens and assumed he'd taken the sleigh back to the stables. That doesn't make any sense though as the inspector was still here."

He smiled, and I knew he didn't hold it against me. "Blunt was rather crafty there, and you mustn't blame yourself. He released the horses and must have hidden out of sight at the front of the house. You're certainly not to blame. I never imagined such a possibility until I had him in mind as a suspect."

"Well, thank you, Grandfather. That makes me feel a lot better." I didn't know what else to say, so I opted for, "Merry Christmas."

"Merry Christmas, my boy. I'm sorry that we won't be sharing it with the rest of the family. I promise that next year will be different."

"It's not all bad," I insisted. "At least we might miss Boxing Day at my grandmother's house now. She never lets me have second helpings. And there's still New Year's Eve to come." As he'd recently acknowledged my role in solving the crime, this was the perfect moment to announce my plans. "I was rather thinking I might have some friends over to Cranley for a party, in fact."

His face turned deadly serious then, and he placed a weighty hand on my shoulder. "The more the merrier. *Ubi bene, ibi patria.*"

I didn't like to tell him that my Latin wasn't good enough to know what he was talking about, so I nodded my thanks as he opened the door to the sitting room. He wandered in ahead of me, and I stood to marvel at that festive scene. Our group of no-longer-suspects sat around a green baize gaming table with my brother, enjoying a hand of bridge. Someone had restored the Christmas tree to its original location and a huge array of neatly wrapped presents had been placed beneath it.

Mother was sitting on the chaise longue with Horatio Adelaide, munching on cubes of crystallised ginger and dried fruit to tide them over before breakfast. Marmaduke had found a penny whistle and was serenading the dog, and the only thing I felt that I really lacked for was my father. I was soon distracted though, as there was a musical knock on the door just then and I went to open it before poor old Halfpenny had to hobble up from the kitchen.

"Good morning, Master Christopher," Todd said, full of the joys of Christmas. "I bring good tidings. Several wise men are on their way, and they're confident they can have everyone on the road by this afternoon."

The cheerful chap had brought a smile back to my face. "That's wonderful, Todd. And I'm so glad you're safe. I have some rather good news of my own."

He paused for the briefest of moments before replying. "Don't tell me… you've found the killer."

"That's right!" I was most impressed by his deduction.

"Let me guess. The culprit is…" He shook the snow from his ski boots as he thought. "Inspector Blunt."

"Oh my goodness." I was truly flabbergasted. "How could you possibly know that?"

He looked rather astonished himself. "It was a joke, Master Christopher. I was going to say Delilah, but I thought that the inspector was just as unlikely. It wasn't really Blunt, was it?"

As he unpeeled his outer layers, I described everything that had occurred since he'd left Mistletoe Hall. When the tale was told, he didn't look as though he believed a word I'd said.

The police had commandeered an extra sleigh from a neighbouring farm and turned up in their neat blue uniforms to make sense of the carnage that had occurred. With no more snow forecast, they were free to explore the forest and soon discovered poor Ogilby's body, really not so far from the house.

After a truly scrumptious breakfast, we went to pay our respects to the poor chap, but it was a horrific sight. The police had to cut him down from the tree and I came to wonder whether that evil had passed from generation to generation of the Schoolcraft family due to blood or upbringing. As hard done by as Blunt had portrayed himself, the man was a savage.

Once the police had finished interviewing the other guests, people began to leave. Todd took Dicky Prowse and Idris Levitt back to their cars in the sleigh and, once Marmaduke and I had taken a good hour to fashion one of the most sophisticated snowmen ever built – complete with deerstalker hat, Japanese Samurai armour, an eye patch, a Chinese opium pipe and a carrot for a nose – it was time for my friend to leave.

"I'll see you for New Year's Eve, eh Chrissy?"

"I'll be there with bells on," I told him, before realising that this didn't make much sense as I was the one organising the party.

He stepped forward and spoke in a conspiratorial murmur. "I'll smuggle some rum in for us."

"No, you won't, boy," his father told him, as he marched from the house to load their bags on the sleigh. "But maybe Lord Edgington will allow you a glass of champagne if you behave yourself."

My grandfather was standing on the steps to the house, quietly observing the scene. Horatio waved up to him and he nodded in that slow, silent manner of his.

To my surprise, Marmaduke's father put his arm around him. "Come along, boy. I think the two of us should have a bit of a drive before heading home. There are some nice spots around that I've never shown you before. If we can get up to the top of Cleeve Hill, it will look spectacular in the snow. You can see for miles."

My classmate was even more shocked than I was by his normally frigid father's warm tone and affectionate embrace. I had to hope that Horatio Adelaide had learnt a lesson from John Fletcher Schoolcraft's mistakes and, from now on, would do better by his son. They were arguing again by the time Todd cracked the reins to send the horses off through the snow, so it was clearly too soon to tell.

"We must stay one last night," Grandfather told me once we were back in the lounge with my family and Miss Bowen – as I supposed Sophy Viner would now be known.

"Oh, what a shame," I said in my most sincere voice. "That means we'll miss Boxing Day at Grandmother's house."

Mother slapped me around the back of the head (affectionately). "Not if we set off first thing in the morning."

Having pretended to be sad at the idea of not seeing my slightly witchy grandmother, I now had to pretend to be happy. I don't think anyone believed me.

Albert had barely said a word all day and was looking thoroughly love-stricken as he hung at the side of his new infatuation. For her own part, Sophy/Millicent looked similarly dazed to be – until her family appeared to divide up the estate, at least – the mistress of Mistletoe Hall.

"I can never thank you enough for all that you've done," she told my grandfather that afternoon, as we took drinks around the Christmas tree.

There were a few officers milling about the place, with Tom and Jerrys in hand, but the prisoner from the key room had been escorted off the grounds. I was not sad to see the back of Isambard Blunt.

Lord Edgington offered a gentle smile. "Nonsense, child. You played your part after all. That was some fine acting you exhibited over dinner. We wouldn't have been able to set the trap for Blunt, without you."

This was another point that I felt needed raising. "Grandfather, what would have happened if Blunt had gone in search of you first, instead of Miss…" I didn't finish the sentence as I didn't know which name to use.

"He would have found an empty room. I sent Miss Bowen to the servant's quarters to ensure she was safe."

"How remarkable," Albert replied, though I was uncertain whether he was referring to my grandfather's subtle plan, or his new love's beauty.

I rather wondered if my brother had met the woman he would marry. After all, Sophy (or Millicent or whatever name she selected) was now the heir to a grand estate. Even more importantly, from Albert's perspective, she had lived an impoverished existence and might well have lower standards than many of the women who had previously broken his heart. I felt confident that she would either snap up the soppy fellow, or realise what a drip he was and send him on to the next girl. Such is love.

There was still a sumptuous dinner to be enjoyed, but first it was time to distribute the presents.

"I'm afraid I didn't get anybody anything," I had to admit.

Mother gave a loving tut and handed me a pile of gifts. There were tags on each one addressed to Grandfather, Albert, Delilah, my mother herself and, perhaps most surprisingly, Miss Millicent Bowen. I must say, I have very good taste and everyone seemed to enjoy my choices immensely. Albert just adored his red cashmere scarf and Miss Bowen said that she appreciated the first edition of Elizabeth Barrett Browning's 'Sonnets from the Portuguese'. Delilah instantly snuffled up her pound of pork belly and Mother gave me a big hug in return for the garnet bracelet she'd purchased for herself on my behalf.

I saved Grandfather's present until last.

"I hope you like it," I told him, feeling a tad nervous that he would not.

"That's very generous, Christopher." His eyes sparkling with just as much excitement as mine, he carefully opened the gold paper package to reveal a pair of glossy silver cufflinks.

"Them, I mean," I rushed to correct myself. "I hope you like them. I never have been very good with pronouns."

He laughed at my pretence and raised one hand to make an announcement. "I actually have a little something for each of you. If you'll wait just one minute."

Possessed of the strangely youthful energy that occasionally took hold of him, he rose from his chair and sprang from the room. My mother engaged in polite conversation with Miss Bowen to pass the time, and I silently pondered what surprise the great Lord Edgington had prepared. I didn't have to wait long to discover the answer.

There was a heavy knock on the door and I was about to get up when it swung open for my jovial grandfather to come dancing into the room. He was dressed in a long green gown with a white fur trim, and he wore a crown of mistletoe on his head. We couldn't help but laugh at him.

"Who on earth are you supposed to be?" Albert demanded.

"He's Father Christmas, obviously." I was fairly certain on this point; he had a bulky sack on his back and the perfect white beard for the part.

"I was thinking of something a little more pagan," the old chap explained. "But he'll do."

When his sidestepping jig had concluded, he took a seat in his usual chair beside the fire and called us forward, one by one, to receive our bounty.

I was thrilled to receive some nice leather gloves, but unsure why he'd decided to give me a map of central London. Everyone else looked just as pleased with their presents – even Albert, whose only present was a painting of Cranley Hall that Grandfather had produced for him – and, when it seemed they had all been distributed, he reached into the burlap sack one last time.

"Christopher, your gifts symbolise a few of the exciting adventures we'll be enjoying over the next year," he said, by way of an explanation.

"And I have one last trifle for you."

It was not a mere trifle – which actually would have been a rather wonderful present as I can think of few things that are quite so tasty – but a large, flat box which was wrapped in the same festive paper as the other gifts.

I eagerly ripped it open to discover a sheepskin pilot's jacket and matching aviator hat. I looked up at the others and wasn't the only one struggling to understand his thinking.

"Really, Grandfather," my brother began. "Of everyone I know, Chrissy is the last person I could imagine going up in a plane."

Lord Edgington's words from six months earlier came back to me, and I looked at the mad old chap in the long green coat.

"Not a chance," I told him. "No. No. No."

He sat back in his chair with a smirk on his face. "Oh yes, Christopher. Yes, yes and, once more for luck, yes!"

The End (For Now…)

We hope that, wherever and whenever you're reading this, you have a sensational Christmas and a very happy new year. From Benedict, Marion and Amelie Brown

READ THE OTHER LORD EDGINGTON MYSTERIES TODAY...

- **Murder at the Spring Ball**
- **Death From High Places** (free e-novella available exclusively at benedictbrown.net. Paperback and audiobook available at Amazon early 2022)
- **A Body at a Boarding School**
- **Death on a Summer's Day**
- **The Mystery of Mistletoe Hall**
- **The Tangled Treasure Trail** (Coming Spring 2022)

Check out the complete Lord Edgington Collection at Amazon.

The First Lord Edgington audiobook, narrated by the actor George Blagden, will be released this year with the subsequent titles to follow early in 2022.

Get another

LORD EDGINGTON ADVENTURE

absolutely **free**…

Download your free novella at
www.benedictbrown.net

"LORD EDGINGTON INVESTIGATES..."

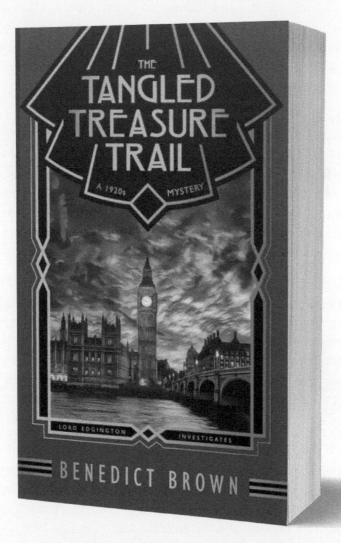

The fifth full-length mystery will be available in **Spring 2022** at amazon.

Sign up to the readers' club on my website to know when it goes on sale.

ABOUT THIS BOOK

This is my third Christmas mystery (two novels and a novella) and I think that, by this point, I don't need to prove how much I love the season. I am a kid at heart, and spending my life coming up with silly stories brings out that side of me even more. The difference between this book and my Izzy Palmer Christmas mysteries is that, with Lord Edgington, I get to indulge my love of history, too.

It's rather nice to write a Christmas story without the mention of a single flashing reindeer or oversized inflatable snowman. In this book, I really wanted to luxuriate in the mistletoe, holly branches and pine wreaths that would have made up the majority of decorations in the early part of the twentieth century, and so I made Chrissy just as obsessive about decorating as I am. It's no exaggeration to say that my mother and I could spend two hours picking out a tree at the farms near us in Surrey, so Christopher was comparatively reasonable in that respect.

When searching for a place to set the mystery, I came across the town of Tenbury Wells, which is known for its mistletoe celebration. As mentioned in the story, that part of England has had mistletoe auctions for hundreds of years. It even has a mistletoe festival – with a Mistletoe Queen and parade. Though they are a modern invention, I couldn't resist reimagining the festival as a more ancient event which our heroes witness on their way to Mistletoe Hall.

Tenbury Wells is a bit further north than the Cotswolds, but I visited my friend in the area this summer and decided to write what I know. I'd been there as a child and it really is a fantastically picturesque part of the world, complete with some of the most beautiful villages and views in England. It is also the home to Edgington's contemporary Major Heathcliff Lennox and his creator, Karen Baugh Menuhin, who graciously showed us around her home region.

I picked the village of Snowshill as the setting for this book, mainly for the name, but it turned out to be a fortuitous choice. Snowshill Manor is an absolutely fascinating house and many of the rooms in the book were inspired by the real place. It was owned by an eccentric artist, architect and poet called Charles Paget Wade. He set about redesigning the gardens and restoring the house to hold the incredible collection of artefacts he had amassed. This includes the twenty-six suits of samurai armour which Chrissy is so scared by, rooms full of instruments, automatons, bicycles, and all sorts of contraptions – all of which you can still see if you visit today.

Another important element in these books is the golden age of motoring. I don't actually know much about cars – and rarely remember to pump up the tyres on my own modern one. But my father loved classic cars and had some interesting vehicles when he was young. At the time he was dating my mother, he drove a British racing green Triumph TR3 from the 1950s. He eventually sold it to a friend for scrap and, thirty years later, we saw the exact car, with the same number plate, on the front of a classic car magazine. It really is one of the most beautiful sports cars and, as these books are devoted to my lovely dad, I thought he would have enjoyed reading about all the models that Lord Edgington acquires.

After managing to write six novels and two novellas in less than a year, it's time for me to have a holiday but Lord Edgington will be back in the spring.

If you loved the story and have the time, please write a review on Amazon. Most books get one review per thousand readers so I would be infinitely appreciative if you could help me out.

THE MOST INTERESTING THINGS I DISCOVERED WHEN RESEARCHING THIS BOOK...

I'm pretty sure this section of the book is going to get longer with each new release, so here goes...

I really enjoyed investigating past Christmas traditions in my research. For example, Christmas pudding played an important role in family celebrations at the turn of the twentieth century. It was the custom for all members of the household, including servants, to give the mixture a stir and a small silver coin was placed within it to bring luck to the finder. A Christmas pudding is also eaten by the Cratchits in 'A Christmas Carol' and Dickens goes into a lot of detail about it, but I didn't have time to mention the scene as I'd already enjoyed their consumption of the goose.

Thanks to Lord Edgington's advanced years, the Victorian age stands tall over the story, and no one influenced the modern celebration of Christmas more than Queen Victoria (and maybe Dickens himself!). She and her German-born husband helped popularise many traditions, including the Christmas tree and Christmas cards. Much like Lord Edgington, she was also very hands-on with her servants, and, on Christmas Eve, the royal family would go below stairs to distribute gifts to their staff, even before they opened their own presents.

In 1927, a request was sent to Buckingham Palace to reveal the recipe of the Christmas pudding that the king was served. This recipe was published widely and used by the Empire Marketing Board to promote ingredients from across the British Empire. The recipe, which the royal chef, Henry Cédard, provided, was enough for a household of forty people.

Here it is in its original form, which had to be slimmed down by four-fifths for normal families...

THE EMPIRE CHRISTMAS PUDDING

according to the recipe supplied by the King's Chef Mr. CEDARD, with Their Majesties' Gracious Consent

1 lb	Currants	Australia
1 lb	Sultanas	Australia or South Africa
1 lb	Stoned Raisins	Australia or South Africa
5 ozs	Minced Apple	United Kingdom or Canada
1 lb	Bread Crumbs	United Kingdom
1 lb	Beef Suet	United Kingdom
6½ ozs	Cut Candied Peel	South Africa
8 ozs	Flour	United Kingdom
8 ozs	Demerara Sugar	British West Indies or British Guiana
5	Eggs	United Kingdom or Irish Free State
½ oz	Ground Cinnamon	India or Ceylon
¼ oz	Ground Cloves	Zanzibar
¼ oz	Ground Nutmegs	British West Indies
¼ teaspoon	Pudding Spice	India or British West Indies
¼ gill	Brandy	Australia · S. Africa Cyprus or Palestine
½ gill	Rum	Jamaica or British Guiana
1 pint	Beer	England · Wales · Scotland or Ireland

WRITE TO THE EMPIRE MARKETING BOARD, WESTMINSTER, FOR A FREE BOOKLET ON EMPIRE CHRISTMAS FARE GIVING THIS AND OTHER RECIPES.

I've seen blogs of modern chefs trying to create it, and it is no longer easy to source the ingredients from specific places in our globalised world. Henry Cedard, the king's chef, sounds like an interesting guy too. Born in France, he served the king for over thirty years, including a trip to the front line. At the time of his death in the thirties, a year before the king died, he was at the top of his game and received a salary of £2000 per annum (£145k in modern money). I was surprised just how much £1 was worth in the twenties and had originally slipped £20 in the envelopes the killer sent to the Mistletoe Hall staff, before discovering that would have been an exorbitant amount (£1243!) and changing it to £2.

In relation to the cranberries Chrissy does not enjoy, I don't know for certain that they were available at the time in Britain. If you'd have found them anywhere, though, Fortnum & Mason would have been the place to look. This beautiful, upmarket food store is still around today and, among its claims to fame, it was the first shop to sell Heinz baked beans, way back in 1886 when such imports would have been considered a grand luxury.

Probably the first thing I looked into in my research, though, was mistletoe. Kissing under the mistletoe dates back to the 16th century, but it became popular with servants in late 18th-century England. As is, perhaps, no longer the case, the custom allowed young men to kiss any woman standing underneath a bough of mistletoe. I rather like another part of the tradition that suggests people would remove one berry for each kiss that was claimed and, once they were all gone, there'd be no more kisses.

It was considered bad luck to refuse someone's kiss, or let the mistletoe touch the ground until Candlemas, when decorations were taken down. Some people would even leave the mistletoe hanging all year. We have our own tradition in my family. On the first weekend of December – before our annual Christmas party when I may or may not dress up as a far too skinny Father Christmas – we go searching for Mistletoe around our village. My wife and I take it in turns to make a fool of ourselves climbing trees with a pair of secateurs and then, with our bounty claimed, we stop off at a friend's house on the way home to share the love (or the mistletoe at least).

The Christmas rose is so known because of a legend that it grew in the snow when a young girl burst into tears when she had no gift to give the baby Jesus. Which makes me wonder…does it snow in Bethlehem!? There is incidentally a very similar story about the origin of the poinsettia – which I couldn't include in this book as it would not have been associated with Christmas at the time and mainly became famous in America later in the century thanks to the efforts of one enterprising family.

Another great story about the Christmas rose is that, as it always bloomed around the 6th of January, which was Christmas Day in the

Julian calendar, when they tried to change to the Gregorian calendar and it didn't bloom, they immediately switched back, and those superstitious Britons didn't adopt the modern calendar for another two hundred years. It might just be a myth, but I like the idea of a flower having such a big impact on history.

The garden of Snowshill Manor, which Mistletoe Hall was inspired by, was designed in the early twenties and is laid out as a series of outdoor rooms. It has many pavilions and terraces, as described in my book (though I added a few of the creepy sculptures to stand out more in the snow) and it even has a model village. The quote on the arch at Snowshill is not the one Chrissy discovers. I chose instead to include something that the owner, Charles Paget Wade, wrote. "Mystery is most valuable in design: never show all there is at once," not only sums up his plans for his elaborate garden, I thought it a fitting reference to an interesting man and also something worth keeping in mind when planning a whodunit.

Moving from Snowshill to snow, there was plenty of it in the winter of 1925, though not perhaps the Arctic inundation described in my book. There had been a series of harsh winters in the preceding years, but terrible liars like me take liberties with these things and Britain rarely has snow right up to your middle. That being said, there was indeed "notable snow" in November, January, and even May in the Cotswolds that winter.

Cars and motoring have become rather important to this series and so I thought I should check what the speed limit was in the 1920s. This inevitably meant that I read more than I needed to about the history of speed limits, but it is rather interesting. The first speed limits established in Britain were 4mph in the country and 2mph in the town but there was a caveat to this as any car was required to have a man with a flag walk sixty yards ahead to warn pedestrians and horses of the oncoming danger – it was hardly high-speed motoring and, by the turn of the new century, it had risen to a pacy 20 miles an hour (evidently with no man running in front of the vehicle).

Idris Levitt in my book was inspired by a duo of incredible women from the early twentieth century. First and foremost. Dorothy Levitt, or "the fastest girl on earth" has a very similar background to my Miss Levitt. She was a secretary turned scorcher – a fast-driving female motorist who competed in races and speed trials and was beloved by the press. Along with holding land and water speed records, she was a proto-feminist and promoted motoring to women. She might even be said to have invented the wing mirror thirty years before they were introduced to most cars, as she recommended women carrying a compact with them to watch out for oncoming traffic.

In France, not long before Levitt's fame, Camille du Gast was a rich widow who excelled in just about every sport going, but was known as "the Valkyrie of the motor car". Not only was she the second woman to compete in a motor race, she sounds like a truly incredible person who was the president of the French animal protection charity, helped young women and orphans in Paris – including during the Nazi occupation of France – and survived an assassination attempt, ordered by her own daughter, when she challenged the gang who came to murder her and they ran away.

Dicky Prowse, meanwhile, (apart from having the same surname as the unsung actor behind Darth Vader's mask) is not based on anyone in particular, but I chose to have a cricketer in my book for an important reason. Unlike my previous stories in the "Lord Edgington Investigates…" series, there's more of a class battle at play in this book, which was rather nicely summed up in the world of cricket. There were two kinds of players, amateurs and professionals, with the idea being that gentlemen who played did not need to be paid and so proudly described themselves as amateurs. The rule was actually ripe for abuse and plenty of gents benefitted from their position as players, but, either way, it established two tiers within the sport which were mirrored in society. There were regular matches of "Gentlemen v Players" and the very idea of choosing a team based on social class seems pretty appalling now – though it's probably worth noting that the gents normally lost! This system met resistance after the First World War, but didn't come to an end until 1962.

There are even more songs than normal in this book. I was surprised to discover that the words to "Ding Dong Merrily on High" were only written in 1924, the year before the series is set. The Anglican priest, composer and, rather importantly, bell ringer; George Ratcliffe Woodward wrote the words to fit a sixteenth century French melody. Meanwhile, "The Coventry Carol" is possibly even older and dates back to the time that mystery plays were performed to re-enact the nativity and other blible stories in the middle ages. It tells the incredibly depressing story of the massacre of the innocents. Far jollier is "Gabriel's Message", a Basque carol which made its way into English in the 19th century, the slightly less holy version that Chrissy mentions in the book was taught to me by my father (Kevin Brown, you scamp!) Finally, no Lord Edgington book would be complete without a bit of music hall enertainment, and "The Galloping Major" is a perfect slice. Written by Fred W. Leigh and composed by George Bastow in 1906, it is a very fun song to belt out at high volume and I can't wait to heear George Blagden have a go at it in the audiobook next year.

Last, and probably least… I may be the only one who didn't know this, but shoe sizes in Britain, America and most former commonwealth countries are measured in barleycorns. Barleycorns (the kernel of the plant) are said to measure 1/3rd of an inch, though in reality they can be much shorter or longer. They were also used as a standard measurement of weight upon which the whole English measuring system was based.

I certainly feel much smarter now I know all of that. Let's see if I can remember any of it by the time I write my next book!

ACKNOWLEDGEMENTS

Normally I have someone to apologise to here, but, off the top of my head, I can't think of anyone one I could have offended, so I'm going to use this space to pay tribute to my biggest supporter. I couldn't do anything that I do without my wife, Marion. As well as keeping our house running when I don't have time (terrible lazy misogynist that I am!) she also designs my covers, maintains my website and prepares the books for publication. She is an incredible graphic designer, a loving mother to our daughter and a brilliant wife to me. I am thankful for her every day and, by all rights, she should have her name on the book covers too.

Thank you, too, to my crack team of experts – the Hoggs, the Martins, (**fiction**), Paul Bickley (**policing**), Karen Baugh Menuhin (**marketing**) and Mar Pérez (**forensic pathology**) for knowing lots of stuff when I don't. Thanks to my fellow writers who are always there for me, especially Pete, Rose, Suzanne and Lucy.

Thank you many times over to all the readers in my ARC team who have combed the book for errors. I wouldn't be able to produce this series so quickly or successfully without you, so please stick with me, Izzy and Lord Edgington to see what happens next…

Rebecca Brooks, Ferne Miller, Craig Jones, Melinda Kimlinger, Deborah McNeill, Emma James, Mindy Denkin, Namoi Lamont, Linda Kelso, Katharine Reibig, Pam, Sarah Dalziel, Linsey Neale, Karen Davis, Taylor Rain, Brenda, Christine Folks McGraw, Terri Roller, Margaret Liddle, Esther Lamin, Tracy Humphries, Lori Willis, Anja Peerdeman, Liz Batton, Allie Copland, Susan Kline, Suzanne Winterly, Kate Newnham, Marion Davis, Tina Laws, Sarah Turner, Linda Brain, Stephanie Keller, Linda Locke, Kathryn Davenport, Kat, Sandra Hoff, Karen M, Mary Nickell, Vanessa Rivington, Darlene Riggs, Jill Tatum, Helena George, Anne Kavcic, Nancy Roberts, Pat Hathaway, Jake Chism, Kate Newnham, Peggy Craddock, Cathleen Brickhouse, Susan Reddington and Anny Pritchard.

"THE MYSTERY OF MISTLETOE HALL" COCKTAIL

Now something of a Midwest regional specialty, the Tom & Jerry used to be an extremely popular seasonal mixed drink across the United States. It's said to have been created either by British writer Pierce Egan to promote his 1821 stage play "Tom & Jerry" or by a canny bartender to celebrate the premiere. Its rather involved preparation method makes it a complicated single-serve drink, which is just as well as the Tom & Jerry really is meant to be shared with friends and family over the festive season. It's even featured in "Beyond Tomorrow" (1940) which is one of my favourite Christmas films.

In essence, the Tom & Jerry is a type of eggnog. A batter is made by beating the egg whites and yolks separately and then mixing them together with spice, rum and sugar. For individual servings, place a tablespoon of the batter in a mug, pour 60 ml of brandy (or 30 ml brandy and 30 ml Jamaican rum) and boiling water or hot milk to fill (milk makes for a better result). Garnish with nutmeg. This heart-warming (and very rich) drink was popularized by the aptly named Jerry Thomas, author of the first cocktail book, most famous bartender of the 19th century and owner of two pet white mice called… Tom and Jerry. It also, we must assume, gave its name to a certain cartoon cat and mouse.

Batter recipe:

> **1 kg white sugar**
> **12 eggs.**
> **30 ml of Jamaican rum**
> **1,5 teaspoon of ground cinnamon**
> **1 teaspoon of ground cloves**
> **1 teaspoon of ground allspice**

The idea for the cocktail pages was inspired by my friend and the "Lord Edgington Investigates…" official cocktail expert, Francois Monti. You can get his brilliant book "101 Cocktails to Try Before you Die" at Amazon…

THE IZZY PALMER MYSTERIES

If you're looking for a modern murder mystery series with just as many off-the-wall characters but a little more edge, try **"The Izzy Palmer Mysteries"** for your next whodunit fix.

"A CORPSE CALLED BOB"
(BOOK ONE)

Izzy just found her horrible boss murdered in his office and all her dreams are about to come true! Miss Marple meets Bridget Jones in a fast and funny new detective series with a hilarious cast of characters and a wicked resolution you'll never see coming. Read now to discover why one Amazon reviewer called it, ***"Sheer murder mystery bliss."***

ABOUT ME

Writing has always been my passion. It was my favourite half-an-hour a week at primary school, and I started on my first, truly abysmal book as a teenager. So it wasn't a difficult decision to study literature at university which led to a masters in Creative Writing.

I'm a Welsh-Irish-Englishman originally from **South London** but now living with my French/Spanish wife and presumably quite confused infant daughter in **Burgos**, a beautiful mediaeval city in the north of Spain. I write overlooking the Castilian countryside, trying not to be distracted by the vultures, hawks and red kites that fly past my window each day.

When Covid 19 hit in 2020, the language school where I worked as an English teacher closed down and I became a full-time writer. I have two murder mystery series. There are already six books written in **"The Izzy Palmer Mysteries"** which is a more modern, zany take on the genre. I will continue to alternate releases between Izzy and Lord Edgington. I hope to release at least ten books in each series.

I previously spent years focussing on kids' books and wrote everything from fairy tales to environmental dystopian fantasies, right through to issue-based teen fiction. My book **"The Princess and The Peach"** was long-listed for the Chicken House prize in The Times and an American producer even talked about adapting it into a film. I'll be slowly publishing those books over the next year whenever we find the time.

"The Mystery of Mistletoe Hall" is the fourth novel in the "Lord Edgington Investigates…" series. The next book will be out in the spring and there's a novella available free if you sign up to my readers' club. If you feel like telling me what you think about Chrissy and his grandfather, my writing or the world at large, I'd love to hear from you, so feel free to get in touch via...

www.benedictbrown.net

WORDS AND REFERENCES YOU MIGHT NOT KNOW

Poltroon – a coward

The willies – not as rude as it sounds. It just means something that gives you the creeps!

Kissing bough – a hanging wreath often made of mistletoe. A decoration which dates back to the middle ages, often in the form of a globe.

Favrile – the style of glossy multicoloured glass trademarked by Tiffany's.

Bonce – British slang for your head.

Yorkers – a type of ball bowled in cricket – that's all I know as I'm not an expert, but the dictionary tells me it's a ball that bounces up close to the bat.

Mackintosh – a long raincoat, named after the Scotsman, Charles Macintosh who invented the cloth it's made of.

Eton – the school of princes (literally) Eton is famously one of the most expensive schools in Britain and a disproportionate number of famous British actors, journalists, politicians and, yep, princes went there.

Sir Ernest Shackleton – a heroic Antarctic explorer who got over one hundred miles closer to the south pole than anyone before him.

Scorcher – a new one to me and what a word! It basically means someone who drives fast but was especially used for women like Idris Levitt.

Bilked – defrauded, swindled

Bête noire – common enough, but there's a lot of French in this book, so it means a person or thing that is disliked.

Scarper - escape

Buche de noël – more French (blame my wife!) it's a desert in a shape of a log commonly eaten at Christmas

Dosshouse – in American English, flophouse

Britisher – a Briton, but often with a patriotic sense

Fogey – From Scottish English referring to an army pensioner, it has come to mean any– an old dull fellow.

À voix haute – French for "out loud"

Milieu – French for middle, but can also mean environment or setting

The Met – The Metropolitan Police, the main London police force for whom Lord Edgington worked

William Morris – Victorian Arts & Crafts movement designer and writer

Phizog – face, from physiognomy, hence phiz

Cloche – French for bell (you're learning all sorts from me!) but English for the cover over dishes in posh houses.

Mountebank – a charlatan or conman

Idem – Latin for "the same" – used to refer to something that has already been mentioned

Stinkard – guess!

Swiz – a bit of a con – British slang

Snapdragon – a parlour game in which you had to pick raisins out of a flaming bowl and then eat them. Victorians were crazy!

Jellyfish – coward

Nary – antiquated form of "not" – used for emphasis

Howling fantods – the same as the willies above (the creeps) and a small, improbable reference to David Foster Wallace's Infinite Jest.

Susurration – a whisper. Incidentally, my favourite word in Spanish is "susurrar" which also means to whisper.

Ubi bene, ibi patria – Latin, literally meaning "Homeland is where life is good" which was as close as I could find to Lord Edgington saying, mi casa es su casa.

Hurray for words! Aren't they wonderful?

CHARACTER LIST

Lord Edgington – "The Most Honourable Marquess of Edgington, Lord of Cranley Hall" – The main detective of my series. Retired Metropolitan Police superintendent, owner of the grandest estate in Surrey, and Christopher's grandfather.

Christopher Aloysius Prentiss (Recently turned seventeen!) – Kind-hearted, well-meaning and somewhat sentimental, Christopher is Lord Edgington's loyal assistant.

Delilah, the golden retriever – she is also very loyal!

Violet Prentiss – Chrissy's smart and caring mother

Albert Prentiss – Chrissy's soppy, heartbroken brother.

Lord Oliver Mountfalcon – Long-serving friend of Lord Edgington. He is a retired commissioner of the Metropolitan Police and a hobbyist collector of exotic antiquities.

Inspector Blunt – rival and former colleague of Lord Edgington when he was in the police. He likes his food.

Horatio Adelaide – onetime criminal kingpin turned wealthy landowner and baron.

Marmaduke Adelaide – Chrissy's former bully, turned schoolfriend. Son of Horatio.

Dicky Prowse – Professional cricketer.

Miss Sophy Viner – unemployed governess.

Wentworth Ogilby – Singer

Idris Levitt – "scorcher" or fast-driving female motorist, racing driver and speed record holder.

"Hilarious" Harry Crump – stage comedian and clown.

Todd – Lord Edgington's chauffeur and all-round helper. Mixes a mean cocktail and is always on hand when action is needed.

Halfpenny – Cranley Hall's Footman.

Alice – Cranley Hall's maid and Chrissy's (former) one true love.

"Cook" – Henrietta – Cranley Hall's somewhat experimental cook.

Patrick Driscoll – Cranley Hall's head gardener.

The Three Williams – Chrissy's best friends at Oakton academy.

CPSIA information can be obtained
at www.ICGtesting.com
Printed in the USA
LVHW090715181221
706563LV00019B/508